Dangerous Art

Dangerous Art

By DC Fidler

Published by DCFidler Publishing

2023

Published by DCFidler Publishing
300 W 5th St #647
Charlotte, NC 28202
DCFidlerpublishing@gmail.com

Printed in the United States of America
by Kindle Direct Publishing

12 11 10 9 8 7 6 5 4 3

Front cover: Pencil rendering of: Schongauer, Martin (1470-1491), *St. Michael* [Engraved print], Original at Metropolitan Museum of Art, New York, NY. Public domain.

Back cover: Pencil rendering of combined photos from Robert James Casey and Donald Carl Fidler: *Saint Michael Beneath the Sea* (2023), Original in the Donald Carl Fidler Private Collection, Charlotte, NC.

WGAE Registration:1363014
Library of Congress Copyright 2023

ISBN: 979-8-9864610-4-5 (paperback)
ISBN: 979-8-9864610-5-2 (ebook)

"Art enables us to find ourselves and lose ourselves at the same time."

- Thomas Merton, American Trappist Monk

Dangerous Art
By DC Fidler

FRANCINE
- September 2021 -

Captain Francine Boult entered the Midtown North Precinct Police Station, wishing to erase images from the previous day. After a judge released a white supremacist, the ankle-monitored man bludgeoned a Chinese-American grandmother to death in a hardware store. The woman's grandson rushed the killer from behind and chopped his spine in half with a pick ax.

Yesterday had been one win and loss for the bad guy; one loss and win for the good guy.

Francine had quit tallying sum totals for the days, weeks, months, or years, telling herself that on this brand-new day, only the present moment mattered.

She once explained to an elementary school class that walking into a police station is not like a job of arranging melons on shelves and carting cardboard fruit boxes to dumpsters. It is a job of witnessing the worst of humankind's atrocious acts and the best of humankind's struggles to seek justice.

Francine forced a pod of Sumatra dark roast coffee into the station's coffee maker as she listened to a rookie TV reporter dramatizing on *Breaking News*.

"Early this morning, an unidentified man was found in Hudson River Park. This marks the park's seventeenth heroin death this year. Police refuse to reveal further details to John and I, but me and John will keep you updated."

Francine scowled at the grammar-slaughtering broadcaster and abandoned her to browse morning homicide reports as one last spurt of black liquid filled her NYP blue and gold mug. No cream. No sweetener.

Planted among reports was a birthday card signed by fifteen detectives beneath her command. It was a card for a two-year-old with an oversized, sparkly blue number two that was now preceded by a black-marker-scribbled four. She recognized the childlike printing of her second in command, Detective Aaron Galanis. His penmanship had frozen at a first-grade level, a quality she dwelled upon on days she was irritated by him, anyone, or anything, desiring to rap his knuckles with a ruler—or tase him.

It was true Francine was turning forty-two today, but strangers appraised her as being in her late twenties. Genetics. Diet. Exercise. Great sleep despite an illimitable stream of grisly cases.

She appreciated the squad remembering her birthday, unlike Jasmine who apparently forgot.

Last year, her twenty-four-year-old on-again-off-again lover threw her a surprise party at the station, but recently, Jasmine had been shunning public appearances.

Francine suspected Jasmine's cause for lying low was Father Possatto reprimanding the two of them before his mega-congregation when they approached communion holding one another's hands.

"Not in God's house, you don't."

Francine refrained from mentioning her suspicion that the aged priest singled them out because Jasmine had begun sporting a crewcut.

Every three or four months, Jasmine would leave a break-up note and crawl back a couple weeks later, smelling of fragrances unlike her own. Most of Francine's friends would have kicked out such a mate, but a noncommittal relationship suited Francine. No permanent mate. No kids. No pets. She was governed by unmitigated devotion to her job, comparable to her commitment to school in early life. Growing up, she felt little allegiance to family and friends. That changed after serving four years in the National Guard, learning to depend upon and protect others.

As Francine passed the detective desks, she paused to decipher one report. She approached Aaron, set down her coffee, and spoke while thumbing through pages. "Precinct Ten, Pier-64-Park Case. I just heard this on TV. Anything I should know?"

Aaron winked. "Happy birthday. Doing anything exciting?"

"At forty-two, all excited horses have left the barn, but thank you. Fill me in."

"There was a card clasped in the victim's hands." Aaron forked over evidence in an air-tight baggie. "Similar to the card found on Precinct Fifteen's Union-Square case three months ago."

"How similar?"

"Same print. Same lamination. This guy's hands were folded as if he were already laid out in a casket. Same with the Union-Square fellow."

"Who in the tenth is lead detective?"

"Sergeant Garfield."

"Did Garfield trace the source of the card?"

"I did." Prepared and eager as a boy scout, Aaron referred to his notepad. "Avery 8371 business cards for home printers: $5.27 at Office Max. Epson Xp-4105 all-in-one color inkjet printer: $69 at Walmart. Scotch Thermal Laminator from Amazon: $29. All of those in tens of thousands of homes and offices."

"Any cell phone on the body?"

"According to Garfield, it's likely swimming with the fishes on the bottom of the Hudson—and that's a quote."

Francine tapped a knuckle against her lower teeth.

Aaron sighed. "I know what follows teeth tapping."

"I'll oversee Garfield. You assist. Have Garfield call me."

As Francine disappeared into her office, Aaron groaned. "Damn it. Yanked out from under me." Paraphrasing his mother's favorite Commodores' song, he sang beneath his breath, "Once, twice, three times a lady thief."

Francine read and re-read the message on the laminated, business-size card. *And He substituted a ram in place of Isaac and destroyed the array of Sennacherib.*

She googled *Sennacherib* and mumbled aloud her discovery. "King of the Neo-Assyrian Empire ... destroyed Babylon ... murdered by his two sons."

Aaron trudged into Francine's office while a gaggle of nosy detectives gaped. He flopped a file onto her desk. "Tox report."

"Remind me who Isaac is."

"Abraham's son. God asked Abraham to sacrifice his only son."

"Rings a bell," Francine said.

"But instead, Abraham sacrificed a ram. That's the total of what I remember from Sunday School. Don't tell my mother."

"What about your wife?"

"I'd be dead meat."

"Uh huh."

Aaron squeezed his nose between his thumb and finger, his habit when eager to change topics. "This guy and the Union-Square fellow have the same tox profile."

Francine skimmed the tox graphs. "Carfentanil?"

"Super toxic fentanyl. Ten-thousand times stronger than morphine. Vets anesthetize large animals with it. Shoot darts at tigers, elephants."

"A veterinarian serial killer? That would be one for the books."

"Rivers of carfentanil precursors are flowing through Chinese markets. Every other crook has a recipe. Russians sprayed it as an aerosol to quickly end the 2002 Moscow Theatre Crisis. Death count: one-hundred-twenty-five."

Francine's left eyebrow raised. "Aerosol?"

"Maybe both these fellows got powder on their skin."

"Fentanyl isn't absorbed through skin. That's a TV myth."

Aaron pointed to the bottom of the page. "Traces on his lips. Along with chocolate icing. Maybe he ate it."

"A deadly drug in the icing? Hm. Could be an accident. More likely suicide or homicide."

"Fingerprint data identified the new victim as a student from Italy. Two cases, two men, similar ages. Casual dress. Two different New York parks."

Francine circled her desk. "Additional victims may have ingested this drug." She sat with a blank look as if they had never been engaged in conversation. "Hm." The few seconds of silence catapulted her into obsessing about Jasmine. At least homicide cases plucked her away from mundane domestic problems. Jasmine's new habit of huffing, "whatever," albeit annoying, could not compete with last week's grandmother with bound hands and sliced throat. And yet, today on her birthday, *whatever* was haunting her.

Aaron squirmed as if eager to punch an elevator button a third time to hasten its arrival. He yelled back while exiting, "I'm taking your 'Hm' to be a go-search directive."

Francine fixated on the plastic-veiled card, pondering why the word *He* was capitalized. The pronoun didn't appear to refer to God. If her Bible-thumping grandmother were still alive, she would explain, apologize for mankind, and conclude with a prayer.

Francine leaned her forehead against her window and stared at the colossal city's skyline, thinking someone is feeding Chinese toxins to New Yorkers. And maybe *He* is responsible.

Suddenly, Aaron and the other detectives entered, followed by Jasmine carrying a cake with lighted candles. Despite being a diverse group, not one serenader could carry a tune.

Francine was not about to reveal she had obsessed that Jasmine had forgotten.

Jasmine aimed a finger at her. "You thought I forgot, didn't you?" She turned to Aaron. "Francine thought I forgot, didn't she?"

There was no way Aaron would side with either woman. He had learned from lessons when his sister and wife asked loaded questions, it is best to simply shrug.

"You did," Jasmine said and held out the cake for Francine to blow out a dozen finger-nail-size flames.

ELISABET

Another dragon was slain. It was time for Elisabet to perform a walk-through of her Manhattan condo. Everything was in perfect order. She glanced back for one last appraisal: heart-shaped wicker baskets, pumpkin scented candles, silk peony bouquets, vegetable-dyed patchwork quilts draped on a vintage-flower couch. She was under no illusion that her fake-country gest offered a genuine experience. A stage-or-movie-set decorator would have declared the scene: *inauthentic.* Elisabet's attention to detail, however, had triumphed for two months in bamboozling the wanna-be-cowboy bachelor she had targeted.

Elisabet had bewitched Beniamino by transforming her jet-black hair into a blond bouffant with bangs and fabricating a Nashville twang peppered heavily with diphthongs. She even developed the ability to speak *one* as two syllables, altering her pitch like a saxophonist slurring two notes.

Elisabet's candy-striper dress of pink and white seersucker stripes, her white-lace apron, and her avouchment that her outfit resembled, "Grandmommie in the kitchen baking buttered rolls," had added crowning touches to execute her seduction.

Nineteen-year-old Beniamino had come from Salerno, Italy to Columbia University on a mathematics scholarship. His heart, however, shrouded hopes of one day moving westward, acquiring a ranch, becoming a cowboy, and settling down with a woman possessing the virtues of the Midwest mother he had yearned for in reruns of *Happy Days*—a much younger woman, of course.

In addition to horses and cattle, he daydreamed of haggling for a Triumph Trophy 500 cycle to straddle like his hero, The Fonz. Beniamino suffered intruding concern that if Fonzie had excelled in math, the leather-jacketed fellow would have followed a Richie-Cunningham trajectory, become a dull accountant, failed at life like Beniamino obsessed was his doomed destiny.

In his early teens, Beniamino had labored to perfect the art of being cool, boosting his Italian accent and over-spending on fashion-model threads to be irresistible to American-tourist signorinas as well as dissatisfied signoras. He had no doubt they craved for him to seduce them, interpreting their body language as begging him for sex.

Elisabet had been the storybook realization of his dreams, walking into his life in the library, a country girl strolling through sophisticated Columbia University, stirring a feeling in him that they were destined to meet.

Now that Beniamino was gone from her life, Elisabet was relieved. She had tired of faking a country-music persona.

She online-shopped condos and phoned her go-to seller-realtor, Karol Whaanga, to flip the country-style residence. Surely, people moving to the Big Apple from Tennessee or bordering states would be thrilled to discover a city abode resonating with a rural, grandparented childhood, no matter how phony. If it did not sell and remained empty, it was of no consequence; her trustee funds were unfathomable.

She slammed the door behind her, strolling into the stage wings of the next play.

What would her curtain rise on next? The staged home of a displaced, discounted wife of a Russian oligarch? A double agent? An equestrian? A beach-volleyball champ?

A computer geek? No. Not that last choice. She had once performed that role.

As dusk settled, Elisabet entered St. Michael's Episcopal Church on 99th Street and Amsterdam. She gazed up at a Tiffany stained-glass pane: *St. Michael's Victory in Heaven*. She was absorbed by St. Michael basking before God in glory after he had cast down the seven-headed beast of darkness.

She had learned to wait until the church emptied before entering to claim the shards of colored glass for herself, apprehensive whether St. Michael would bless or discount her choice for the next dragon to cast down.

Beniamino had been her fourth dragon. She was eager to cast down three more for a total of seven, cognate with seven heads of the beast. But of course, she could only speculate about the saint's masterplan, about what he would bless or condemn.

Tonight, while praying, she begged for protection while eliminating another Satan acolyte. Her prayer was interrupted by a loud crash as something struck the stained-glass window. She first thought that a bird or a stray pitch from a game of catch had slammed into the window, but then realized a truth: St. Michael was pleased with her recent success.

She lumbered onto the street. The night sky was a patchwork of city-lit, orange-grey clouds alternating with patches of deep black space studded with stars.

Tomorrow, she would browse Manhattan bars, scour faces, and initiate small talk with lone and misfit men. Browse the New York Public Library. Sit in the back of cinemas on 42nd Street. Picnic in Central Park. Concoct stories about the men's abominable pasts that grew them into dragons. Although tempted, her standard was to refrain from acting until a target had been clearly identified and blessed for sacrifice.

She heard footsteps following her and pivoted to face the suspected danger, sliding her hand into her coat pocket to assure her combination-tactical-pen-and switchblade was available. The sounds, however, came from a man in his eighties limping with a hip replacement, struggling to maintain balance. Elisabet paused to watch the senior citizen cross the street, making it to the other side seconds before two revved cars with blacked-out windows raced one another over the crosswalk as if it were a NASCAR finish line.

Elisabet preceded onward, feeling spirited that once she identified a worthy beast, she could return to the sanctuary, report to St. Michael, and await his blessing or forbiddance.

KAROL

Realtor Karol Whaanga received Elisabet's call to sell a fourth condo. Karol had never met Elisabet in person. They only associated through phone calls. She only knew Elisabet by the name she gave on the phone: Azza Thornton. All monies were deposited into accounts using that name.

Four months ago, during their third phone conversation, Karol had broached the topic of the elaborately clashing styles of Elisabet's condos. Elisabet's voice had become as frigid as a cold-blooded soap-opera villain. Today, Karol treaded on eggshells, cloaking her curiosity.

Karol detested undeserved, harsh reprimands, recalling childhood memories when her second-grade teacher summoned her to the front of class, slapped the desk with her ruler, and screamed, "Cheater." Not true, but as a child, whenever Karol was confronted, she held her tongue and wet herself. As a grownup, when confronted by loud adult tirades, her husband, Sol, had coached her to absorb fumbling assailants' tantrums as gifts, view them as fodder for studying wishes, goals, and maturity—or lack of. Her Māori husband, Sol, had been the most peaceful and handsome man she had known.

Although Elisabet's theatrical condo designs seemed bizarre, Karol was more perplexed—even alarmed—that the three previous times Elisabet requested her to sell a condo, her phone numbers differed. The three times Elisabet instructed Karol where to mail checks, the PO boxes differed. Today was a fourth phone number and a fourth PO box.

Karol had twice attempted to call Elisabet, but

automated messages announced the phone numbers were inactive. Burner phones? Of course, she would never ask.

Her suspicion warned of unscrupulous issues, but unlike her pre-real-estate life of chasing all things curious, these days, she worked overtime to ignore clues and allow others to unravel mysteries. Mostly.

Was Azza—if that actually was her name—a drug dealer? A whore? On the lam? Karol googled the name. Azza was listed as an Arabic, Hebrew, and Urdu name. She even hit upon a male rapper named Azza.

Karol's phone rang, interrupting her obsessing about her mercurial customer. It was her son's school. Karol explained Bram was absent due to a stomach ache, but the call was about more than today's absence.

She marched into Bram's room where her thirteen-year-old lay with his pillow hugged around his head. She was certain he had overheard her conversation and would fake he was clueless.

"Bram. That was Principal Breitenstein."

A smothered groan sounded beneath the pillow.

"I can't understand you. Sit up."

Bram removed the pillow and sat up as slowly as their Labradoodle Betsy approaching when scolded.

"Principal Breitenstein said you are disrespectful with your math teacher."

"Ms. Critcher is an imbecile."

"Because?"

"She yells at me to write out all my reasoning in solving her stupid equations. I told her I do it in my head and get the right answers one-hundred percent, but she screamed that I'm inappropriate. Threatened to fail me. I wrote out an equation and asked her to solve it in her head."

"Did she solve your equation?"

"Are you kidding? But don't worry. I only thought what

I wanted to call her. I never said it out loud."

Karol thought about how she had been a timid student, but that Bram took after his father. Whether deceased or missing, either way, Sol was not present to help with parent-child dissensions.

"I have to take the train into Manhattan and assess a condo. You're going with me."

Bram wrapped the pillow around his head. "I'm sick."

"Uh huh. And as soon as I leave, you'll be well enough to stray. Get dressed."

Much like a child ripping paper off a gift, Karol was eager to behold the style of the fourth condo, certain it would be extravagant, dramatic, humorous, entertaining, or all of those.

She tried to imagine what Azza looked like. The woman's accent wandered. In college, Karol had taken a theatre course led by an excellent voice coach. New York was a fascinating mine of accents. Today, Azza's accent had a hint of deep South. Four months ago, a tinge of Parisian. Prior to that, Azza had vocalized a Seattle accent and later a San Diego accent. Most people could not distinguish the difference, but Karol could.

She had become interested in accents during college when a nose-pierced sorority girl heard Karol's Brooklyn accent and whined, "Why can't all Americans speak English the way it's supposed to be spoken like Californians do?" Karol chuckled, feeling proud she had been assertive, even before marrying Sol. "I'll quiz Queen Elizabeth about that and get back to you." The girl's grimace had asked, *who the hell are you*, and had pulled both feet up onto her chair, signaling, *we're through.*

Karol was spellbound by the fourth condo. She thought it looked staged for *Southern Living Magazine*. Or a house trailer forced to look like a dollhouse antebellum parlor.

Bram held up a black-faced, red-haired Raggedy Ann doll. "What's this?"

"Something racist from past eras. Put it back."

"You'll never sell this place with that creepy thing staring at people." Bram stuffed the relic into a trash bin.

Similar to the previous three residences, sheets, towels, washcloths, dishes, glasses, utensils, pots, and pans remained. Unwrapped new bars of soap, new rolls of toilet paper, and little bottles of shampoos sat on bathroom shelves. Rugs had been vacuumed and floors mopped, but neither a vacuum cleaner nor a mop was to be found. She thought, Azza must have hired hotel-type cleaners.

Although clean, walking through Elisabet's condos made Karol feel fouled, a second sense she would have honed in on in her past, questioning the precise reasons. But thirteen years ago, she had chosen to shelve over-active curiosity and focus on real estate.

This dwelling, like two previous condos located in Manhattan neighborhoods, was near a park and facing west. She asked herself, what's special about facing westward? New Jersey?

She searched closets, shelves, cabinets, and beneath furniture for left-behind objects. Nothing.

Being a single parent who felt unflinching duty to shield her only child, Karol felt icky about exposing Bram to such enigmatic bailiwick.

Bram reported he sensed a spell hanging over the indecorous chambers. "This lady's like guilty of a major crime or like an accomplice to something that's like super evil."

"Don't be silly, honey. She's a tad unusual, but she sounds very sweet on the phone."

Bram grimaced as if his mother had screeched her

fingernails across a chalk board. "Right. You think everybody's sweet."

Karol flung open the curtains and allowed west sunlight to stream through the bedroom window. Moments earlier, when she had peered beneath the bed, she had not restored the bedspread to cover the side.

With sunlight spotlighting the bed, Bram detected something glittering where a bed slat joined the frame.

Upon inspection, it was a St. Christopher medal. Its chain was lodged in a breach. He tugged it free and held up the medal for sunlight to divulge a well-worn name on the backside. *Beniamino.*

Before his mother noticed, he pocketed the charm.

CENTER STAGE

Eleven women sat in a folding-chair circle on the stage of a shuttered theatre. Stretched extension cords supplied electricity to a half-dozen antique pole lamps that cast silhouettes onto a crumbling-brick upstage wall. If someone were to view the scene from the slanted, seatless auditorium, one might suspect that either a reading or a rehearsal of a gothic play was transpiring.

Elisabet entered late with her head wrapped in a solid black scarf and her body covered in an ankle-length black dress that others assumed she had inherited from past generations or had purchased for a few dollars at a thrift shop. Her black slippers appeared scuffed and formless as if a ballerina had discarded them into a trash dumpster after a thousand-too-many performances.

No one in the group had heard her voice other than her infrequent mumbles of, "terrible" and "unforgiveable." She always departed as the others began taking a break for bottled water and oatmeal cookies, turning her head downward enough that she appeared to be nothing more than a heap of moving black cloth.

It was impossible for anyone to identify her. No one knew her name, age, or details of her life, just that she attended every third or fourth weekly meeting of their group: The Daughters of Boudicca. They assumed she valued something from their gatherings and discussions as much as do silent people sitting on park benches year after year, devolving to become park scenery as much as the statues.

Lavender stood to present material she had scribbled in her decades-old Columbia University notebook. No one questioned if Lavender was her official name. Many participants elected to remain anonymous.

Lavender waved her notebook with slow deliberation as if it were a heavy book full of sacred commandments. "This information was passed along to me by my sister-in-law in Chicago."

She dragged her finger from line to line as she spoke. "My sister-in-law's daughter is a freshman studying at Loyola University, majoring in theology and considering to become a nun. A man earning his masters in theology there, had a reputation for luring young freshman and sophomore women into getting severely drunk, having his way with them, and bragging to his buddies about his conquests. She heard rumors that the man also siphoned money from church donations to support his lavish lifestyle. He completed his masters in theology and is now here in New York in a Catholic seminary. One of my niece's older friends is now here and reported that this same man, a deacon, who can fake being charming, seduced one of the few women admitted to the seminary. He takes photos of his passed-out victims, including my niece. He threatened to post the compromised photos if anyone reported him. One of my niece's former classmates took that news hard. Killed herself."

"Awful," Elisabet murmured with her hands veiling her eyes.

No one spoke for several minutes. "Criminal behavior," Lavender said.

"Complicated to prove," another woman said. "We know how that goes. Nothing ends up being done."

A self-appointed leader asked, "Is this criminal immersing himself in a local church community?"

"I have his information here." Lavender circulated one-page flyers. "His name, address, and the name of the church. He should be easy to find."

Another woman glanced at the leaflet and nodded satisfaction. "The heads of this church may ignore us, but when members of the congregation read these flyers, they won't."

"Thank you, Lavender," the leader said. "Who wants to report next?"

Florence, a new member of the group, raised her hand, speaking too softly in the manner people whisper the word *cancer* as if normal-volume speech would cause the disease to spread.

Lavender appeared annoyed as she strained to hear. "Please, speak up, Florence. I know this is your first presentation, but some of us have poor hearing."

Florence cleared her throat and began again. "A woman in my building confessed to me that her husband ties her to the bedposts. He threatens to hit her if she refuses to cooperate. He has his way with her by … by you know … from … from behind. He's rough. Injures her. She never complains to him. She refuses to allow doctors to examine her."

Group moans emitted from the attendees.

After much thought, the leader spoke. "This sounds like a situation that is suited for a domestic abuse team. Social workers can offer refuge while legal possibilities are explored."

While another presenter began sharing a report from a Daughters of Boudicca branch in New Orleans, Florence, feeling embarrassed that her report had been brushed aside, excused herself from the room.

As other women talked, Elisabet glanced at the vacated chair. Florence had left behind a flyer. Elisabet had come late to the gathering and missed discussion of the man identified in the flyer. She read about Ernest Farthing from Alabama. Two women had claimed that when they were juniors in high-school, Ernest had led them beneath the football-game bleachers and forced them to perform oral sex on him.

Elisabet slid the flyer beneath her robe-like clothing and blended into the theatre's shadows as if by magic she had come from nowhere and returned to nowhere.

SILENT MUSE

Dressed in blue jeans and a leather jacket, Elisabet slipped into the back pew of St. Michael's and scowled at an altar boy on the church dais replacing each individual candle on a legion of candelabras. The nine-year-old boy's meticulousness annoyed Elisabet.

She was eager to approach her beloved stained-glass St. Michael in private and reveal news of the man identified to her in the group discussion.

The boy was undermining her design. She wanted to snap her fingers and make him vanish.

Foremost in her thinking, was the image of the young Catholic deacon on his way to achieving full-fledged priesthood. Targeting him was a wise choice in many ways. In addition to the man deflowering potential nuns, she sensed St. Michael must feel aggrieved about modern clergy stuffing their own pockets with God's money.

As a child, Elisabet had traveled with her grandmother to visit lavish cathedrals and museums in New York and throughout Europe. Most dispiriting was St. Peter's Basilica in Vatican City, the biggest blemish, a spit into God's eyes. Or so, her grandmother had pontificated.

Gargantuan, palace-like buildings housed statues and paintings of people wailing and contorting while nailed to crosses and tortured in the flaming netherworld. The images had infiltrated Elisabet's childhood sleeping and waking hours.

Nothing her family offered palliated her agony, until one day in the Louvre, her grandmother nodded at Raphael's painting of St. Michael slaying the dragon, his foot crushing the dragon's neck as he raised his sword to the sky. Her grandmother had seated her on a bench and wrapped her arm around Elisabet. "He fights for keeping you and me, good people safe, holding evil at bay, serving God's will."

Upon return to her parents' home on Long Island, she had built a secret altar in her closet to her protector.

Once the earth rotated enough that sunlight ceased backlighting church windows, the altar boy appeared blissful—until he spotted Elisabet. He began dawdling like a reluctant captive marching to the guillotine, not walking down the aisle as do high-spirited folks initiating a wedding, but up the aisle as do snobbish relatives at weddings' conclusions, holding chins too high, showing off privilege as they depart first, forcing others to wait and watch.

He gloated as he forced Elisabet to wait and watch. She had intruded upon his privacy, and as he neared, he glared into her. A game ensued of who could best stare daggers at the other with unrivaled disdain. The boy passed her, paused at the bright red front door, and glowered back.

Elisabet turned her back on him and waited until she heard the door click. She rushed to the altar balustrade and knelt.

With no doubt of the superiority of her sacrificial selection for her archangel, she hurried through her presentation of describing the deacon. At conclusion, she appeared as pleased as a maestro completing the best rendering ever of Beethoven's *Hammerklavier Sonata*, anticipating thunderous acclamation.

But the sanctum remained hushed.

She waited longer, pulling at hair strands of her newest wig.

Still, the vast hall remained quiet.

Elisabet was dumbfounded. She was certain she had

identified a worthy beast, one that deserved more than being exposed by a one-page leaflet listing his transgressions. Was her beloved Michael forsaking her?

Rejection gnawed at her until she remembered Florence's flyer in her jacket: Ernest Farthing and the accosted high-school girls. She clutched the flyer, turned to St. Michael, and closed her eyes in prayer. "Please inform me if this other man is a worthy beast. Do I have your blessing to seek out this creature from Alabama?"

For minutes, she remained kneeling with eyes closed until hearing a clamor above and behind.

She looked upward and spotted a pigeon trapped in the vaulted ceiling. The panicked bird was flapping its wings so fiercely that feathers were dislodging and floating to earth. The bird suddenly calmed and sat upon a beam.

The young man from Alabama, she thought. This bird may be a sign, but a hesitant sign, a weaker sign than I am accustomed. I feel cast off, Michael, but I'll seek out this sinner and pray you come to me with a clearer blessing.

She exited, but unlike the altar boy, she accelerated along the carpeted path, shoving open the red door so fiercely that it banged against the outer stone wall. She fled, feeling unfulfilled and bewailing as much as a jilted bride.

SEEKING A DRAGON
- October 2021 -

Elisabet, choosing to dress as nondescript as possible, followed Ernest Farthing, a young, clean-cut business-type leaving his work and proceeding to the Regal Cinemas Complex on 42nd Street. She waited for him to exit, tailed him to 10th Avenue, a right turn north, and watched him descend into a basement club, Bare Marlon's. She gawked at a poster of two men, naked except for white T-shirts. They were piggybacking on a small motorcycle, a moped even smaller than a Harley Davidson Sportster. The rear guy's bare butt cheeks were drooping off the slender seat.

The venue's subterranean steps were guarded by an offensive-tackle-size bouncer dressed in drag. Hair puffed higher than Elisabet's previous blond bouffant. Enough eye shadow for a clown.

Rather than disappointment, Elisabet laughed out loud. This guy definitely was not Ernest. He could not possibly be the beast Florence's flyer had identified nor the man she had followed to the cinema. All the same, she had been smitten by this young man wearing no tie and his top shirt button fastened. She thought how her keen intuition should have flagged he was the wrong guy, gay or insecure and working overtime to impress. Oh well. He would never know what smutty fun he had missed or that he had escaped death by drugs.

She retraced her steps to the cinema and stared across the street at men exiting a triple-X-rated movie house. The flickering marquee stated *Navy Sluts* was playing, starring Gloria Titts. She fantasized how that would be an exciting role for herself. She scrutinized the poster.

Woman in a white jacket with navy-blue epaulettes. Brass buttons. White skirt. Fashionably short hair. Clean scrubbed face except for the lightest touch of lipstick and eyeshadow. A serious frown announcing, *no crap from you guys.*

Suddenly, well-groomed, mid-twenties Ernest exited the Regal and strolled across the street and into the plaster-cracked movie house. His head was bowed as if saddled with guilt his grandmother might catch him.

Was he theatre hopping? Maybe he became horny watching the single-X-rated movie at the Regal and began craving a triple-X flick.

She would wait him out. Triple-X movies were certainly not epics.

After twenty minutes, beneath the marquee missing every other lightbulb, a trio of young military men emerged. The threesome behaved as if on shore leave after being cooped up in a submarine with too little oxygen for too many months. Intoxicated. Slapping one another on the backs. Yelling as if trying to surmount battlefield gunfire and screeching aircraft furor. "Can you believe what Titts could do with her tongue?" "She can tongue me any time she wants." "I've had better." "You're full of crap."

Elisabet had her fill of the sots, feeling relieved when her target exited the movie house. Whether St. Michael had given her a clear sign or not, she was drawn to the shamed lad and followed him.

The potential swain continued walking with head low, leaving behind the three partiers staggering into the nearest pub.

Elisabet's beast entered a Hell's Kitchen beer, wings, and pizza joint with a few outside tables, a small inside bar for takeout, and a half-dozen empty booths. Business was predominantly takeout with enough standing room for a dozen patrons to splatter pizza sauce on themselves, enjoying they had purposefully strayed from the formal theatre district and landed in a real-New-York-City experience.

Ernest placed his order and sat in a booth.

Elisabet approached. "Are you familiar with the food here?"

Ernest jarred as if his little sister had walked in on him misbehaving in a bathroom. "Uh … Yeah." And then rapidly added, "I live around the block."

"What's tasty?" Elisabet asked. "I'm meeting a friend. She's in the Marines. She's late and I'm starved. My first trip to the Big Apple."

"Oh … Uh …" Ernest blushed and Elisabet surmised she had transported him back to earlier moments lusting for nude and compromised Gloria Titts.

Still staring at the table top with hands in pockets, Ernest mumbled, "New York pizza. Can't go wrong."

"Do you come here often?"

"Uh … Every couple days. So, pretty often … I guess."

"What do you recommend?"

"They have one of New York's rare coal-fired ovens. Makes crusts crispy. Generous olive oil going in, coming out. Pepperoni and mushroom toppings. Simple. Nothing fancy."

"Simple. Not fancy. Sounds like me."

Ernest looked up. "Pardon?"

"I teach third grade. But my friend, Marguerite, is in the Marines. I'm simple. She's complex. Makes for a perfect friendship. She's a little loose if you know what I mean."

The lad perked up.

"She should be here by now. You look like someone who

would fancy military women."

Ernest's sudden sweating revealed Elisabet had again cued him to relive hot moments of *Navy Sluts*. He mumbled, "Uh … Guess so. Depends on the woman, I guess."

"Simple or complex?"

"What do you mean?"

"Simple women or complex women? Which is your preference?"

"Uh … Never thought about it."

Sure you haven't, Elisabet thought. The abuser of girls beneath football bleachers is playing innocent. But I know his type. She leaned down, forcing eye contact. "Have you ordered?"

He held up his ticket. "Seventy-six."

"Takeout or inhouse?"

"Uh … I ordered a beer. Drink it here. Eat here."

"Sounds good. Think I'll do the same."

Elisabet paused, waiting for an invitation. The invitation never came.

She pictured her new hair style: short and dirty blonde or brown. Minimal makeup. Marine uniform.

Tomorrow, she could check out a book on Marine women. Had to be Marines, not Navy. Even if this guy is a sinful beast, he desires to be directed—commanded.

Googling would probably be sufficient.

She would follow Ernest again from his office. This already was fun.

She departed without a salutation.

RUG-RATS OR ANGELS

In the past, it had become customary for the station detectives to come alive whenever Jasmine strolled into their nest, smiling and winking at the cluster of men and women.

The detectives always appeared mesmerized as if a celebrity dressed for a gala had made a grand entrance, expecting them to yell comments from the sidelines.

"Hi there, sunshine. What's up? "Wow. I adore the new hair glitter highlighting your crew cut." "What did we do right to earn this honor of your company?" "Help yourself to fresh baked cookies celebrating Freddy's promotion."

Today, however, looking preoccupied and withholding usual pleasantries, Jasmine maintained a tight grin and waded past her admirers.

Francine's door was ajar. Jasmine faintly knocked, cautiously opened the door as if it were booby trapped, and checked to assure Francine was alone and not on the phone. Without looking back, she gently pushed the door closed with the heel of her pink and aqua sneaker.

"Well," Francine said with a warm smile, remaining seated at her desk. "Didn't expect a midtown visit today."

"I was thinking."

"Uh oh."

"We've been together how long?"

"Twenty-three months as of yesterday—off and on."

Jasmine took in a deep breath before announcing, "I think it's time we consider having a child."

Francine reacted to the unbroached topic as if someone had dropped barbells onto her chest. She was barely able to breath in and out to speak. "What?"

Francine's startled response alerted Jasmine to tread

cautiously. "Before you say anything, think about it. You and I adore all our friends' children."

"You adore them. I tolerate them."

"You always look like you adore them."

"Look like. To make our friends feel good."

Jasmine sat to think for a moment, and then crossed her legs and straightened her back as if she were a TV guest seizing control of a talk show. "Are you saying you fake it?"

"Uh … not a kind way to put it. But in a nutshell, yep. I fake it."

"Wow. Not what I expected."

Both women focused on objects in the room rather than one another.

Jasmine eventually stood and broke the silence. "Don't concern yourself. You'll never have to lift a finger. All I ask is that you tolerate my child. I had pictured us raising a child together, but I guess that's out. I'll do it solo while you stand on the sidelines and fake you adore my child."

Francine rocked back in her tilt chair, her standard position for taking command of office situations. "You need to think this through practically."

"Absolutely I did. I'm twenty-four. I'm not waiting longer. I'm ready now."

"I'm forty-two and childless. Not because I'm waiting, but because my job demands too much to wake in the middle of the night to feed or rock a rug rat."

"Rug rat? Well, this is going downhill fast." Jasmine censored herself from spitting out expletives she was thinking and paced the well-worn carpet path in the center of the office. "You won't be bothered to feed or rock anyone. I'll be responsible for all childcare chores. I'll love and dote on the child I'm raising. But never again refer to my angel with an ugly word or tone. Got that?"

"It's obvious you are skimming over reality. You are around the house far less than I am."

"Completely false. You're not home enough to know when I am or am not home. You're out loving that you get to chase New York's vermin."

"You should keep a calendar. Chart your activities. Pubs. Nightclubs. The women you sleep with, coming home smelling of cheap perfume."

"Oh my God. Are you accusing me of being unfaithful?"

Francine bit her lip and remained motionless.

Jasmine placed her hand on the doorknob. "I'm going to raise a child and you can either deal with it or toss us onto the street. Your choice."

"And exactly how are you going to do that? Have a child?"

"Really? Well, let's see. I could adopt. Or I could find a surrogate father—artificially or jump in the sack with one of my many man friends who would be more than happy to share a bed for the one-night deed."

"Share a bed? Oh. And I guess you would make sure you didn't enjoy the deed. No passion. No sweet talk. Just fucking."

Jasmine froze as do defendants on the stand when prosecutors attack with blindsiding evidence. "My child will share my DNA. That removes adoption from my list. I want to know exactly who the father is. That removes anonymous sperm donors from my list. I have handsome men friends with solid DNA. Men who would create a fantastic child with me, directly or indirectly."

"Let's sit down and talk this through calmly. Go across the street and grab a drink and talk."

"I'm through talking with you about necessities of my heart."

Jasmine yanked open the door forcefully enough that it

slammed against the doorstop. She stomped through the station, stupefying her fan club with her reddened face, pout, and swift exit.

Francine quietly closed her door as station detectives shrugged to one another, all thinking it would be wise to avoid Francine for a lengthy period of the day.

Or days.

MUSEUMS ARE TEMPLES

Dressed in her Marine dress uniform, Elisabet strolled through the cloisters of the Metropolitan Museum of Art, remembering visits with her grandmother. Several times, they had gazed at a five-by-six-foot canvas, the 1600's masterpiece: *The Abduction of the Sabine Women.*

Ten-year-old Elisabet had studied the painting at length sitting by her grandmother's side and listening to her story. The women were about to be snatched away and raped by soldiers and by Romulus, the first king of Rome.

Elisabet's grandmother had unveiled a parable while pointing her cane at the vivid figures. "The women were pure in that moment, but within seconds, they would no longer be pure. That quality would be stolen from them as the men had their way with the innocent women, forcing them to do something against their will."

Elisabet felt she had stepped into that painting, similarly to how she felt about a photo in her grandfather's study. It was a famous photo from the Vietnam War in which a young man was being shot by a pistol aimed at his temple. Elisabet had sat on her grandfather's lap as he had said, "That youthful man remained alive for only a split second longer. But that moment is frozen-in-time for you and me to view repeatedly. For as long as we want."

The painting captured women in a pure state and the photo captured a man in an alive state. Both conditions would abruptly end for the people in the art, but the moment of ruin would eternally linger for spectators, solidifying in their minds the very moment they shut their eyes or turned away to disengage.

Both images imprinted in Elisabet, slithering into her memories and nightmares.

Elisabet knew that remembering the excursions with her grandmother and talks with her grandfather would be souring. In preparation, she arrived at the museum ready to soothe herself with art from Florence.

She entered another gallery, sat on a bench, and retrieved her art book from her MET Museum cloth bag, a book of paintings housed in the Uffizzi gallery in Florence.

She turned to where she had bookmarked a particular painting and read the caption. *Judith Beheading Holofernes, a 1600's painting by the woman artist, Artemisia Gentileschi.*

Two women had pinned a man to a bed. Judith was holding the man's head while her maid sliced his throat with a long sword. The man was conscious and open-eyed as his blood dripped and soaked a white sheet.

Although this art also captured an afflicting moment, Elisabet found this art to be alluring. She reviewed the painting's story. *Judith had seduced and pleasured the Assyrian General who had besieged her city. She was plotting to rise up as a warrior and seek revenge.*

Elisabet gently rubbed her fingers over the photo of the painting, feeling grateful to have found a painting that became a muse for her to seek justice in a debauched world.

Once Elisabet felt inspirited, she strolled into another room of the vast complex and sat upon another bench.

Ten-year-old Rhonda stepped away from her fifth-grade classmates and teacher examining a canvas of a woman artist instructing a young girl in art.

Ronda crossed the room and stood beside Elisabet, curious about the uniformed woman.

Ronda inhaled deeply while mustering bravery. "Excuse me, but are you in the Army?"

Elisabet jarred out of her trance. "Oh … Uh … Military yes, but in the Marines."

Rhonda sat beside the woman and stared at the painting of a girl looking at herself in a hand mirror.

Elisabet became intrigued by the girl's lengthy stare. "Do you like this painting?"

"It's dumb."

"Oh? … Why is it dumb?"

Rhonda pointed at the art. "See the girl looking at herself in the mirror? Now look at the girl in the mirror. Her reflection's not looking back at her; it's looking at us."

Elisabet nodded approval. "Good eye. Not everyone spots that detail."

The girl asked, "Who painted that?"

"The artist? A woman two-hundred-or-so years ago. Elisabeth Le Brun. She painted her younger sister."

"Why did she paint her that way?"

Elisabet leaned back, her mind flooding with museum memories. "My grandmother introduced me to this painting. She said that in our heads, we see who we think we are. In mirrors, we see who we are … But sometimes, if we are fortunate, we see beyond."

"In a mirror, you have to see yourself. Right?"

Elisabet paused, recalling fervent outings with her grandmother. "What do you see when you look in a mirror?"

The girl stared at the floor. "The scar on my forehead."

"How did you get that scar?"

"I fell on the ice and slid into my best friend's skate."

"Ouch … Do you see your beautiful, long hair?"

The girl looked at Elisabet and shook her head. "Just the scar."

"Then your girl in the mirror is different from the girl you are. I hope the next time you look in a mirror, you see your lovely hair, see all the beauty you possess."

"What did you see in the mirror?"

"When I was young?"

"Uh huh."

"Well … for a long time, I didn't see anyone. My mirror remained blank."

"But it's a mirror. You have to see something."

"I think your class is leaving."

The girl stood. "Thank you for your service—My dad says I should always thank people in the military."

ADULT CHESS
- January 2022 -

Months later, when Francine entered the nest of detective offices, Aaron greeted her like a doorman standing at attention, disposed to assist. "We have another carfentanil death. Hands clasped around a similar card. This time closer in our backyard. Upper midtown."

"Another pier park?"

"Hudson Park again. Pier 84. Three days ago."

"How long since the Pier 64 homicide?"

"Four months."

"And the Union Square Park case?"

"Four and a half months before that."

Aaron tagged behind Francine as she ambled toward her office, tossing questions over her shoulder. "Why would there be that specific time lapse?"

Aaron relished moments when he accurately anticipated and prepared answers for Francine's rapid-fire questions. "Time enough to groom her victims. Game playing. Teasing them." He was especially fond of springing unforeseen intel. "A Circle Line security camera on Pier 83 captured our victim and a woman staggering into the park, drunk enough to not be wearing their winter coats."

The coup de grâce was being able to slam-dunk a punch line. "The woman holding up the guy, was a Marine."

That fact snatched Francine's breath. "Women Marines? That should narrow our data base."

"Fourteen thousand."

"Thousand? Women made more progress than I realized. What's the nearest Marine base?"

"Not close. Arlington. Quantico. We have two Marine

recruiting stations in Manhattan: Times Square and 125th Street."

"Any facial recognition?"

Aaron shook his head. "It was dusk."

"Nametag?"

"Not recognizable."

"Any women serving at Quantico?"

"At least a hundred. They recently made network news claiming discrimination by the good-ole-boy network."

"Pissed women." Francine stifled a grin, but Aaron saw her suck in her cheeks. Caught.

Francine cleared her throat. "Was our victim military?"

"No. Ernest Farthing. Age twenty-four. Moved from Alabama to New York two years ago. Tenth Avenue near 47th Street." Aaron handed over the victim's biography.

Francine retrieved uncased reading glasses from her jacket pocket and read aloud. "Accounting intern. Metropolitan Tax and Accounting. Broadway near 42nd Street."

"Walking distance from Ernest's apartment." Aaron pointed to a middle paragraph. "Been interning there eight months. Fifty-two employees. We're thinking homicide locations correspond to victims' addresses."

"Description of our woman Marine?"

"Short brown hair. Most likely Caucasian. Typical Marine uniform. Dress. Not combat."

"Coffee shops, bars, ice-cream parlors, porno shops our victim frequented?"

"Pizza joint on Tenth. A dive with gourmet pizza."

"Like most New York pizza," Francine said. "Anyone there remember our woman Marine?"

"It's not kosher, but I dangled a handful of twenties in front of the bastard proprietor. Struck out. Joseph volunteered to have a talk with him out back."

"I won't ask." Francine sighed and stuffed her glasses back into her pocket.

"Learned the woman went by Marguerite." Aaron held out a pencil rendering. "We got a sketch, but any block I walk, a hundred women look like her. Joseph pried out of a pizza chef that Marguerite sounded like she was from Maine—he worked a boat up there one summer."

"Chocolate icing on the victim's lips?"

"Oh yeah. On his fingers too."

"I want this woman found." Francine entered her office, closed the door, and phoned Jasmine. "You wanna help on a case?"

"Three months with your mouth sewed shut and suddenly you want my help? The world must be ending."

"Shut up. I helped your sister last week when you were at a loss."

"You helping me. Not me helping you."

"Do you know any women in the Marine Corps?"

Jasmine couldn't help but chuckle. "No. But I'd love to."

"Behave or I'll hang up. Ever see women in midtown who are Marines?"

"Now and then."

"I think one's poisoning men in Manhattan."

"Does she need help? I have free time."

"Why am I bothering?" Francine asked.

"Because even though you're mad at me, you know I frequent spots you would detest—and of course, I'm smarter than you."

Francine bit her lip, not wanting to encourage another round in the sparring ring. She mumbled, "Drinks at St. Cloud Rooftop? Wear our coats and stray out onto the roof for a winter nighttime view?"

"Wow. Better than make-up sex."

Francine rocked back in her leather tilt chair, smiling

as she savored a moment of Jasmine's voice rejuvenating with playfulness. "Six-thirty?"

"I'll rush out and buy a frilly dress."

"Six-thirty then."

Francine started to hang up before more smart remarks avalanched, but Jasmine squeezed in machine-gun-firing comments. "Ground rules. I won't involve you in having a child. You won't involve me in talk of misfits and scum crawling out of their caves."

T or S

Aaron was at his desk editing an incident report when he spotted Francine balancing an overly full coffee cup. "Hey boss."

As she approached Aaron, Francine sloshed a bit of coffee over the rim. "Please, stop calling me boss."

"It reminds me to be respectful. Here. Look at a summary I'm preparing."

Aaron held out a page. Francine licked coffee off her fingers before accepting it.

Aaron pointed at the second paragraph and Francine read it aloud. "Two of our victims, Union Park and Pier 64, were accused of domestic or sexual abuse but received nothing more than a slap on the hand."

"I couldn't find anything on Ernest T. Farthing on Pier 84." Aaron handed Francine a second page. "However, I was able to dig up dirt on a Mr. Ernest S. Farthing from the same county in Alabama. Police said there were many rumors of him abusing high-school girls. Never any charges. Maybe this case was mistaken identity by our killer. Almost identical names. Two guys from the same county. Cousins maybe."

"Wow." Francine read and reread the second page.

Aaron fidgeted as if urgently needing to relieve himself. "Motive gone awry? What do you think?"

"Our killer could have confused the names. Rather a stretch. But something doesn't follow. All our victims had come from scattered locations, right? It would be impossible for someone to know all of their backgrounds."

Aaron held his breath for a few seconds. "Maybe our killer had access to criminal records."

"But if your assumption is correct, these men didn't

have successful charges against them—at least not that we could find. So … How would someone learn their histories?"

"Not magic," Aaron said. "I called police in their hometowns, home counties, and asked if these guys had anything shady, or suspicious, or anything in common going on that could possibly make them targets."

"Yeah. But you already knew they had been murdered. What if you didn't know that fact? How could you have identified them and learned about them beforehand?"

Aaron paced a circle around Francine. "I couldn't."

Both detectives sighed over hitting another dead end.

"Maybe the worlds just rotten enough," Francine said, "that everyone has something shady in their past."

Aaron had the expression of a little kid at Halloween who had been given advice instead of candy.

Francine always felt bad when she deflated Aaron's idea balloons—which happened routinely.

"Well," Aaron said, "Back to the drawing board."

"Wait." A faint grin spread over Francine's face as if a switched-on light had revealed a clue. "Maybe you're not off base. We just have to ask the right person. I think I know somebody. Can't promise, but let's roll the dice."

A GROUP OUTLIER

Francine invited Jasmine to meet her at a bar where fashions ranged from tuxedos and evening gowns to ripped blue jeans. Ages ranged from looking like they would be required to show IDs for entry into R-rated movies to looking like an assisted living facility had arranged an assisted outing.

"Canadian Whiskey neat," Jasmine said.

Francine held up two fingers to signal the same room-temp drink for herself.

As they raised glasses to toast, Jasmine quickly spit out her thoughts. "To friendship. Despite irreconcilable differences about raising a child and you buying me drinks whenever you want something."

Francine paused, smiled, and before they clinked glasses, said, "I love you always see through me. Makes me feel understood."

They drank and studied eclectic patrons as if just discovering they were not alone.

Francine waited until Jasmine looked into her eyes. "I have a problem."

"I'm so relieved you finally realize that."

"A work problem, smarty. A mystery actually."

"Oh," Jasmine said, making sure she appeared bored.

"There is a woman who kills young men. The young men as it turns out, were abusive to women, which we're pretty sure but not positive may be a motive." Francine leaned back and passed time sipping her iceless drink.

"And?" Jasmine asked. "Am I to cheer or pretend I'm alarmed?"

"Be curious. How could the killer know about abusive histories of men who moved to Manhattan from diverse places scattered around the world? Ranging from Alabama to Italy."

Jasmine waited for Francine to cease sipping and stalling, and then interrupted the tranquil scene. "And that's it? That's your mystery?"

"That's my mystery I cannot solve."

"Have you ever heard of criminal records as I believe you and yours call them?"

"None of these men were ever charged."

"Oh." Jasmine studied two women at the opposite end of the bar, both highly intoxicated with hands roaming all over one another. "There's a group. A group of women who meet regularly. Trade information about abusive assholes whom no one in the ranks of the law gives a fuck. And so, those men believe they are sanctioned to continue their habits."

"A group?"

"A secret group."

"Does this group have a name?"

Jasmine tried to stifle a grin but gave way to chuckling. "A secret name."

"And have you attended this group?"

"Months back. Once. It was too depressing. Women wallowing in misery." Jasmine shuddered. "I never returned."

"Any idea how we could get eyes and ears into this group?"

"The women in this group are not killers. They're not mean. They're nice. Everyday people who want the world to know."

"The world?"

"Work places. Schools. Voters. Yes. The world."

"And what if a not-nice person infiltrated this nice group?"

Jasmine took time to think about that. "Such as your killer?"

Both women sipped in silence, having no ice in their drinks to swish and clink.

They signaled for a second round.

A PEAK BEHIND THE CURTAIN

Francine was accustomed to sighting Father Cardoza wearing his Roman collar at departmental dinners, funerals, and baptisms. She was discombobulated when the former basketball Goliath and former Special Forces icon greeted Aaron and her at the precinct, wearing an official blue jacket with NYPD insignia. It struck her that if she could talk this behemoth servant of God into accompanying her on missions, dressed in police attire, desperadoes would melt into the pavement.

Francine turned to find Aaron standing, mouth agape like a four-year-old spying his Marvel hero. Within a second, he blurted, "Oh my God. You have to have played football or basketball—or both."

Francine wanted to duck beneath a table.

Father Cardoza replied with deadpan face and low voice. "I bowled on my high school bowling team."

"Oh." Aaron stared at his feet. "Yeah. That's good. Grandmom took me bowling a couple of times. Good sport."

Forget the table. Francine now desired to crawl beneath the floor boards.

"Both," Father Cardoza whispered.

"Both what?" Aaron asked.

"In college, both football and basketball. All conference championship." He chuckled. "Sorry. Couldn't resist."

Aaron's face reddened. "I knew it."

"Now," Cardoza said, turning to Francine, "I understand you have questions about a biblical story."

Francine motioned for the two men to follow her to an interview room and sit. She set a photo on the table of the laminated card found on the Pier 84 victim.

Only requiring a glance, Cardoza nodded. "These scrambled fragments refer to an archangel, St. Michael. As legends go, he aided Abraham to spare his son by substituting a ram for Isaac. Other versions tell of Abraham having the character to spare his own son. Many stories, many variations."

Cardoza pointed at the last phrase. "This refers to King Sennacherib. Historical data confirm Sennacherib was a powerful king of the Neo-Assyrian Empire. He destroyed the fabled and archeologically studied city of Babylon. He further besieged Jerusalem, the ruling city in the Kingdom of Judah. But this note found on your victims contrasts historical evidence, suggesting that *He*, meaning St. Michael, destroyed the powerful ruler before he had a chance to approach Jerusalem, an idea consistent with ancient Judean texts. Judeans were resolute to have the cosmos remember events in their favor, demonstrate they were powerful. Archeological research, however, shows that unlike the myth, Jerusalem was indeed surrounded by King Sennacherib, trapping the inhabitants like caged birds while he laid waste to the surrounding countryside. King Sennacherib lived to rule a vast empire—until two of his sons murdered him. He died at the hands of family, not God's archangel St. Michael."

Francine pointed at the card. "Why is the *He* capitalized?"

Both Cardoza's mouth and eyes smiled. "Ah. *He* is capitalized for God as well as all archangels. *He* in this conflation of ideas, represents St. Michael, the archangel who cast Satan out of Heaven, Satan who is sometimes referred to as the beast or the dragon. A dragon sometimes artfully depicted with seven heads."

"Wow," Aaron muttered, like a child amazed by

grandpa's bedtime whoppers. "Seven heads on one dragon."

Francine tapped Aaron's arm to shush him. "Where might we seek St. Michael?"

"You'll find the chief of all angels and archangels in Revelations 12:7-12. Battling with Satan."

Aaron appeared disappointed. "Oh. In the Bible."

"Well," Cardoza said, "there are churches around the globe named for St. Michael. Two here in Manhattan. One with stunning Tiffany glass windows depicting the angel of angels."

BLAKE POLISHES THE BRASS

After an unfruitful investigation of The Roman Catholic Church of St. Michael on 34th Street, and learning that St. Michael's Academy for girls on 33rd Street had closed in 2010, Francine and Aaron headed north to 99th Street.

On the drive, Francine noticed Aaron dozing off. "This case keeping you awake at night?"

Aaron snapped to. "Oh. Sorry." He rubbed his eyes. "Colt woke me several times last night."

"Three years old. Isn't that old enough to sleep through the night?"

"Not when an older sister shows him dad's old DVD of *Superman*. He repeatedly asked to watch baby Superman lift the Kent-family car and then ran around wearing a towel cape, upset he couldn't lift furniture. Nothing I said consoled him—or got him to sleep."

"Influence of movies."

"My brother became a lawyer because of Gregory Peck as Atticus Finch in *To Kill a Mockingbird*."

"Hm." Francine tried to recall movies or any art profoundly influencing her. She sighed, recalling her mother had selected art to match colors of her shag carpets.

Cardoza had been correct about the Chapel of Angels in St. Michael's Episcopal Church. Aaron was entranced like a kid in a candy shop, scanning dramatic Tiffany chandeliers accentuating the nave and apse.

Museum-quality, stained-glass windows commanded the cathedral. Seven Tiffany lancet windows depicted St. Michael in Heaven. Francine and Aaron had viewed images of St. Michael, but unlike Cardoza's art books and the Internet depicting St. Michael battling, this rendering cast St. Michael in brilliant divine light, extolling triumph after the downfall of rebel angels.

Aaron blurted out, "Clearly this fellow's gotta be the good guy."

Francine hummed a sound of agreement. "If this capitalized *He* is your good guy, perhaps victims were targeted as dragons, disciples of Satan. I wonder which deadly sins our killer attributed to them?"

Examining the seven glass panels, Francine mumbled, "I count seven archangels but don't see a dragon with seven heads."

Aaron combed the sanctuary art for dragons but found none. "Cardoza said the beast had seven heads. Following warped logic, I'm betting we'll eventually uncover seven dead dragons."

Francine scanned side windows for clues. "Any more precincts reporting positive carfentanil tox screens?"

"We're combing through older cases. Possibilities are Riverside and Marcus Garvey park deaths."

Francine's focus gravitated to St. Michael's youthful face. She was drawn to his upward gazing, his sad eyes longing in harmony with her own unspoken yearnings. Swimming in Michael's eyes evolved into both a wish and apprehension that he might speak. As disconcertment swept over her, she became conscious of her own thinking, feeling tension in her shoulder muscles. She quickly stepped out of herself, pivoting to join Aaron marveling at the apsidal chancel with its white Vermont marble altar and massive Tiffany mosaic. Their shared inquest settled Francine quicker than a double shot of Milagro Silver.

A nine-year-old boy, sporting a backpack, entered through a side entrance and snatched their attention. As they watched, he momentarily disappeared into a transept, emerged draped in a choir robe, and set about polishing brass pedestals.

Francine approached the boy, clearing her throat to elicit his attention. "Pardon me. Is the minister here?"

"You mean the rector?" the boy asked. "He'll be here in an hour."

"Are you here alone?"

"Why?"

Francine pulled out her credentials. "I'm a police detective and have some questions for him. But you know what? I bet you can help us."

The boy trembled and stepped back. "I'll have to ask the rector."

"A simple question. Just wondering if you ever saw a woman Marine in here."

"Why?"

"She's a person of interest in a case we're working on."

"I don't know what that means."

"The woman may have information. It would be helpful for us to talk with her."

The boy shrugged. "I was told not to cause trouble."

"No, no. No trouble. In fact, you'd be helping lots."

The boy pointed at Aaron. "Is he a policeman too?"

Aaron displayed his credentials, and the boy pulled them to his face and studied them carefully, his frown revealing he did not understand some words.

Aaron pocketed his ID. "What's your name?"

"Blake … Blake Ricci."

Francine squatted so her head was lower than the boy's. "When was the last time the woman Marine was in the church?"

Blake shrugged and spoke with a meek voice. "Two months. Maybe three."

"Did she say anything? Speak to you?"

"She sat in back. Stayed quiet. Stared at me."

"I imagine that felt uncomfortable."

Blake nodded and stared at the carpet.

"Can you show me where she sat?"

The boy pointed a finger at a rear pew and withdrew the digit quickly as if it might get bitten.

"Every time?"

"Uh huh."

"How often do you help out here?"

"Two afternoons."

"Every week?"

"Uh huh."

"How many times did you see the woman?"

Again, Blake shrugged. "A handful or so."

"Was she wearing military clothes?"

Blake scratched his nose as he answered. "Uh huh."

Aaron jumped into the inquiry. "Combat uniform or dress uniform?"

Blake flinched at Aaron's intrusion. "A white jacket."

Francine resumed questioning in a gentler voice. "And did that woman stop coming around?"

Blake nodded.

"Anything else you remember about her?"

The boy shook his head but then added, "She fidgets. Plays with her fingers like this." The boy demonstrated drum rolling left-hand fingers while tapping the back of the hand with his right index finger.

"Very specific, Blake. Good eye." Francine retrieved her address and phone number card and handed it to the boy. "Can you give my card to the rector?"

Blake examined the card, eyeing it as carefully as if bidding for a treasured baseball card.

"Please ask the rector to call me. It's important that you do that. Can you do that for me?"

Blake nodded and placed the card on the altar railing.

"You've been enormously helpful. Thank you." Francine stood up straight. "You look like a diligent worker, Mr. Blake Ricci. A responsible helper. I wish I had someone like you to polish my silver and brass. Keep up the great job."

Francine and Aaron were a quarter way up the aisle when Blake called to them. "Other women sit in that exact seat."

Both detectives glanced at one another and reapproached Blake.

This time, Aaron knelt to the boy's height. "What do the women look like?"

Again, Blake shrugged but answered. "One I guess, looked sort of like a country-western singer. One was a Marine. This week there was a woman with weird hair. Super red and green."

The two detectives said little as they left, not wanting to worry the boy with the possibilities swirling in their minds.

As they opened the bright red front door, a nun was entering. Aaron stepped aside and held the door open as the sister nodded gratitude and proceeded toward the sanctuary.

Once on the sidewalk, Francine pointed diagonally across Amsterdam Avenue. "That's Frederick Douglas Park. My nephew used to play soccer there. On the other side of the park is the 24th Precinct Station. Let's pay Deputy Inspector Lazelle a visit. Ask him to order a stakeout."

While they advanced to the 100th Street Station, the nun entered the central hall, seated herself in the rear pew, and began praying.

Blake was bent over, preoccupied polishing the brass base of a communion altar. When he stood erect, he witnessed the lone nun. Her familiar hand movements and glare made him stiffen. His heart began speeding while he stared. He eased out a side door and jetted to the front of the church, searching for the two detectives, panicking when he could not locate them.

Inside the church, Elisabet, dressed in the nun's habit she had procured should she lure the deacon, approached the altar and knelt at the railing. "St. Michael, forgive me. I am still waiting for your blessing to pursue the deacon."

She looked up at Michael's face and detected disappointment in his upward gaze. "I can see I failed you."

As she bowed her head, in her peripheral vision, she spotted something white contrasting the dark wood of the altar railing. She turned her head and sighted the calling card.

She scooted on her knees to the card, plucked it to her chest, and surveilled the premises. Before reading it, she moved to a front pew and cupped her hands around the card as if protecting a sacred treasure from vile elements. *Captain Francine Boult. Command Officer. Homicide Squad. 54th Street, Midtown North Precinct.*

Elisabet looked to her archangel. He did not move. He did not speak.

Once again, she knelt and prayed to her protector. "This person, Captain Boult? Is she friend or foe? Are she and I on the same side in combatting evil? Enlighten me if I should enlist her to be on our team."

Elisabet waited with eyes closed. A side door swung open as if a brewing storm had sucked it open. Through the opening, she heard glass from a mobile tinkling in the wind, and then crash onto the cement steps.

Feeling at peace, Elisabet whispered, "Thank you my archangel." She tucked Francine's card into her habit and strode into the night.

Outside, Blake breathed relief when he spotted the detectives strolling toward their unmarked car, both talking on their cellphones.

"Hey," the boy yelled, racing to the officers. He was out of breath enough that he expressed himself with staccato speech. "The lady came back. I'm sure it was her, cause she sat in the same seat and fiddled her fingers exactly like the other women did."

Aaron was excited enough that he shouted. "Is she still in the church?"

"She left a couple of minutes ago. I saw her heading toward Broadway."

"Damn. She's probably on a subway by now." Aaron punched a number into his cellphone. "I'll put out a call. You said she has red and green hair."

"Not now. She's dressed like a nun."

Francine and Aaron looked at one another, unable to speak for a moment until Francine mumbled, "Shit. We held the door open for her."

THE BARRACKS CONDO

Although Karol had flipped four previous condos for the woman she knew as Azza Thornton, this was the first time her client had left behind personal items.

There were multiple women's Marine combat and dress uniforms, three men's business suits, numerous shirts and blouses, and piles of men and women's under-garments, socks, shoes, and sweaters. Unlike previous Azza condos, there were used soap bars, linens, pans and dinnerware, sheets on the half-made bed, and food in the refrigerator.

Karol ascertained that Azza had left in an urgent rush. She felt put upon having to clean up after a person who surely was wealthy and spoiled.

On the dressers and shelves were framed photographs of uniformed men and women from various military branches, representing three, possibly four generations. On one wall hung an oil portrait of a colonial-looking navy officer, possibly from the Revolutionary War.

Karol was disgusted after finding unwashed underwear and socks beneath the bed. She always hired the same crew to thoroughly clean, but this time, she would warn them to bring far more trash bags and be prepared for bad smells. She pondered if she should ask them to donate discarded garments to charity, keep the rejects for themselves, or dispose of them.

In her years as a real estate agent, such issues had never existed—well, maybe the time a client had lived with three untrained, undisciplined cats in her Brooklyn flat. That had been a salvage-type horror scene.

As Karol entered the bathroom, she found used toothbrushes, razors, and makeup strewn about. Even if there had been a fire evacuation, the condo would not have appeared so chaotically abandoned.

Karol walked into a room that all previous owners had designated as a second bedroom. Now, Karol found herself staring at a fitness club. There was a large treadmill, a stationary bike, a rowing machine, and a medicine ball. One wall had shelves from floor to waist high, filled with assorted weights, jump ropes, yoga mats, dumbbells, foam rollers, resistance bands, suspension trainers, and other exercise tortures. A chin-up bar and gymnastic rings dangled from the ceiling.

On the phone, Karol recalled that Azza had a type of New-England accent and lacked sounding rushed or alarmed, ruling out experiencing chaos or panic about moving.

Something was amiss, but she could not put her finger on what.

Karol searched for anything with specific identification for either Azza or her live-in boyfriend or husband. She found no credit or business cards, and no restaurant receipts that often list customers' names when paying by charge card. She also did not find magazines or utility bills with Azza's or anyone's name.

Karol was discomforted by discovering herself snooping through drawers and cabinets as if she were trying to build a case to attack her client's integrity. That was not her job. She was paid to place residences on the market and match buyers to venues.

In the past, with Azza's odd tastes in decorating, Karol had worried she would be unable to find interested parties. She soon learned there were ample eccentric humans flooding the city to match with Azza's choices.

This condo, however, would be more of a challenge. Trading out furniture and bringing in typical staging furniture was usually a pain, but this tenement would require unreasonable hours of effort and expense to neutralize.

There was one closet off the workout room that was locked. She checked her condo keys, but none fit. She phoned the high-rise building's management desk. They reported they had no keys to the internal workings of residences. Since the condo was officially on the market, however, they offered to send one of their property handymen to break into the closet if Karol signed to assume responsibility. Although that seemed ridiculous, she agreed.

Jamal arrived with a toolbox. He was a college student working in the building part-time.

"Are you sure this is okay?" Jamal asked.

"The office said it was fine as long as I sign papers assuming responsibility."

"Oh yeah. These ones." The boyish handyman plucked a paper from his jacket's inside pocket and Karol signed it.

"Aren't you going to read it first?" Jamal asked.

"No more than I read my credit-card agreements." Karol scribbled her name illegibly and returned the paper. "Okay. Now you can go to it."

"My supervisor said to remove the hinges rather than risk splintering wood where it latches."

"Sounds good to me."

Jamal appeared pleased when he tapped his screwdriver beneath a hinged bolt and the bolt easily pried up and out.

"Wow. I could have done that," Karol said.

Jamal wiggled the door off its hinges and leaned it against a wall.

They both peered in.

Inside the closet was one simple knee-high shelf with

two candles. Above the candles on the back wall was an unfamiliar religious icon. On the floor was a small doormat-like rug.

"Well, that's interesting," Jamal said, whispering as softly as if they had stumbled into a miniature church.

Karol studied the worship room, glanced around at the body-building menagerie surrounding them, and looked back into the closet. "Quite a contrast."

Jamal inhaled as strongly as if he had been holding his breath to set a new record. "Maybe it's a time-travel or a universe-transport closet."

Karol did not need to look at the rookie handyman. "You and my son would get along splendidly."

She was relieved Bram had not accompanied her.

ONE MUST DEAL WITH OBSTACLES
- February 2022 -

After receiving St. Michael's blessing, Elisabet was eager to join forces with Captain Boult and right the world from evil forces lurking behind innocent faces. She and Captain Boult could seek out the deacon for starters.

She slid on one of her grandmother's ankle-length black dresses, donned one of her elderly-woman gray wigs, and powdered pale foundation over age crevices she had created with liquid latex. This was an identity she sometimes used to browse museums. She thought it was a fitting presence for entering St. Michael's Church and requesting a blessing to pursue her target: a man of the cloth.

As she approached the church's bright red doors, familiar doors she had passed through for several years, she was stopped by a man's voice sounding from behind her.

"Pardon me, ma'am."

Elisabet pivoted to face an overweight, late-middle-aged NYC officer, a man out of breath from merely scampering a short distance.

"Good evening, Officer."

"Sorry to bother you, but there's been trouble at this church days back. I'm required to check IDs of people before they enter. A formality."

"IDs Officer?"

"You know. Any ID with some type of photo. Driver's license and so on."

"Oh." Elisabet stepped closer to her obstacle, squinting as if her vision was not acute. "Will my Medicare card work?"

"Uh …" The officer removed his hat and wiped sweat from his brow. "I don't believe medical cards have photos—but I'm not positive about that."

"I'm pretty sure it does," Elisabet said, opening her matching black purse and spilling papers, tissues, pens, and breath mints onto the sidewalk. "Oh dear."

"Here. Let me help." The officer knelt as slowly as a reluctant circus elephant.

As smooth as a well-rehearsed ballet glissade, Elisabet was upon the man, swiftly retrieving her tactical pen from inside her dress and jabbing the anodized-aluminum tip into the carotid area of the officer's exposed throat.

The man was rendered disoriented, giving Elisabet seconds to extend the tool's switchblade and plunge it into the man's opposite carotid. The officer collapsed forward.

Elisabet calmly surveyed the premise for other officers and gathered her papers. She checked her clothing to assure it was free of blood, but detected dark-red splatter on her shoe.

She thought it best to approach St. Michael at another location and beg for absolution. She discarded her shoes in an outside construction trash bin. As she fast-walked toward the subway, she heard a voice behind her yell, "Pauly? I got your Reuben. Where are you?"

As if she had never been at the church, Elisabet Norgaard blended in with the evening crowd on Amsterdam Avenue.

She took the Broadway local southward to begin her pilgrimage to the Church of St. Michael the Archangel on 34th Street. She needed to check in with her saint and assure the execution was justified. Would the archangel be shocked by her assumptions and actions? Demand repentance or retribution? She had killed a man with no knowledge of his history. Was it merely because he challenged her? Was it her acting out of selflessness to serve her saint?

People on the subway stared at her: an elderly, barefoot lady. She hung her head low and contorted into the smallest possible size as if she were nude and not wanting voyeurs to spy.

If police were barricading St. Michael on 99th Street, they could also be on the prowl at 34th Street. Across the street from the church, she ducked into a smoke shop at the base of a brick apartment building, fearing to approach or enter the century-old house of worship and risk confrontation by another officer.

Staring out the shop window at the church squeezed among super-high-rise glass buildings, she felt St. Michael was under attack. He would understand if she communicated from across the street, but the noise from people selecting tobaccos and vaping flavors drove her outside.

She leaned against the base of a Doric column and meditated, hoping she could reach her archangel. She heard a disturbance across the street. A mutt dog with an almost hyena look was glaring at her like she was a squirrel it had been stalking. The animal growled, displaying clinched teeth as hair on its back stood erect. It abruptly postured as if capable of pouncing across the busy road to devour her.

She closed her eyes and all sounds dissipated. She felt sudden freezing air pelting her from all directions.

She opened her eyes to see a normal scene of people walking about as they would on any evening.

The bizarre moment sent a clear message: St. Michael was displeased. She must endure torment if she were to be vindicated.

She hailed a taxi rather than summon her family

chauffeur. She did not want to risk their driver witnessing her attire and makeup. He would be sure to gossip with the house staff.

Once she was safe and in comforting clothing within the glass walls of her penthouse, she dismissed the staff and bolted all doors. She silenced her cellphone and disconnected the landlines.

She sterilized her switchblade with alcohol, spread a thick towel on her dressing-room floor, lay on her back, bit down hard on a multi-folded washcloth, and pricked her abdomen, inflicting multiple shallow but painful punctures.

EVIL RESIDES OVER LEFT SHOULDERS

At the murder sites, the only fingerprints or DNA—
including DNA in victims' saliva—matched victims. No
woman of any shape or form returned to sit in the rear
pew at St. Michael's.

Recognizing that the trail of the serial murderess had
vaporized, Francine and her crew became as dispirited as
losing teams in locker rooms at halftime.

Knowing the trail had grown cold and that the woman
Marine was a fleeting phantom, Jasmine lost faith she
could aid her friend with her case. She had grown fond,
however, of meeting Francine for midtown lunches. She
made a habit of arriving early at the station, enjoying
rock-star adoration from the tribe of detectives, including
five women, all tripping over themselves to chat a
moment. Jasmine felt Aaron was the most alluring. He
was the only detective she bothered to learn by name.

She pondered if the gang truly enjoyed her, or were
simply pleased for her to invigorate their commander
enough to transform her into a tolerable human being.

On a New York Monday with record-breaking warmth
for February, Elisabet arrived at the 54th Street Station.
Imbued with a Louisiana Bayou accent and a plain-
clothes suit, she introduced herself to Lane and a second
receptionist. "Hey y'all. I'm Sergeant Madeline Winters
from Baton Rouge. I apologize deeply. I know I'm two days
early, but I got a appointment to see Captain Boult on
Wednesday about a Louisiana case and was praying she
might could fit me in today. One of our parolees raped and
strangled two twelve-year-old girls. Poor things was
innocent little cousins visiting their senile grandmother's
cotton farm. So, you can plum see why I'm eager to get a

move on. The suspect's sister lives here in Manhattan, and he called his girlfriend back home from a Manhattan payphone. I ain't seen a payphone thing in years."

"I love your Louisiana accent," Lane said, thumbing through her log.

Elisabet winked. "And your Big Apple accent is cute as a ladybug."

Lane frowned, doubting any insect could be cute. "I don't see you listed on the captain's schedule."

"Paperwork in Baton Rouge is slower than winter molasses. And here I stand pestering you two days early." The flimflamming impersonator leaned elbows on the counter, pretending to be straining to peek at the log.

Lane shut the book. "The captain just left to grab lunch next door or I would—"

"That was her I just passed? Them two ladies going out that there door?"

Lane tightened her lips and faintly nodded, realizing she had violated protocol.

"Tell you what, honey. I bothered you two girls a bunch too much. Let me wait til Wednesday's paperwork crawls in here. Much obliged. You two have a good day, hear?"

Elisabet had shammed a low-budget-movie Southern accent for entry into midtown's detective world. She was hell-bent on shedding it.

Exiting the station, Elisabet glanced at DaTommaso Ristorante next door, crossed 54th Street to the National Market, purchased tomato basil from the soup bar, and slurped while eyeing the Italian restaurant. She had spare time to devour a prepackaged salad and a small stack of Nutter Butters before she spied the two women departing the restaurant. She recognized them because while passing them at the station, she had been struck by the attractiveness of the younger one with a crewcut.

She wondered if the two women were sisters, but then observed them embrace and kiss long enough that sundry New Yorkers turned heads to stare.

Elisabet judged the short-haired woman was accustomed to snatching more of the world's treasures than she merited, but then again, the woman resembled Elisabet's heroine, Joan of Arc, someone who challenged everyday norms and dedicated herself to fighting for justice.

She assumed that the older, professionally-dressed woman disappearing back into the station was Detective Boult. The crewcut woman, however, lingered, made a cellphone call, and proceeded toward 8th Avenue, wearing self-assurance like it was a knight's jousting armor.

Would St. Michael accept either woman as a covetous sinner worthy of sacrifice? Or would he prefer the three women form an alliance? Three sisters with a shared heart, swimming against the current to fight for justice. Joan of Arc had been canonized for such dedication.

Elisabet tailed Jasmine several blocks and into Taverna Santorini, a Greek pub populated by female couples. She observed Jasmine walk directly to a young woman whose body was coated in tattoos and embellished with ear, nose, and eyebrow piercings. Immediately, they kissed—much longer than the kiss with the captain—and with Tattoo practically climbing into Jasmine's lap.

Once they came up for air, Elisabet looked to where Jasmine was nodding. Both women giggled and appeared infatuated with a waitress who was as clean-cut as a royal—except for one skinny streak of bleached white hair with soft purple borders. Elisabet watched Jasmine fan her face with both hands as if cooling hot passion.

The couple-coveted waitress approached Elisabet. "Hey. What's happening? You're new here. May I fetch you some nosh or a bevvy, Luv?" All spoken with a British accent.

Ah, Elisabet thought. I know precisely how I shall dress and how I shall speak if I choose to befriend Crewcut.

Both Captain Boult and the crewcut woman drew her interest, but Elisabet knew that in the end, Michael would command with whom to ally and whom to sacrifice. Otherwise, like Joan, if Elisabet made rash decisions, she risked burning at the stake.

MEDIEVAL CRUSADER GALS

Burning to share pivotal news of coming upon Captain Boult and her crewcut lover, as well as eliminating one of Satan's disciples who had tried to block her, Elisabet Norgaard ached to return to St. Michael. She was exuding rhapsody like soda foam exploding from a shaken pop can. Francine's card on the altar railing had led her to the couple—her fondest find—and she had uncloaked one of Satan's agents spying on the church.

She felt agitated she was not able to step inside her hallowed temple. She calmed herself by uprooting memories of weekend excursions with her grandmother, remembering lessons that St. Michael camps out in a plethora of world venues, including New York's Metropolitan Museum of Art.

Elisabet, dressed in her best private-schoolgirl clothing, admired herself in a full-length mirror. But at her age, the outfit made her look like a schlocky porno star. She tore off the clothes, popping buttons and ripping a pocket.

She settled for the garb of a sheepish secretary on lunch break, complete with a dime-store white blouse and eyeglasses with a string holder dangling from her neck.

The Metropolitan's information-desk lady consulted her computer and printed a list of various St. Michael artworks on exhibit.

Elisabet first inspected the museum's Cloisters, winding through medieval and Byzantine art, coming upon *St Michael Defeating the Devil.* Her printout informed her: *Tempera and oil on wood created in the 1400s by the Spaniard, Master of Belmonte.*

She was struck by the archangel's cold, preoccupied,

feminine face and the overwhelming brutality of a spear thrust into Satan's mouth and exiting his throat. She grimaced at the devil's grotesque, rotted-gray-brown body with extra pairs of eyes and mouths on his chest and legs, perhaps representing the seven heads of the beast.

At least Elisabet had procured youthful and handsome dragons, peacefully transitioning them into a better dreamworld, cuddling their heads on her lap as their breaths slowed.

Elisabet left the Cloisters to search for Michael in other galleries, locating the 1475 limestone French statue of her saint. She treasured she could circle her three-dimensional, armed warrior and enjoy him as much as stumbling upon an old friend at cocktails.

Although Michael's right arm was missing after five centuries of manhandling, his left arm wielded a damaged sword stabbed into the dragon's mouth. The agonized beast's tentacle was squeezing Michael's leg. Elisabet considered herself fortunate. Her adversaries had neither fought nor struggled.

In another gallery, Elisabet viewed a 1701 French bronze plate with Michael's sword held to the sky as his foot crushed the prone Satan.

In Gallery 516, her heart hastened when she beheld *Saint Michael Overcoming Satan*, a bronze statue by British sculptor Edward Wven.

Reading information on her printout, she was disheartened to learn that the 1842 sculpture was not original. It had been based upon a plaster sculpture created by John Flaxman in 1822, later to be carved by him in marble for Lord Egremont. Elisasbet's contempt softened when she learned that Flaxman's work had been based upon an earlier authority: Raphael's eight-foot-tall, 1518 painting exhibited in the Paris Louvre, the very masterpiece that Elisabet's grandmother had selected to calm her fears and launch her missions.

She felt driven more than ever to return to the Paris bench she and her grandmother had sat upon, a place where she felt grounded, a place where she could observe the purity of St. Michael and exult in knowing her saint had directly inspired Raphael to capture his likeness.

One of her grandmother's sermonized phrases lodged in her brain, much like a relentless TV-ad jingle refusing to fade. *Behold God's triumph over evil. As we all must.*

She felt unfulfilled as the various works of art failed to achieve the profundity of the 99th Street church's stained glass.

Elisabet referred to her printout. There was one last artwork listed on the second floor: an 1879 oil painting by French artist Jules Bastien-Lepage: *Joan of Arc.*

Elisabet was vexed that a non-Michael canvas was contaminating her list. At least it promised a glimpse of her heroine, Joan.

Entering Gallery 800, she witnessed an oil-on-canvas creation larger than Raphael's.

Joan of Arc was portrayed as a peasant teenager standing in a garden, appearing to be adrift in a sea of awe. The descriptor stated that Joan's expression was one of *spiritual awakening.*

As Elisabet eased closer, she realized why this painting had been included. In the background among the trees, her beloved St. Michael appeared as a dim premonition entering and dominating Joan's thoughts.

Apparently, Michael had entered Joan's life in much the same manner he had wedged into Elisabet's heart. Most people feel music. A fortunate minority feel words. Elisabet possessed a rarer gift. She felt her life to be penetrated and stewarded by art.

She and Joan were akin. It was once again time to shed her skin and transition anew.

From this heartbeat forward, she and Joan would be twin sisters as destiny had intended.

Elisabet had entered the Metropolitan as Elisabet, dressed as the simplest of secretaries. She abandoned the slender, hall-like gallery, descended the marble staircase, crossed through the Great Hall, and with head held high, strode onto Fifth Avenue, feeling renewed as if she were a peasant girl clad in decorous armor, a gladiatorial pillar confronting evil.

Elisabet now had two companions, Captain Boult and Crewcut, to aid her in slaying two more dragons. Afterwards, her North American campaign would be complete and she could reward herself by returning to the Louvre bench of her childhood.

A ROLL OF THE DIE
- March 2022 -

Elisabet sat on her high-rise, glassed-in penthouse balcony overlooking Central Park, typing on her grandfather's ancient Underwood typewriter. She was careful to wear gloves when touching the paper and a mask when proofreading her copy, not risking leaving fingerprints or DNA.

She considered various offenders whom the women's group had discussed and narrowed her choice to four specific men. She paced as she considered which names to present to St. Michael, trying to anticipate offerings he may dismiss.

For persons dismissed by St. Michael, she would impel Captain Boult to pursue them. She selected two nominees she considered appropriate and rolled a die to allow the universe to decide which. Odd for a former Utah carpenter/championship wrestler and even for a former Tennessee tobacco farmer. Both men had accepted positions as stevedores in the Port of New York and New Jersey.

The wrestler had blackmailed his neighbors into forcing their underage, adopted daughter to marry him, and the farmer had swindled thousands of dollars from a fund raiser for an elementary-school girl diagnosed with leukemia.

When both men relocated, they had changed their names. The Daughters of Boudicca, however, had contacts who helped their New York branch track the men they had labeled: *scumbags.*

Elisabet rolled the die. The former wrestler won—or surely in his eyes he would declare he lost.

Elisabet typed and revised her letter five times.

Dear Commander Boult. Below you will find the name and present job location of a man who blackmailed his neighbors to force their fifteen-year-old daughter to marry the man. Once the girl reached the age of consent, the man declared they were no longer married, changed his name, and moved from Ogden, Utah to New York City. I wish I could take matters into my own hands, but I have a busy schedule. I know you stand for justice and I admire your superb work. I shall be in touch with additional names. I pray you will appreciate my gift to you. I have high hopes for you.

Elisabet read the letter to herself, read it aloud, let it rest, read it a final time, and while still wearing gloves, attached a self-adhesive stamp, and mailed it from a mailbox in lower Manhattan.

Three days later, Francine opened the unsigned letter, skimmed it, and immediately showed it to Aaron. After a moment of mutual panic, they dropped the letter and envelope into a plastic evidence bag, sealed it, and had the lab examine it for ricin or other toxins.

They had no doubt as to the identity of the author.

AN ACTOR IS AN ACTOR IS AN ACTOR

Francine summoned Aaron, two other midtown detectives, and the lead detectives from the four precincts of Elisabet's murders.

She rolled a white board into a conference room and set yellow pads and markers at each seat as if running a General Motors board meeting. A side table was set up with water bottles, sodas, coffee, pretzels, various cheeses, crackers, and carrots with ranch dip. She avoided providing donuts and cookies.

After everyone gathered, Francine opened the meeting. "Welcome all. You are now part of an inter-precinct investigation task force. I invited Agent Lin Jia from FBI's Behavioral Analysis Unit Two—Crimes Against Adults—to consult with us. Lin? Good morning and welcome."

Lin stood. "Good morning, everyone. On this particular case, Detective Boult will remain the local commander and Sergeant Garfield as lead detective. We at the FBI shall work in parallel, keeping our doors open to you for any consultation or resources, and hope there will be a free exchange of intel."

The group of detectives, many with mouths filled with snacks, mumbled, "Welcome."

"I have shared all intel with Agent Jia." Francine walked to the board. "Okay then. Let's dig in. What do we know about this criminal, other than being a woman?"

"I'm not even sure about that," Sergeant Garfield said, prompting others to chuckle.

"I think it's safe to assume woman." Francine appeared stern enough that smiles converted to enforced gravity. She wrote *Woman* atop the board. "What else?"

"We believe she killed three men: Union Park, Pier 64, and Pier 84."

Francine wrote the locations on the board.

A second participant spoke. "She changes her identity each time. Drastically."

"That's according to your typed summary from interviewing a nine-year-old boy," Garfield blurted out. "My boy is his age—not even reliable telling me what happened at school."

Two detectives chuckled.

"Gentlemen," Lin said. "We rely on community tips for much of our most important intel. No matter their ages."

The two jeering detectives quickly strutted stone faces.

Francine scribbled *Identity shifts* on the board.

Aaron raised his hand and Francine grinned. "We're not in school, Detective Galanis. Talk over one another if you have urges to be heard. Allow thoughts to flow freely."

Aaron interlaced fingers of both hands across his chest as if blocking them from moving. "You and I saw the suspect dressed as a nun—with fair confidence it was her. She's about five-eight. Probably in her thirties."

Francine scribbled those observations.

A detective added, "She lures men, establishing a relationship of a few months with them. Likely sexual."

"Drugs them in parks," another said "Peaceful deaths. No signs of struggle. No blood. No guns or knives or bruising."

"I imagine she holds them as they die," Garfield said. "Resting their heads on her lap."

Lin's interest piqued enough that he paused from scanning photographs. "Why do you think that?"

"Imprints in the grass and snow," Garfield answered. "The victims' heads were lying in imprints the size of someone's butt."

"Romeo and Juliet," Detective Ted Mateo blurted out, eliciting disapproving moans from attendees.

"No. Don't dismiss ideas," Francine said. "Ted, what prompted you to say that?"

"Juliet loved her dying—just-dead Romeo. Held his head in her lap. She was tender with him."

"So, you're thinking maybe our killer loved these men?"

Aaron mumbled, "Or had mixed feelings they were dying."

Francine scribed *love* and *ambivalence* on her board, and paced a moment until Ted spoke again.

"I'm thinking maybe our suspect selected men aching to change, to be loved by a woman who sensed what they desired, but perhaps a type of woman they had difficulty winning."

"Their dream woman," a sad-eyed detective whispered.

"Much like why we go to movies and plays," Aaron said. "To meet, hang out with people we may not be able to know in real life. We pay for a moment to be with someone we can't expect to like or love us."

Ted added, "Or a moment with someone we wish we could be, but never will."

"Superman in a cape," Francine said, glancing at Aaron. She wrote on the board: *Selects dissatisfied, yearning young men. Fulfills their wishes.*

One detective shook his head. "That makes me and every man a target. One-hundred percent."

"Some more than others," Garfield mumbled.

"Say more," Francine coached.

"Look around you. Check the faces of men slinking out of porno theatres, or wannabe sports heroes exiting stadiums, or men we see in parks lusting after pretty women they can't have. All day long, I see men with aching desires stamped all over their faces."

Francine wrote: *Desirous, inadequate-feeling victims* on the board. "Are we on track, Agent Jia?"

Lin nodded. "Keep tossing out ideas, see what sticks."

Francine circled the room, taking as much time as changing a movie reel on an old-fashioned projector. "Why does our suspect seek guidance from a saint?"

After prolonged silence, Aaron spoke. "We all do. Jesus. Mohammed. Church saints. Deceased family-member angels. Sports or military heroes we turn into our personal saints. Somebody who has our six. Somebody—"

Garfield interrupted. "Heroes, idols—saints as you will—start when we was kids. For years, mine was Batman."

"Batman?" Ted yelled out, snorting mid-laugh.

"Who was your hero?" Garfield asked. "Robin? Someone in second place?"

"Okay, officers," Francine said. "Try to appear slightly professional for Agent Jia." She wrote on the board: *St. Michael*, and turned to her think-tank. "We know that saint allegedly saved a son from a father about to execute him. Saved Isaac from Abraham."

"So," Garfield said with a tentative voice. "Maybe that same saint saved this killer from a home full of psychos. And by the way, we Catholic cops usually have a St. Michael visor clip in our cars. Patron of police. We're pretty darn fond of that guy."

"Lots of criminals had abusive homes," Aaron said. "Maybe her father or other family members abused her."

Another detective added, "Lots of us were abused, but we didn't become criminals."

Ted mumbled, "No. We went into law to fight criminals."

"Wow, this is a bunch of psycho-mumbo-jumbo," another detective said, retrieving a second soda from the food table.

Everyone quieted, reviewing childhood tragedies in private.

Garfield broke the silence. "I just think this bitch is a psycho. Simple. She fell off the deep end."

As Garfield refreshed his coffee, Francine encouraged him. "Keep going."

"This lady demon hates herself. Hates who she is. She couldn't get what she wanted as she looked, as she acted, as she was. So, she became a fraud."

"An actress," Aaron said.

"A fraud."

Aaron shrugged. "Same thing sort of."

Francine refereed. "Actresses are socially accepted. Frauds are not."

"But if she believes what she's doing in the moment," Ted said, "it's real for her. Not play acting. Right?"

"Like I already made clear," Garfield said, continuing his tirade, "a psycho." He swirled his finger around an ear to signal, *crazy*, causing him to spill coffee. "Damn it. How is playing arm-chair shrink getting us closer to solving this case?"

"Our other leads are failing," Francine said. "I'm hoping if we step into her shoes, we'll open a door. What do you think, Agent Jia?"

"I agree," Lin said. "Try to see through her eyes. It's evident that you and your team know plenty about this killer. Maybe you could stare at her saint. Sense what she sees in him. Try to identify other art that calls her."

"Hm," Francine hummed. "Study art that consumes our suspect."

Garfield chuckled. "Sure. Maybe the saint will step out of the painting like a frigging Disney cartoon character and come to life, talk to you, solve our case."

BEWARE OF STEPPING INTO ANOTHER'S SHOES

Francine and Aaron again approached Father Cardoza for more information about St. Michael.

Cardoza welcomed them into his church office where the two detectives were spellbound by his ornate, Edwardian-legged desk.

Cardoza noticed and said, "It was a gift from a wealthy parishioner to my predecessor."

He wrote out a list as he talked. "In case you did not know, there's a St. Michael statue sitting outside of our 34th Precinct stationhouse. You'll find the archangel holding a downed policeman beneath his wing. Sculpted to honor two slain officers. And there's the Peace Fountain in Morningside Heights, showcasing the struggle of good over evil—St. Michael winning of course."

He reached into a side drawer. "Here's a copy of a list of St. Michael art in the Met—some currently not on display, but if you ask politely, who knows? I prepared this list for my deacon students. Pieces from around the globe. That's pretty much all I have to offer off the top of my head."

During the weekend, Francine, wearing street clothes, took subways to 86th and Lexington and walked the last few blocks to the Metropolitan Museum of Art.

She purchased a MET paperback, clipped on a guest badge, and zigzagged her way to second-floor galleries. She first laid claim to the bench before Joan of Arc in Bastien-Lepage's magnum opus.

She knew she could not possibly see the art through the killer's eyes, but hoped if she opened her heart to experience beyond what her eyes saw, perhaps new understanding would bubble up from within.

At the start of her day, she had not anticipated sitting in the dark on a beautiful day in the company of Joan of Arc. She was stunned at how much Joan resembled Jasmine with her cropped hair and manly clothes. She felt that in this moment, she was able to connect with art more open-hearted than in past years.

Francine focused on the girl's expression. It was different than she recalled from seeing in Cardoza's art book, different enough to believe the child-warrior's features had morphed. It is well known that museum art staff touchup paintings time to time. She believed *restoration* was the proper term. As far as she knew, however, restoration did not include license to alter.

Francine consulted her museum-shop paperback for historical context. *Medieval teenaged martyr.*

She took a deep breath and focused on Joan's upward gaze, a gaze that felt identical to the angle that her own eyes fixed upward upon Joan's face. She felt that both she and Joan were longing as if there were something at a distance that was eternally craved but eternally unobtainable.

Francine contemplated the similarities of their two lives. When is art a mirror; when is art a threshold?

The biographical section of her paperback stated, *A military leader who transcended gender roles.*

Those were hallmarks she and Joan shared.

Born to a propertied peasant family.

Another similarity. Francine's family had worked on rural Indiana farms, owning little more than a meager lot and a four-room cabin. "Modern peasants," she mumbled.

If Francine had not entered the National Guard and been eligible for military assistance programs, she would never have attended college, never developed a passion for police work.

Amnesia lifted as she recalled how her mother had glowed when boasting to neighbors. "Our little Frannie is a stickler for justice. My girl stubbornly argues for decency til she's blue in the face."

Now here Francine sat, canonizing a French savior, a sixteen-year-old girl who had led battles to rescue her nation from the English. A girl who at nineteen was burned at the stake for refusing to yield from wearing men's clothing, flaunting cropped hair, professing her actions were governed by visions.

Francine found it enchanting how assertively this piece of art spoke to her, resonating with her intimate sense of self. She hungered to step into Bastien-Lepage's imagination and sit with Joan, meet up with her in a patisserie or a brasserie and swap stories and counsel. What glorious wisdom Joan might offer.

If museum visitors were coming and going, Francine had no awareness. She was suspended in a different sphere. Time and space had violated everyman's laws. She felt the painting crafting missions, obligations, demanding pledges from her. Not with words. But a knowing that dances in the recesses of existing. A knowing formed in ancient animal hearts. A knowing that baked in earth's creatures as they scratched marks on cave walls, beat rhythms on hollow logs, and streaked ochre on faces. A knowing that refused to go extinct when tribes and cities were incinerated. A knowing capable to rise from ashes time and time again and command.

Francine scribbled as fast as a madwoman in the margins of her museum paperback. *I am falling under the spell of art dancing with nature. Art is holding me captive, nodding toward my destiny.*

An intruding children's tour with echoing giggles yanked Francine from her immersion.

As she departed, she turned for a last look. She felt lighter on her feet, feeling heartened as if Saint Joan had her six.

Francine turned in her visitor's badge, exited the art temple, and strode into sunlight, relishing her deep journey into art. Never before had she allowed art to become so personal. She felt changed, sparked to explore the unknown, embrace the noble, and confront the vile.

She recalled having a passion for art in kindergarten, but at some point, she had forfeited drawing stick figures and filling in empty spaces with whichever 48-crayon color suited her. But why? Had she endured a family trauma? A personal trauma? Shut down her imagination for an unknown reason?

Had the massive painting been magical enough to put her in touch with her younger self?

She stopped to sit on a Fifth-Avenue-Park bench, ignoring bus fumes, people feeding nuts to sidewalk squirrels, taxis honking for no reason.

Francine pondered if art had changed their suspect, put her in touch with her true self, but instead of the joy Francine was bathing in, art had raised the woman's fears to the surface, brought out drives to avenge, envy, and destroy.

Perhaps art frees the souls for some and dooms others to eternal hell.

What about the artists who depicted St. Michael with Satan? What were their intentions? What drove their obsessiveness to render good attacking evil with such perverse images? What buried, haunting horrors lived deep within them, leaped out onto their canvases and embedded into their plaster to penetrate the hearts of beholders?

Francine felt closer than ever to understanding the

woman killer. She felt elated for a moment, but then despair, realizing that even though her attempt to understand her transgressor's motives was healing her own heart, understanding did not promise to prevent future transgressions. That left her feeling half fulfilled, half empty.

Francine sauntered along the edge of Central Park, admiring magnificent trees with rich foliage thriving among asphalt and manmade pinnacles. She was seeing the city as a newborn gazing with fresh eyes.

She felt rejuvenated as if for decades she had been a groveling caterpillar, followed by being imprisoned in a chrysalis, and now holding the promise of blossoming into a winged butterfly.

ST. CHRISTOPHER

Arriving home late from work, Karol opened her son's perpetually shut door.

Bram shouted even before he startled. "Geez, Mom. "Knock. You know the rule. Knock."

"Look at this mess." Karol looked behind the door, expecting to find a rumpled boogieman or sloven ogre contributing to the trashscape. "The scrap yard behind JD's Auto has less garbage scattered on the ground than your floor."

"I have the same amount of crap I've had since I was eight. Why you busting my case? Bad day at work?"

Karol did not appear angry at the smart-mouth remark. Bram was uncertain if her expression was one of exhaustion or one of despair. Either way, she appeared ready to surrender.

Karol opened her purse and pulled out a frayed, overly-folded newspaper clipping. Only it had not been clipped. It was ragged, carelessly ripped from neighboring stories.

She held it out to Bram. "This was in your pocket. I've asked you time and time again to empty your pockets before you toss clothes in the hamper. Shreds of paper embed in our clothes. Damage the washer. What is this anyway?"

Bram snatched the wrinkled scrap. "A news story. Did you bother to look at it? Probably not."

Karol examined it, pretending she had not read it. *Another Park Murder.* "Standard news rubbish. I've warned you about polluting your soul with such trash."

"God almighty."

"Bram! You know better than—"

"I'm sorry. I'm sorry. But it's not rubbish. It's the *New*

York Times."

"Not every story in *The Times* is worth—"

"God all—Never mind, never mind."

Karol tilted her head back, raising her chin so she looked like a preacher in a pulpit glaring down at a sinner. "I want you to go to church with me this Sunday."

"And I want you to read newspapers. Not be a turtle afraid to come out of its shell. But neither's going to happen, is it?"

"If I had talked to my parents the way you—"

"Your parents? My grandparents I've never been allowed to meet? I think you disqualified yourself from deserving to shove that story down my throat."

"You'll listen to it as long as you don't clean your room, don't go to church with me, and keep reading trash."

"You should read this," Bram said. "The police are requesting help from the public to solve a string of murders."

"What does that have to do with us?"

Bram extracted the St. Christopher from a drawer and dangled it before his mother.

Reaching for her reading glasses, Karol asked, "What's that?"

"A St. Christopher."

Karol looked perplexed. "Like Catholics wear?"

"I found it."

"Oh, dear God. Please tell me you aren't becoming Catholic."

"Really, Mom? I f‑o‑u‑n‑d fucking found it."

"You don't have to—"

"You've been selling condos to a psycho."

"I told you she's very—"

"Sweet. I know. But there's a name engraved on this. The name of the guy murdered in Hudson Park."

"I don't understand."

"He had to have been in her condo. *Beniamino*. Not exactly a common name. Coincidence? I don't think so."

"Could be coincidence. Lots of strange—"

"Yeah, yeah, yeah. And you're sure the world's a sweet place. I'm contacting the police."

"You absolutely will not. You're constructing an outlandish, comic-book fantasy. You read smut and like I feared, you polluted your mind. Now give me that thing."

Bram stuffed the charm back into his pocket.

Karol yelled, "You're grounded."

Bram smirked. "And what? You're going to stay home from work and guard me? I don't think so. By the way, thanks for teaching me which trains run to the heart of midtown."

"I'll enlist friends to watch you."

"You don't have friends. Not even at church."

After recovering from the jarring accusation, Karol said, "Sonia's my friend. We play mahjong or go bowling every Thursday night. I'll check with her."

"You asked her once before, and she told you never."

"Oh." Karol paused to recover again. "Wouldn't hurt to ask again."

I hate you going to Sonia's place at night. It's not safe."

"Mahjong and bowling are the safest games on earth."

"You know what's only one building away from Sonia's place, Mom? The Westside Rifle and Pistol Range."

"The what?"

"20th Street. Same block as Sonia. People fire all kinds of weapons inside and walk out onto the street. Who knows what they carry outside." Bram slapped his hands together. "Wham."

Karol startled. "I don't think so, honey. Are you certain that shop's on Sonia's block?"

"It's not a shop, Mom. It's a place where people actually shoot. Jason Weiman's father goes there. Took Jason for his birthday. I was invited but you wouldn't let me go."

Karol searched for a drawer with enough space to stuff her son's stray socks. "Well, I've never seen anyone carry a gun onto that street."

"You never noticed the building much less what anyone was toting."

"If that area was dangerous, Sonia wouldn't live there."

"Whatever. Stay happy living in your fog."

Karol's mind raced to construct a list of people who might supervise her son, but she despaired, realizing that other than Sonia, she avoided socializing, barely knowing her senile neighbors or the community-college dropout across the street who appeared to have gang affiliations.

Karol scooped up a mound of T-shirts and gym socks from a chair and sat, thinking the chair had not seen daylight in years.

Bram read aloud from the paper scrap. "Two men found murdered in parks on piers 64 and 84, overdosed with a super-potent form of fentanyl."

Bram tapped the pocket protecting his evidence. "You remember the name on this St. Christopher, right?"

Karol shrugged.

Bram huffed and trudged onward, reading to his mother. "Both men were recent residents of Manhattan. Beniamino Moretti—recognize that name, Mom? Here's more. Beniamino Moretti, age 19, was a Columbia University student from Salerno, Italy. Ernest Farthing, age 24, relocated from his hometown of Falkville, Alabama, south of Decatur. Surveillance video captured a woman Marine entering the park with Mr. Farthing, making her a person of interest."

Bram stared at his mother. The color had drained from

her face. Bram's demeanor shifted from standing his ground to looking like he was yearning to cuddle a whimpering beagle puppy. "Are you okay?"

Karol shook her head. "It scares me when you snoop around trying to play detective."

"I like solving mysteries."

"I know all too well." She paced to the window and back. "If you promise not to do anything stupid, I'll share more about the woman—but you have to promise."

Not looking at his mother, Bram mumbled, "I promise not to be stupid."

"I'm holding you to that."

Karol sat silent for a moment until Bram yelled, "So, tell me for gosh sakes."

"I'm thinking how to phrase this." Karol scooted forward and then backwards in her seat. "You know the most recent condo, the one I'm selling now?"

Bram nodded, knowing that prompting his mother was annoying but the only method that would succeed in gaining more information.

"Well, her most recent condo is decorated in a military motif. Heavy on women Marine paraphernalia."

It took Bram a moment. "Holy shit."

"Bram."

"Sorry." After digesting that news flash, Bram stood and spoke fast enough he tripped over his words. "That's a slam dunk. We have a duty to contact the police—you have a duty."

"You know how after your father ran off while overseas, it became overwhelming for me to deal with police. I swore off all police and legal types til the end of time."

Bram talked in his head, reviewing how his mother not only avoided police, but avoided teachers, book clubs, his soccer coaches, his scout leaders—all people. "Did her other condos have Marine junk?"

Karol covered her face with her hand as if it were a sun visor. "You're not going to let this go, are you? So much like your dad: obstinate."

Bram heard her words opposing his curiosity, but also detected her tone of voice softening and a slight grin speaking admiration and encouragement. "You gotta tell me more, Mom."

"Very well." Karol took a deep breath and sat up taller as if invited and honored to read a story to a circle of kindergarten children. "Azza Thornton drastically transforms the look of where she lives. Changes her phone numbers, her accents. On the last call she sounded like people in that Maine movie I love so much … uh … uh—"

"*Mooseport*. The one you probably watch in your sleep."

"*Mooseport*. With that guy from *Everybody Loves Raymond*."

"Yeah, yeah, yeah." Bram thought about his mother's astute observations for a moment. "Mom, you have to be the one to talk with the police. I can be there beside you. Hold your hand if you want. I promise."

"I can't. I won't. And you won't either. This woman could come after you—after us."

Bram shuddered. "She doesn't know where we live, right?"

"She knows my office address. She could easily—"

"Shit."

Shit indeed, Karol thought. The room was quiet long enough that she became aware of traffic noise outside, Bram's clock ticking, a dog down the street barking. She leaned over with elbows on knees and whispered as if the alleged murderess were in the hallway. "It's best if we forget we know anything."

"Hell no."

Karol withdrew into her own head, a condition that Bram knew sometimes lasted for hours.

Bram weighed several possibilities before speaking. "When Philip Pease cheated in fifth-grade U.S. History, you encouraged me to tattle on him."

"I never pushed you to tattle. But you magnificently did what was right. Made me proud. I still am."

"That didn't end well."

"What do you mean?"

"Mrs. Pease told Philip's friends' mothers. They told their sons. The gang cornered me and gave me a little talk. A black eye and a bloody nose."

"You said you hit a tree skateboarding. You lied to me."

"I wanted you to think I made a good choice." Bram leaned back with interlaced fingers cupping the back of his head. "Yep. Now Philip's my best friend. Weird how that goes, huh?"

Karol studied Bram's latest art pinned to the wall: a man playing chess in Washington Park. "I'll find you a frame for that. It's one of your best." She stared at her ring finger, wishing the strong Māori man who had whispered vows into her ear and slid that symbol of eternal love onto her finger were here to help raise their son.

She wanted to pat her son's shoulder, but knew he had outgrown accepting even slight touches of affection. "I'm sorry you suffered back then. Good intentions, bad outcome. Eventually followed by a good outcome. Like I always say, life's complicated."

"We have to stop this woman, Mom."

More moments passed. Karol noticed jet sounds from the sky, beeps of a truck backing, cranked-up pounding bass from a passing van. "Let's go downstairs. We need pancakes."

Bram huffed, knowing his mother had retreated into her head to some happy place. "You're not listening, are you? Besides, it's afternoon."

"We need pancakes."

"Pancakes or not, I'm contacting the homicide squad. They asked for help and I'm going to help them. With or without your help."

THE DETECTIVE GENE

Karol marched through Midtown North Precinct's homicide suite directly to Francine's office. Younger detectives failed to notice, but more seasoned detectives stared and gossiped to one another as if spotting a movie or sports star who had been exposed on the morning news for having multiple affairs during the past week.

Karol entered Francine's open office.

"Oh my gosh," Francine said, immediately rising from her chair. "K.C. Whaanga. I haven't seen you in how long?"

"Too long." Karol gestured for permission to sit.

Francine scooted a chair closer to her desk and noticed a cluster of detectives spying upon them. She targeted a frown at them and shut her door. "I had given up I would ever see you again. You know you and Sol are still legends around here."

"Kind of you to say, but I doubt we are legends."

"You definitely are and your unsurpassed reputations dominate office story-telling."

"You look in great shape, Francine."

"Morning stretches now and then."

Karol wrinkled her face. "I'm here with a personal request."

"The same K.C. Always to the point."

"My son is thirteen now."

"Thirteen? Wow, time flies. The last time I saw you, you told me he was seven or eight. You were with Sonia at the range. The time before that, you were pregnant."

"Sol's memorial. Thirteen years ago. I finally accepted that nightmare gathering was a memorial service, not an event marking missing-in-action."

"Iran officials continue to deny Sol had been in Tehran during the Ashura protests. We know he was. I wish additional intel had turned up, but it hasn't."

Francine gave Karol time to resurface from deep remembrances. "Do you and Sonia stay in touch?"

It took a moment for Karol to shift back to the present. "Uh ... Yes. Now and then. We avoid dwelling on past times. Just les sujets de jour. But I'm here to talk with you about my son, Bram."

Francine jarred as if having felt a sudden earth tremor. "Your son? Wow. That is unexpected. Is he in trouble?"

"He is adamant about assisting you."

Francine chuckled with surprise as if she had been asked to build an escalator to the moon. "I can't imagine you could dream I'd permit a thirteen-year-old boy to assist me."

"For better or worse, Bram inherited his father's and my detective genetics—and his father's stubbornness— maybe a bit from me."

"Probably enhanced by you dazzling him with stories of your and Sol's careers," Francine said.

"I have never shared anything about our intelligence careers. For better or worse, he believes I was born a real estate agent and that his dad was an IBM computer consultant. Ran off after delivering a lecture at the Technical University of Athens in Greece."

Francine leaned back in her chair as if sizing up her visitor. "It's hard to believe that in all these years, you never told your—"

"I never let him meet his grandparents or relatives. I feared he would grow up and follow in our footsteps."

"Footsteps don't get better than your and Sol's. Is Bram as handsome as Sol?"

"Girls think so. The boys call him, 'Hawaiian wimp,'

and 'Polynesian nerd,' and crueler labels."

"Kids. Can I get you some coffee?"

"Do you have any in here? I don't want to risk being recognized."

"Really? Did you miss the abrupt silence and heads twisting? Recognition couldn't have been more obvious. I'll fetch us some coffee."

"No need. I'll be brief."

"Of course, you will. I doubt either of us has changed her modus operandi."

"Bram believes he is on the trail of your serial killer."

Again, Francine was jarred, struggling for a reply. "You were serious about his genetics."

"Bram feels a duty to help."

Francine circled her office, pausing to peep through her blinds into the common area while her reasoning was being pulled in opposite directions by fascination on one hand and fear of dealing with the exuberance of a teen boy on the other. "Surely you remember my impatience with kids."

"Impatience is a mild term for what I recall. You once declared all teenage boys as having super-sex hormones cooking on steroids."

"I actually said that? Sounds too poetic for me."

"You, and I, and Sol were swigging down shots of Courvoisier at O'Malley's."

Francine chuckled. "You may try, but you haven't put this place behind you. But even shoving my prejudices and emotional swings aside, I don't have time to spare for children playing cops and robbers."

"My son is on target—not that I as his mother would dare admit that in front of him. But I am asking you to hear him out, act grateful, and then discourage him from crime solving until he's older and studied the law or intelligence and moved up through proper channels—God forbid.”

“Wow.” Francine walked to the window for the city view that always expanded her thinking. “You were a strong, legendary intelligence case officer.” She returned to her desk. “I would have thought you would be proud, want to encourage him, approach me as a team. Mother and son.”

“I lost Sol. I don’t want to lose Bram. For his sake and mine, please be kind, gentle, but set absolute limits. Guide him back into his few remaining years of childhood.”

“Wow again. So, you’re asking me to play along as if I’m some child-nurturing, warm, fuzzy—but at the same time restrictive—mentor. You must have forgotten the cold bitch I embrace being.”

“Point out one person in this domain who does not see through your façade—other than yourself.”

Francine tried to stifle a grin, but warmth leaked through her eyes.

Karol planted her elbows on the desk and leaned forward as if she were pressuring a suspect. “I’m looking at your face and see enough kindness to rest my case. With you, Bram will be in the best of hands. He of all people will see past your poor acting skills. But you must confront him with the reality that he is a child, not ready for adult dangers.”

“Does he know you are here?”

Karol’s snicker and frown proclaimed, *absolutely not.*

“How do you know he’ll even approach me?”

“He may be my over-protected son, but he’s also his father’s son. He’s on a mission. He’ll find you.”

“How do you expect me to act?”

“I expect you to be you. Live up to the legend I’ve heard you’ve become.”

"From whom?"

"Thank you for doing this," Karol said. She stood and stepped toward the door.

"Wait. Any chance you can share information your son knows with me now?"

Karol remained with her back to Francine.

"K.C. This woman killed an officer. Stabbed him."

After a moment of silence, Karol fled the department, never glancing sideways or backwards.

Mission accomplished.

DUTY

Jasmine felt irritated by the boy sitting in the station waiting room studying her, quickly looking away and pretending to study objects behind and beside her anytime she glanced his way. After minutes of playing pee-pie, she settled on prolonged staring back at him, determined to catch his eyes, but the lad avoided her until she resumed reading her magazine.

She felt his stare again, and without looking up, she said, "It's rude to stare at people."

"I like your warrior look," the boy said.

Now that they had broken through an undeclared rule of not conversing, of not making normal eye contact, Jasmine said, "Not the first time I've been told that."

"You look like the character in one of my video games," Bram said. "Glitter in your crewcut and a metal-studded leather wrist band. Defined muscles from working out."

"Maybe my muscles are naturally strong."

"You're reading a strength-training magazine."

"So, I am." She assessed the boy's slender body build. Maybe he was envious. "What's your name?"

"Bram. What's yours?"

"Jasmine. What are you doing here?"

"Waiting to show somebody my report."

"A school project?" Jasmine asked.

"Maybe. What are you doing here?"

"Meeting someone for lunch."

"Someone who works here?"

"Maybe."

Bram pulled a notepad from his bookbag and began sketching.

Jasmine returned to her fitness magazine.

Francine entered. "Oh, Jasmine. You're early. I have a quick appointment with this fellow. I'll be with you shortly."

Jasmine stood. "I'll grab coffee and return."

Francine waited for Jasmine to be out of earshot. "So, young man, what is your name?"

"Bram W."

Francine bit her lip. "Well, Mr. Bram W., please follow me to my office."

Once in the commander's office. Bram browsed photos and trophies as if he had stumbled upon his new favorite museum.

Francine sat and enjoyed observing her young acquaintance enter her world, surprising herself that she was not annoyed by his intrusion. Maybe it was because he was K.C. Whaanga's son. Maybe it was because he displayed intense interest. Maybe it was her rebelling against being told to curb the boy's enthusiasm. "I take it you're interested in detective work."

"How do you know that?" Bram asked.

"Guessing that's the case since you responded to our solicitation."

"I'm interested in understanding people."

"Oh." She was surprised by how much she was entertained by his company. "Understanding people's is an essential building block of detective work."

"I read in *The Times* you are focusing on the park serial killer."

"You're to the point." Francine tapped her desk top. "I like that. We did call on the public for information."

"The killer's a woman. A dramatic-actress type. She changes her appearance and the décor of where she lives to attract her victims."

"And you know this how?"

"My mother's in real estate. She sold four different condos that the killer owned and redecorated."

"Why didn't your mother contact us or come with you?"

"She's shy. A loner. I don't know how she even sells anything or manages to shop."

"How many condos did you say your mother sold for this dramatic woman?"

"Four."

"Four?"

"Four."

"There have only been three murders."

"That you uncovered," Bram said.

"I see. That we uncovered."

"Are you including the death in Gramercy Park?"

Francine shuddered hearing the name of a park that brought back painful memories. "Why do you think that death was a homicide rather than an accident?"

"Mom sold a condo for the killer near there. I found it in Mom's notes. And I read the report in the *Times*. Same pattern."

Bram stared through Francine in a way that made her feel he had undressed her defenses. She thought there was no doubt that this was the offspring of K.C. and Sol. "Let's refer to her as suspect rather than killer for now. I'll have my detectives look into the Gramercy Park case."

Francine was fascinated how expressionless the teenager's face became when he chose to throw up a wall. "I appreciate your coming forward." She handed a card to Bram. "This is Detective Aaron Galanis's contact information. I'll ask him to accept calls from you or contact you if he has questions. Do we have your contact info?"

Bram stood. "Does your receptionist turn over forms to you that she forces people to fill out?"

Francine laughed. "Remind me not to challenge you in a chess game. But front-desk forms or not, comfort me that Detective Galanis will have your cellphone number should he wish to reach you."

"Why can't I call you?"

"As you can imagine, I stay very busy."

Bram stepped toward the door.

"One more thing," Francine said. "Did your mother ever mention the name of her client?"

She mentioned it, and I found it in her notes. Azza Thornton. An alias I'm certain."

"Before you leave," Francine said, "you need to realize we're both on shaky ground for you to be here unaccompanied, talking with me or one of my detectives without your mother's permission."

"And you are guessing she did not grant permission." Bram left without looking back.

"To the point," Francine mumbled. "Know where he got that."

Francine spotted Jasmine waiting outside her door, hands across her chest, staring at Bram hurrying along the hall.

Jasmine asked, "A quick lunch?"

"Give me ten. I need to follow up on something."

"Did I really hear you laughing in here? I thought you hated rug rats. Especially boys."

"Shut up. Give me ten."

Francine leaned in Aaron's office. "Grab Ted and come join me."

Aaron arrived with a tranquil disposition of being in a routine experience, whereas Ted arrived with the elated disposition of being in a once-in-a-lifetime experience.

Aaron asked, "How was K.C.'s kid?"

Francine looked at notes she had jotted. "Her son,

Bram, led me to believe that the drug death in Gramercy Park was a murder by our serial killer."

"Her kid did?"

"Bram. Yes."

"And in Gramercy Park of all places. I know that park has special meaning for you."

Francine shut Aaron down with the glare of a fire-breathing dragon about to roast a human.

"Oh. Sorry," Aaron mumbled, jarred from being censored.

Ted perked up. "That's the park with Edwin Booth's statue. The great Shakespearean actor of the 1860s."

"You don't say, Ted," Aaron mumbled, preparing to be bored by another Ted Mateo lecture.

"Did you know Edwin was John Wilkes Booth's brother who assassinated Lincoln?"

"Did not know that, Ted."

"Yep. He sure was. Edwin had to beg President Andrew Johnson to let him have John's body to bury him in their family plot."

"Gentlemen," Francine said. "Can we focus on this century's deaths in our backyard?"

Aaron nodded agreement and Ted appeared bewildered that neither detective was enthralled by his historical saga.

GARDEN STATUE
- April 2022 -

Elisabet Norgaard was lounging in her floral-print, satin sleep robe when her morning charwoman, Beatrice, entered the penthouse library and served morning coffee and croissant aux amandes.

"Will there be anything else, Ms. Norgaard?"

"Thank you no, Beatrice," Elisabet said, reaching beneath the desk. "I'm fine for the rest of the morning. Have a pleasant day."

Beatrice nodded, having been lectured to never curtsey before Elisabet in contrast to etiquette with former family members.

Elisabet pressed a hidden button, and a large computer screen raised out of the Edwardian-legged table. Searching the *New York Daily News* for homicides, she found the story of police asking for information about an Alabama man overdosing two months before in Hudson Park. *Foul play suspected.*

She also searched the *Daily News* for police seeking help in less serious investigations. *Wanted: Suspect for Shoplifting in Midtown. Manhattan police seek help in identifying a female suspect of repeated shoplifting at numerous local bodegas. Clerks report she alters her appearance and accent, sometimes using aliases such as "Azza." The suspect appears to be a white female with a slim build, about five-foot-seven. If anyone has information to help identify the suspect, please contact Midtown Precinct North at 212-555-8400.*

"Fuck," Elisabet yelled. "Bodegas my ass." She marched in circles among floor-to-ceiling books until kicking over an end table, sending a voluminous French art book sailing into the base of a globe.

She yelled to the walls of books. "I only use that name with my fucking sales-realtor. That evil woman has finally surfaced to reveal her intelligence to connect the dots. No more hiding behind sugary language and nonsensical baby talk, Ms. Karol Whaanga. It's time I call upon you."

Elisabet phoned the number of Karol's realtor company. "Hi. This is Captain Boult. Ms. Whaanga has been marvelous in helping my new recruits at the Midtown Precinct find perfect housing in Manhattan, matching neighborhoods to spouses and children's needs. We want to reward her with a garden sculpture. She's always bragging about her garden—but be sure not to tell her. It's a surprise. The statue's a heavy outdoor piece. It would be inconsiderate to drop it off at your office and stick her with the task of hiring movers to transport it."

"I didn't even know Karol gardened," Jacqueline, the receptionist, said. "What a wonderful gift, but I'm not really supposed to give out home addresses. Company policy. I apologize, Captain."

"Oh, that's fine. Sorry to bother you. The museum needs to deliver it this afternoon."

"Museum. Oh my. I bet it is nice."

"I'll have the movers leave it on the sidewalk in front of your building. As I said it's rather large."

"Oh dear … Uh … Well, maybe it would be simpler if you delivered it to her personally."

A WORTHY SACRIFICE

Elisabet approached the Peace Fountain next to the Cathedral of St. John the Divine in Morningside Heights and knelt beneath the bronze sculpture of her Archangel Michael. He was frozen in the moment after he had decapitated Satan with his sword and was plunging Satan's body into the depths while a peaceful lion and lamb observed.

Although the fountain was quiet, no longer offering cascading water, traffic noises were enough to overshadow Elisabet talking aloud to her saint.

"I found a worthy sacrifice, Michael, but of course shall await your blessing. My find is a woman realtor who despises all that is holy and is out to destroy our mission."

Tourists and other visitors walked by, comforted that the woman was praying, asking for forgiveness or protection as many guests did with the bronze sculpture.

Elisabet stared into the heavens and waited. Dust, leaves, plastic bags, and paper cups suddenly lifted from the park grounds and chased one another in a whirlwind circling the fountain.

"Thank you, Michael. I shall not fail you."

NOT EVERY HOUSE IS A CASTLE

Sitting at her kitchen counter, Karol checked emails on her laptop. She opened one from a colleague and shrieked, "Sensational."

Her yell superseded Bram's earbud music, interrupting his sketching Captain America from memory. He jerked off his head apparatus. "Why are you screaming?"

Karol pointed at her screen. "One of my colleagues, Bertram Finley, answered the email I sent asking if he remembered selling the condo near Gramercy Park. He did. Described Ms. Thornton perfectly—well, the way she sounded on the phone at that moment."

"What the hell are you doing?"

"Helping you, honey bunch."

"Have you flipped? You do everything in your power to keep me safe from the tiniest dangers."

"I do not."

"Every time I start to cross a street, you grab my shoulder like I'm a frigging three-year-old."

Karol waved her no-cursing finger. "You said Captain Boult distinctly told you to call her if you learned more about Azza Thornton. Now you can suggest to the captain that she should interview Bertram."

Bram screamed, "This is my case. Not yours."

"Oh. Your case. I see."

"Detective Aaron Galanis said for me to call him if I learned anything. He didn't say for me to have my mother call him. There's no way in hell I want you involved and screw it up."

"Screw it up. I see." Karol checked the timer on the oven. "Roast is almost done. Just to remind you, Ms. Thornton got me to sell five condos. She already involved me."

"Five?" Bram asked. "I thought it was four."

"Did I say five?" Karol asked, placating with her hands. "Four. Five. Whatever."

"Detectives don't throw up their hands and whine, 'whatever.'"

"Maybe not, honey, but listen. Although I sold Azza Thornton's condos for her, she purchases her condos from other realtors. Each time a different realtor. One of them was Bertram Finley."

"Fuck. I can't believe this."

"Bram."

"What did you do? Wade through every real estate sell in New York? That would be an insane job even for first-class detectives."

"For your information, closure-real-estate records for buildings and houses list both the seller and buyer realtors. Since I sold condos for Azza, I looked up who had first sold those same condos to her—even though she used varying aliases."

"Whatever." Bram pouted, mumbling to himself about his own mother subverting his spy world.

"I'm trying to help you, honey—with something I don't approve of but something it's clear you love. I'm a mother. I want to make you happy."

"You are so far out of your league."

"I gathered helpful information. Do you want it, or not?"

"You won't be glad you helped if she finds out and comes after us."

"How many times have I said that to you? And you're just now getting that? We could already be in danger."

"Odd you said that. Come look at this." Bram peeped through the living-room blinds. "I didn't want to tell you this and freak you out, but the past two days there's been a car sitting out front."

"Cars sit out there all day long."

"Not this one." Bram motioned for Karol to peep through the blinds. "See next to the phone pole?"

Karol squinted. "The black car?"

"See how the windows are tinted."

"The light's not good."

Bram opened the front door and Karol grabbed his arm. "Wait. Where are you going?"

"I gotta know." Bram marched out the front door and toward the mystery vehicle. Immediately, it sped away.

Bram yelled at his mother peering out the door. "Did you see that? Somebody's spying on us."

"Probably someone got lost, or pulled over to make a call, or is bird watching like I sometimes do."

"Wow, your world's a nice place. I'm going to call Aaron."

"What's his last name again?"

"Detective Aaron Galanis." Bram stormed upstairs to his bedroom, yelling as he slammed his door. "Don't interrupt me."

Moments later, the doorbell rang and before Karol could walk from the kitchen, Bram rushed down the steps two at a time, yelling, "Let me get it."

He swung open the door in time to see a special delivery man climb into a curbside van and drive away. Bram looked down and spotted a bakery box on their stoop.

Karol joined him. "Oh look, honey. Something from Brooklyn Sweets. I bet it's a payback treat from Miss Abernathy down the block. I baked her a peach pie last week when Mitsy, her puppy, was run over. Poor thing."

Bram unfastened the lid and opened it cautiously, apprehensive a Jack-in-the-Box or a snake might spring out.

Karol laughed with delight. "Oh look. My favorite. Cupcakes with chocolate icing."

"Wait," Bram screamed and shut the box lid. "Chocolate icing was how Azza Thornton poisoned those men. I'm calling Aaron to analyze this thing."

BIG BROTHER IS WATCHING

Karol detested cellphone interruptions while she was compiling complex lists. She was wading through swamps of numbers, judging and comparing: square footage of kitchens, home-owners-association fees, which schools accept which neighborhood kids, what childcare is available, which buildings are pet friendly, what bus and subway routes are close by, and a zillion other factors.

She did not recognize the calling number. If it was another robocall—the eleventh of the morning—she was prepared to scream one of three curse words she allowed herself.

She answered with an irritated tone. "This is Karol Whaanga. How may I help you?"

The caller's voice was familiar: their receptionist. "It's me. Jacqueline."

"Oh, sorry. I didn't recognize the number."

"Adam ranted we've been busy enough to add a third landline. Ms. Featherstonehaw—or however you pronounce her name—called to ask if you can move her appointment up an hour on Thursday."

"Why didn't she call me?"

"She lost your number."

"Couldn't you give her my number?"

"I tried, but she said she was in a hurry and she'd call the office later this afternoon."

"Good golly, wolly. Fine." Karol consulted her phone calendar. "Tell her that'll be fine. Anything else?"

"That's it—oh. How did you like your big gift?"

"What big gift?"

"The statue."

"What statue?"

"For your garden?"

Karol's voice registered confusion. "My garden?"

There was a long pause on Jacqueline's end. "Oh no."

"What?"

"A uh, a uh … a Captain—let me look up the uh … a Captain Boult asked for your address so she could have a museum deliver a statue—"

"Oh shit."

"Did you just curse?"

"I'll call you back." Karol ended the call and searched for the precinct's number.

Karol was thankful that instead of rotating through a litany of recorded messages, an actual human answered. "This is Midtown Precinct North. How may I help you?"

"Is Captain Boult there?"

"Who's calling?"

"K.C. Whaanga. I need to speak with her promptly."

"She's in a meeting."

"Tell her it's an emergency."

"One moment."

Karol only had to wait twenty seconds for Francine to answer. "Hi K.C. What's the emergency?"

"My agency said you called for my address to deliver a gift for my garden. A statue."

"I know nothing about that."

"There is no statue. There is no garden. I think Azza Thornton called my agency with a ruse to get my home address."

"Oh my God," Francine said. "Are you certain there wasn't a mix up?"

"She's clever. She sought my home address."

"I'll order a Personal Security Detail. Are you and Bram both at home?"

"Bram's at school. He usually walks home. I'll call the

school and have them hold him until I get there."

"Do you have anywhere else you can stay? If she killed an officer and lied to get your address, she'll try something more. This weird woman has a psychotic thing going with St. Michael."

"You mentioned she stabbed an officer," Karol said.

"A fast death. Much like a professional hit."

"I don't know where we could—"

"I'll arrange a hotel. Order our security detail to stay close."

"This is all happening so fast." Karol's confused tone transmuted to an alarmed tone. "Oh my gosh. Oh my gosh."

"What?"

"Bram spotted a strange car with tinted windows parked outside our house more than once. When he walked toward it, it sped off."

"Let's move you out of there fast."

"I thought going into real estate would be safe."

"I had already planned to move you."

"Why on earth?"

"When you called, I was in a meeting with Detective Galanis."

"Bram's helper, Aaron, right?"

"Aaron received the results back on the cupcakes delivered to you. Bram was right. They were poisoned."

Karol had to sit and have her world go silent. She had done everything to protect her and Sol's son. Not allowing him to ride his bicycle beyond their yard for years later than neighborhood children were permitted to race bikes any and everywhere all hours of the day and night.

"K.C.? Are you still there?"

"Oh. Uh yes … It's just that this is so unexpected."

"What time does Bram's school let out?"

"Three o'clock."

"Which school?"

"Midwood High School on Bedford Avenue."

Francine reached for her log of officer assignments. "I'll call Midwood and let them know I'm sending two officers to pick up Bram. You stay in the house and pack until Bram and my people get there. Do not leave the house. Got that?"

BETTER THAN A HALL PASS

The times Bram had been called to the principal's office had been for a host of misdemeanors—misdemeanors by his account. Incidents such as trying to commandeer a science class in which Bram considered Mr. Broyhill's lecture on galaxy formation to be embarrassingly antiquated. Did the guy read current issues of *Scientific America* or only issues he found rotting in his grandparents' attic?

Today, Bram had no clue why he had been summoned to Principal Breitenstein's office. It had been days, maybe even a week since he had irritated a teacher or been tardy due to forgetting the order of his classes.

Bram noticed two police officers in the office sitting with their backs to him. Oh my gosh, he thought. This must really be bad, but then he recognized Aaron and dread converted to exuberance.

"Aaron? What's going on, man?"

Aaron leaned closer to whisper. "Your hunch about the cupcakes was on target, my friend. The icing tested positive for carfentanil. The carrier had responded to a call and acquired the bakery box from a pigtailed woman in a checkered dress dashing out from Brooklyn Sweets and handing him the box and cash. We arranged protective custody for you and your mother."

Bram appeared alarmed. "Custody?"

"Police assigned to guard you and your mother."

"Really?" Bram yelled with enough enthusiasm to turn heads of other students waiting for hall passes. "Do I get to ride with you?"

"Absolutely."

"Flashing lights and siren?"

"We're doing our best to go unnoticed."

Bram nodded toward the batch of students staring at them. "You're doing a great job with that."

Aaron turned to the principal. "Are we cleared to take him?"

Principal Breitenstein peered over his reading glasses. "His mother gave her okay. By all means. Please."

WE SHOULD ALL BE FRIENDS

When Aaron entered the precinct station, Francine was antsy and frowning as if she had been waiting for him for days. "Did you get them settled?"

"Snacks for Bram, healthy meals for K.C., Netflix, Wi-Fi for laptops, shifts of two officers at a time."

"Thank you." Francine tapped a folded letter against a clinched fist.

"What's that?" Aaron asked.

"A second note from our disturbed fan."

Aaron blushed as if a grade school friend had excoriated him for being friendly to the school's most unpopular girl. "Please tell me she's not demanding we investigate another person for her."

"A janitor at a kindergarten."

"I don't even want to know." Aaron's tone swiftly shifted to anger. "What's this creep want? Us to invite her to join our squad? Be her best friend?"

"She's psychotic."

"She's worse than psychotic. She's … she's … We need Superman to transport her to another galaxy."

Francine stepped back. "Are you rubbing off on Bram, or is he rubbing off on you?"

Aaron mumbled, "I couldn't think of the right word or phrase."

Francine laughed, adoring Aaron's typically fresh honesty. "That's because there is no correct concept."

Aaron pondered possibilities for a moment. "Do you think she's really that crazy or is toying with us?"

"Doesn't matter. She kills people. We don't need to spin our wheels trying to understand or figure out what to label her mind set. We just need to stop her."

BEYOND THE BIG APPLE

Bram sat on the edge of his hotel twin bed, reviewing life and how this was the first time he had slept in the same room with his mother since he was four. This sucks, he thought. Why couldn't NYPD spring for a two-bedroom suite?

Karol returned to their room after consulting with one of the officers. "Benjamin's going to accompany me to the coffee shop."

"Ah. First name basis with our detail. You're growing social skills."

Karol was too exhausted to spare facial muscles to react. "Do you want anything? A muffin? Juice?"

"Nope."

"I'll be back in a few minutes."

"Take your time. I'm having a blast being stuck in this box. Did you know our bathroom is four-and-a-half tiles wide by twelve tiles long?"

Karol was not about to invite Bram to tag along. They both needed the break.

Bram leaped off the bed and yelled, "Wait a second."

Karol stopped mid-threshold.

"Why did Captain Boult call you K.C.?"

"She did?"

"On the police car radio. Twice."

"Huh. Guess you'll have to ask her."

Bram waited a moment and peeped out the door to assure his mother was out of sight, ignoring the second officer watching him.

He opened his mother's laptop and typed *Azza* in the search box. Several choices appeared. There were two condos near Hudson Park, a condo overlooking Gramercy

Park, and a fourth condo bordering the Union Park area. He found his mother's note to herself about recently searching condos sold to Azza by various realtors. Finally, there was information about an earlier transaction, one not in New York State but in New Haven, Connecticut. The entry preceded the dates of the Manhattan murders.

Bram startled when he thought he heard the doorknob click, but the door did not open. He closed his mother's laptop, crawled on top of his bed, and searched on his laptop. Had there been a similar murder in the New Haven area close to the date his mother sold that condo?

After half an hour, Karol returned. "I brought you orange juice."

Bram uttered, "Uh huh," and continued searching.

"I'll put it in the mini fridge, unless you want it now."

Another "uh huh."

"Well, you're obviously lost in cyberspace. Let me know when you land."

No response.

"I said let me know—"

"I heard you." After a silent minute and Bram remaining fixated on his laptop screen, he asked, "Have you ever heard of Beaverdale Park near New Haven?"

"Not that I remember. Why?"

"Nothing."

Karol mumbled, "Of course. Nothing. A dangerous word: nothing."

"Did you ever sell real estate there? New Haven?"

"Two or three times, I think. Why?"

"Nothing."

Karol checked her hair and makeup in the mirror, frowning that hotel lighting accentuated lines in her face. "I think I'll go back down to the coffee shop. See if there's something rather than nothing."

Bram continued scrolling.
"Are you listening to me?"
"No."

LEAD WITH WHAT'S IMPORTANT

Bram sat in the precinct waiting room, sketching in one of his dozens of unlined-paper notebooks. He was sitting near the window, preferring to draw in natural sunlight.

Jasmine entered and Bram looked up in time to see her glare and mouth the word *fuck*.

Bram halted sketching and waited until Jasmine sat. "I can read lips, you know."

Jasmine dismissed the comment with a shrug. "You here to see your little detective friend?"

Bram buried his head in his sketching. "Yep. You here to see your little detective friend?"

Jasmine tried to suppress a grin, but Bram obviously had the gift to tease her into a better mood—much like her brothers had always been able to do. "Yep."

She watched him sketch for a minute and then attempted to be more social. "What are you drawing?"

"The officer who drove me here."

"Your mother didn't drive you?"

"She hates to drive. She insisted one of our all-day-long bodyguards transport me."

"Well, you certainly are getting special treatment."

"I have a foot escort every day. Causes a big stir at my school. But it was cool being driven here today. I hate public transportation."

"Me too," Jasmine said. "Getting stared at. Smelling God knows what."

Jasmine did not want to appear overly curious, but she was. "Can I see your drawing?"

Bram rotated his sketch.

"Oh wow. I know him. That's Travis."

"You can recognize him?"

"Duh. You captured him perfectly. Well, except you made him more dignified. He'll love it."

Bram placed his notebook on the magazine table, carefully tore out the page, and handed it to Jasmine. "For you."

"Oh. No, no, no. I can't take your Travis drawing."

"I have two more of Detective Hogan. Here. This one's yours."

Jasmine's face flushed as if she were back in eighth grade, and a classmate she was fond of annoying had sprung forth with a bouquet of wild flowers.

Aaron poked his head in the door. "Hey, cool guy."

Bram leaped up from his seat, grabbing all his belongings in one smooth move. "Hey, wild guy."

Jasmine watched the two males exit, feeling a hole in her heart. She and Francine had recently been missing the jubilation she just witnessed.

Francine soon entered, and in a flat monotone, asked, "Ready?"

***

Aaron ushered Bram to the chair opposite his desk. "What's so important you couldn't tell me on the phone?"

"I like to see people's faces. Watch how what I say lands on them."

"You definitely are unlike kids I see all day long glued to their phones."

"I hope that's good."

"And those kids talking in weird, raspy voices. What's up with that? Disdain for everything and everyone?"

"Mom's big on elocution."

"Good on her."

Bram coolly extended his hand like a rap star and they

fist bumped.

"So?" Aaron asked.

"So? I came across an earlier murder by Azza."

Aaron's lighthearted expression took a dive. "You know we're pretty sure that name's an alias."

"Should I refer to her as perpetrator, killer, psycho, or do you prefer bitch?"

Aaron smiled, slowly reconnecting to the task at hand. "*Azza* will be fine. I believe her name earned all those connotations. I'll sit back. Tell me everything."

Bram placed his crossed arms on Aaron's desk and leaned forward with an eager look of being prepped. "I may be wrong, but I believe you guys missed a death in Beaverdale Park outside of New Haven."

Aaron appeared pained as if suffering an emotional punch in the gut. "That's not our jurisdiction."

"It's close by. Connecticut."

"Fair enough. Tell me about it."

"Two years ago, the New Haven police ruled a Beaverdale Park death as an accidental overdose. But the victim's friends said the guy never used drugs. Not even alcohol, cigarettes, or coffee."

"Why do you believe it wasn't accidental?"

"Police reported his friends told them the victim had been dating a new woman for three months. The victim was getting his B.S. in chemistry at Southern Connecticut U. Suddenly, a woman appeared out of nowhere. Claimed to be a pharmaceutical researcher. She never associated with the guy's friends. Squandered him to herself during those months. After he died, the woman vanished. Poof. Same pattern as your four Manhattan cases."

"How did you gain these story-like details about the couple?"

"The *New Haven Register*. Online. I printed the story

to add to my notebook."

"You keep a notebook about murders?"

"Don't tell Mom. She'll freak out."

"Good sleuth work. But at best, your evidence is circumstantial. That means—"

"I know what circumstantial means. Mom said Azza had a German accent when discussing her condo in New Haven. I had to show Mom the online article and pin her down to pry more information out of her. She got really pissed I infiltrated her records."

"Hold on a minute. Are you saying your mother sold a New Haven condo for Azza?"

Bram's faced reddened. "Shit. I skipped over my most important fact. Yeah. Mom flipped that condo for Azza. I should have led with that. Right?"

"It helps."

"I'll do better. Swear to it."

"You're doing fine."

"Mom said that for each condo, Azza had a different accent. Different phone and address info. And back when she dated the New Haven chemist, she had this really cool wooden card table in her condo with the periodic chart engraved into it."

"You saw it?"

"I like chemistry. Mom snapped a photo as an idea for me to make. I never did."

"I thought your mother only handled real estate in New York."

"Why would you think that?"

Imitating Bram's cadence, Aaron said, "I was assuming. I'll do better. Swear to it."

Bram grinned. "Mom focuses on the greater New York area, including some of New Jersey and Connecticut. But she refuses to deal with places on Long Island. Well,

Queens and Brooklyn, but not farther out on the island."

"Why not farther out?"

"I don't know for certain, but I found a shoebox with old love letters and—"

"You read your mom's love letters?"

"I'm snoopy. Always have been."

"And without guilt, I see."

"I think the letters were from my father. He only signed using his first name. *Love Sol.*"

"Does your mother talk about your dad?"

Bram teared up. "I think it would rip her apart. Not that she doesn't want to." He took a moment to calm, not wanting to cry in front of Aaron. "She can't."

"Do you know anything about your dad?"

Bram shook his head and wiped his nose. "Can we talk about something else? About Azza?"

"Sure. But if you ever want to talk with me about more than cases, more personal stuff, know that I'm—"

"I know that. Thank you. But back to Azza. Please?"

"Absolutely."

Bram stretched his arms while regaining composure. "So, the dates of the condo sell and the dates of the Beaverdale Park death are earlier than the Manhattan murders. So, maybe in New Haven, Azza was just getting started with killing. If so, that makes that case more important, right?"

"Why more?"

"The first time tells us why. The ones after that are just copies, missing actions that could tell us what drives her. What's behind her weird patterns."

"Huh." Aaron pushed back in his seat to get a fuller view of the human being across from him.

Bram squirmed with discomfort. "What?"

"You really do have the detective gene like Captain

Boult said."

"She said that?"

"And she's tough to impress."

"I wouldn't call it a gene. Mom is—and excuse me for saying so—is a scaredy-cat wimp in every way. And my dad repaired computers. A solitary kind of job."

"I thought you didn't know anything about him."

"Three things. Computer repair guy. Lived on Long Island. And was Māori—Mom had to tell me that so I could answer the million people pestering me asking if I'm Hawaiian or Pilipino."

"Do you know much about New Zealand and Māoris?"

"Try me."

Aaron burst forth with a laugh contagious enough that Bram joined him.

"Yeah."

Aaron studied the handsome kid before him, trying to imagine the tribulations he must have endured. "Bram's hardly a Māori name."

"Biblical name. I'm supposed to sire lots of kids—or so, my teacher explained to our class."

"Bet that was embarrassing."

"I skipped the next three days."

"So, what should we do with your masterful deducing, Detective Whaanga?"

"I'm hoping you'll tell me."

"Do you really think that was her first kill? New Haven? The kill that reveals the mysteries of this violent, cold-blooded monster?"

Bram slinked enough to appear sheepish. "Not really."

"Ah ha. And why is that?"

"Her pattern in New Haven was too similar to the other cases. I think the actual first kill would differ more, tell a deeper story."

"Huh."

They sat still listening to office music, staring at their own fingers, at the ceiling, out the window.

Aaron interrupted the entr'acte. "What are you doing this weekend?"

"Nothing special."

"I'm taking my three-year-old, Colt, to a minor-league baseball game. He loves them. Especially hot dogs and organ music. Go with us—if it's okay with your mom."

"Sounds like fun. But how does that help?"

"Wow you are focused. But it works for me. Being in a crowd of people cheering and booing suddenly lifts me to see something I couldn't see when I was deliberately concentrating. A rich vision or answer just pops into my mind. Go with us."

Bram hesitated and then nodded hard. "Fine. Anything with a chance of helping."

"And if we fail, we still have fun."

Aaron studied Bram, not detecting a change of expression or a hint of acknowledgement. He thought, this is one tough kid. But fascinating and loveable.

Aaron wished he had known Sol, not just heard about him through Francine's stories. He felt certain Sol would be proud and love this boy dearly.

LADIES AND SECRETS

While Bram met with Aaron, Francine was concluding a meeting with two officers. She escorted Detectives Jenetta and Wyatt out of her office. "I appreciate you two taking the lead to tie the smash-and-grab jewel robber to a homicide. Let me know if you need more support. Great job following a hunch."

As the officers exited along the hallway, Francine spotted Jasmine. "Wow. Haven't seen you in the station for a while. Come in."

Jasmine marched straight to Francine's hot seat, laid a paper on her desk, and sat. "This is a description from three women in the Daughters of Boudicca group. I didn't get to see the woman in question, but they told me about an elderly woman who is always draped in black cloth and attends their group every few weeks. They assume her garb is a Muslim burka. It practically conceals her face. She never speaks, but takes notes and always leaves early, carrying away fliers, handouts, whatever has identifying information about men reported to be abusive."

"Wow." Francine took her seat and studied the multi-folded page.

"I didn't have time to type it."

"I've learned to decipher your scribbles."

"Sorry about the food stain."

"Have the women tried to speak with her?"

"They said they have." Jasmine grabbed a mint from a desk bowl. "She acts as if she doesn't understand English—or Spanish. But they report she appears to be listening intently. And as I said, she takes notes."

Francine smiled at her friend. "This may be our best

lead yet. You told me this group likes to remain secret."

"Demands to remain secret."

"Did you tell them why you had questions about the woman?"

"I told them I'd seen her coming out of a meeting once, acting strange and that I was curious. They volunteered that she worries them."

"Did they become suspicious of you?"

"I've told you, they're nice people. Not vigilantes. They respect law. They don't like how the law is failing them."

Francine moved to sitting on the edge of her desk. "Will you be returning to the group?"

"As your spy?"

"As a concerned citizen."

"It's not my preferred way to spend an evening—or even an hour of my evening. I did this for you."

"Thank you. Do you think they would consider working with us, if you ask them?"

Jasmine stood. "I hope that solved your mystery. Never ask me to do something so repugnant again."

"It cleared up a chunk of my mystery. But it won't help identify the criminal. Unless I—or someone from here—talks with the ladies about the burka-covered woman or intercepts her at a meeting, we're at an impasse."

"Not my problem," Jasmine said.

"When did you attend the group?"

"Wednesday night."

"I haven't seen you for a couple of weeks."

"I've been camping out at Teresa's. She's twenty-five weeks pregnant. Lots of headaches. I promised to be on-call and accompany her if she has any difficulty."

"Very considerate of you. Am I correct assuming she used a surrogate father?"

"Yes."

"She and Sasha must be excited."

Jasmine stared at the floor. "They broke up."

"Oh no. That's a tragedy."

"Similar to the situation you and I found ourselves in. Teresa wanted the baby. Sasha did not."

Francine nodded but remained silent and shifted to skimming Jasmine's report.

Jasmine stepped toward the door and stopped. "I still want a child."

"I know. What are you holding?"

Jasmine unfurled Bram's art and held it up.

"Is that a sketch of Travis?"

"A gift to me from your child detective."

Francine laughed. "That boy is talented. Even though he is snippy, he has a way of wiggling into people's hearts."

"Even yours. Have you informed him about his parents?"

Francine pursed her lips and shook her head. "That's an awkward, uncomfortable situation. I don't like withholding truth from Bram, but I also don't want to betray K.C."

Francine smoothed out Jasmine's report, flattening the page with her hand. "I'll have Lane type this and share with our team. Thank you again. Are you going back to Teresa's?"

"After a few errands."

Jasmine stared a moment and left.

Francine called Aaron. "Can you do me a favor? A favor that will sound like I'm a jealous lover, but it is totally to follow a lead on our serial killer. I need for you to check locations for Jasmine's phone this past Wednesday night. She attended a meeting. It is highly likely our killer uses those meetings to select her victims."

STINGS CAN BE STUNG

Bram trudged downstairs to the kitchen, wearing only boxers. He found Karol with her laptop on the kitchen counter, a coffee mug on one side, and a bowl of yogurt topped with oatmeal on the other.

Karol glanced at her son's mostly naked body. "I've asked you hundreds of times to wear clothing when you wake and stumble downstairs."

"I haven't woken up yet. Besides, it's Saturday."

"I won't attempt to follow that logic."

"Proves I'm not awake. What are you doing?"

"I thought you would be interested in this email." Karol pivoted the laptop for Bram to read.

"It's your laptop. Read it to me."

"That didn't stop you from invading my laptop at the hotel."

"Golly. How many times do I have to apologize?"

"More."

"Whatever."

Karol sighed. "Okay. I'll read it to you. It's from Vincent, one of our realtors. 'Karol. The woman you asked about, Azza, bought a condo from me five weeks ago. Sorry I took so long—'"

"Holy … shoot."

"Ah. Now, you're awake."

Bram clung to his mother's shoulder as he peered over it. "Keep reading."

"'Below is the address of the condo. It overlooks Central Park.'"

Bram pushed away and clapped his hands. "Gotta be her. I gotta give this address to Aaron. You didn't call 'im and tell 'im already, did you?"

"I wouldn't dare do that and face your wrath."

Bram kissed Karol on the cheek. "Where's my phone?"

"In the laundry room. You left it in your pocket."

Bram snatched his phone and raced up the stairs.

Karol yelled after him. "You're welcome."

Karol sat alone, pondering why her client had used the alias Azza to buy the condo from Vincent. She always used other aliases purchasing condos. Had she been careless?

***

With weapons drawn, Francine, Aaron, and three midtown officers eased along the eighth-floor hallway at the Central Park West address Bram had provided—and confirmed by Karol's discrete phone call.

With ears to the door, the officers heard *Fox News* anchors arguing about corrupt government and an ad for car-warranties.

Although prepared to breach the door with a two-man ram or halligan tool, Aaron knocked.

A young man dressed in boxers and a NYU T-shirt, peered out the cracked-open door, immediately appearing alarmed.

An officer kicked the door, ripping off the chain latch.

"Jesus Christ," the occupant screamed as officers threw him to the floor, pressed knees into his back, and pinned his arms and legs.

Francine observed as Aaron dropped onto all fours and screamed into the guy's ear. "Are you alone here?"

"Yes. Yes sir. I'm alone."

"Do you live here?"

"I sublet here."

Francine looked around and breathed easier. "Let him up."

The officers pulled the man to his feet and patted his shirt and boxers.

Francine snatched control of interviewing. "Who sublets to you?"

"A woman."

"What's her name?"

"Sting Charlatan."

Aaron snickered. "Sting? You're shitting us."

"That's what she said—what she wrote on the lease."

One of the officers approached Francine. "You should look at this." She showed Francine the readings on her counter-surveillance tool. "The hidden-camera detector reads positive in every room."

The officer pointed at a ceiling air vent. "We're definitely on air."

Aaron exhaled with puffed cheeks as he double-checked the scanner readings.

Francine slid a chair beneath the vent and climbed up. "I'm accustomed to psychotic criminals and accustomed to smart criminals … Not super-smart, psychotic criminals."

Aaron uncovered a microphone in a lamp. "You know what scares me?"

Francine used a pocket tool to unscrew the air-vent cover. "I know what scares me."

"What?"

"She knows we're pursuing her. I fear her next two kills will be her last in New York. She'll move on to other locations."

Aaron pulled on rubber gloves and used sterile tweezers to extract a tiny listening device. "Well, there's no doubt she knows we're close."

Eyeing a staring camera lens, Francine frowned. "And now she knows what each of us look like."

***

Overlooking Central Park, at her home-base penthouse, Elisabet Norgaard studied her video feed. Rather than alarm, she felt amused and intrigued by confirming that the detective hot on her tail was none other than Captain Francine Boult, the person St. Michael had blessed to become her intimate friend, but the person who had failed her. Failed St. Michael.

Elisabet smirked, knowing she also had eyes and ears on new bodies: Detective Galanis and three other detectives.

It was also clear that New York City realtors were her enemies. She had no doubt her go-to realtor, Karol Whaanga, was collaborating with other realtors against her.

It had become clear watching Ms. Whaanga respond to the cupcake, that she had a teenage son. And after tailing Captain Boult, it was clear she had a lover.

There was no need to set her sights on Captain Boult and realtor Karol Whaanga. Death is quick. Suffering concludes. For them to lose a loved one, however, would inflict eternal suffering.

She needed to seek St. Michael's blessing before refining her plans.

THREE STRIKES AND YOU'RE OUT
- May 2022 -

When Aaron arrived at the precinct, Francine was waiting outside his office with an unopened letter. "I think this is from Azza. No return address."

Aaron appeared surprised. "You haven't read it yet?"

"I wanted to share the fun."

Aaron invited Francine into his office and sat. "With her history of gift giving, I prefer to be sitting when I learn what is wrapped and hiding inside."

Francine sat facing Aaron, their knees almost touching. They both slid on N95 masks and plastic gloves.

Aaron examined the envelope and saw that it was addressed to both Francine and to himself. He held onto the envelope for a long time, fighting to conceal his rush of emotions. "Did not expect my name to be included."

Aaron used his four-inch, serrated pocket knife—good for home defense—to slice open the envelope's upper ridge. He extracted the letter and unfolded it. "Ready?"

Francine minimally nodded.

"It's brief. Typed. No heading. Unsigned." Aaron read aloud, "You and your team have failed to deal with the Utah child marrying man and failed to deal with the kindergarten janitor. I lost faith in you. I will send you two more names. If you do not deal appropriately and expediently with bringing about justice, you will be made to suffer. Do not be concerned about your own safety. Placing you in danger is not justice. Be concerned for those you love."

The pair of detectives sat in silence for a moment until being interrupted by Lane.

"Pardon me for barging in, Commander, but K.C.

Whaanga is on the line for you. She says it's urgent."

"Did she say what it concerns?"

"Just that she received a letter."

Francine took a moment to consider the many possibilities. "Thank you, Lane. Captain Galanis and I will take the call in my office."

"Yes ma'am."

Francine and Aaron looked at one another for a moment and then walked together to the commander's office.

"Hello K.C. I have you on speaker phone so Captain Galanis can join us. We just received a letter too."

NATURE AND ART – TRUTHS OR LIES

If you asked Francine for her reason, she would have stuttered, faltered, drawn a blank. There was no reason, no intent.

It was a lovely spring afternoon when she completed a guest lecture to professional-studies students at Columbia University.

The chance to lecture had been a welcomed diversion from the park-killer case. She was exhausted from months of hitting perpetual dead ends. Although Bram had provided a promising clue, following the clue had backfired. And although Jasmine had provided promising information to solve a mystery of how victims were selected, the information was no help in identifying the suspect.

For the ninety minutes of lecture and discussion, Francine had not once thought about the recent third letter from Azza. She assumed that *loved ones* included Jasmine, Bram, and possibly Aaron's family. She could only assume that all of them were being stalked.

She was in no hurry to descend back into the hell hole of agonizing.

Once into fresh air, rather than descend below ground and rush to catch the number one back to work, she strolled toward the Hudson River, stumbling upon Sakura Park. The man-made oasis was demarcated from bustling avenues by an ivy-festooned wall. Pink cherry blossoms in the Japanese garden were still in bloom, prime time for meandering on paved paths coursing through rolling terrain.

She had begun the morning pressuring herself to memorize clever phrases for her lecture, rehearse canned responses for likely questions, and fret over how to tackle the ubiquitous kindergarten-level question that always popped up: "Do you carry a gun?" Most often followed by someone on a back row smiling smugly and announcing, "British police don't carry guns."

Coming upon a gazebo, she sat on its concrete steps, enjoying magic of a metropolis that had mastered the art of plunging guests into nature's embrace, tendering a reprieve from paperwork and murders.

Soft petals floating to earth and warm sun flickering on her face rivaled tranquilizing steam of a Turkish bath she had indulged in as a gift from her niece.

She closed her eyes and inhaled deep breaths, not wanting to waste a molecule of refreshment awarded by the garden.

Visions of childhood holidays and visions of Jasmine lying beside her caressed her soul. Slowly, her cherished montage dissolved into the reminisced image of Bastien-Lepage's garden illuminating Joan of Arc.

Francine watched her mind's theatre as the Sakura and Joan-of-Arc gardens merged. She was beside Joan, beside Jasmine, the three of them stretching toward thin air, longing for the beyond.

The pleasant moment shifted as Francine felt crowded by other presences, by faintly focused, floating women intruding upon her dreamworld.

Francine opened her eyes and the illusion faded like mist in sun.

She called on her cellphone. "Hi Lane. Can you tell Aaron to meet me at the MET right away. I want him to view a painting with me."

Lane's voice filled with excitement. "Oh my gosh. You're purchasing a painting from the MET? I've never known anyone who could do that."

"No, no, no, Lane. I want Aaron to examine a painting with me for clues to a crime. The answer could be in one of the MET paintings, however, I wish I could afford a MET painting—probably costing millions."

Lane sounded tenuous. "Oh. Okay. I'll tell him."

"I know it sounds insane, but this case is insane. I prefer to stroll over to the museum and savor more moments of spring, but it's a fifty-or-sixty-block hike."

Francine crossed to Claremont Avenue and hailed a cab to the Metropolitan Museum of Art.

At the MET, Francine claimed her spot on the bench before Joan and the celestial garden. She did not dare tumble too deeply into the painting, guarding against descending into the art abyss that had likely swallowed their suspect's sanity.

She remained aware of museum visitors coming and going, people coughing, an infant cooing, the hall elevator bell ringing, followed by trampling feet as spring hordes squeezed into one of New York's most treasured landmarks.

Joan resembled Jasmine. Cropped hair—at least for that era. The same dreamy expression of wanting to be somewhere else or with someone else. Light skin as if she were a Scandinavian who had never burned in sun.

An elderly woman approached from behind. "May I help you, dear?"

The woman was hunched over from years of bending to avoid pain from pinched nerves and strained tendons, crippled by wear-and-tear leading to inflaming arthritis.

"Do you work here?" Francine asked.

"I'm what they call a volunteer curator." The woman flashed a small badge on a lanyard and stuffed it back into her buttoned grandmother sweater. "A role our Women's Art Appreciation Society initiated in the 1920s."

"Do you know this painting?" Francine asked.

"The Bastien-Lepage masterpiece? It's celebrated throughout the world. Mind if I sit?"

Francine gestured for the trembling lady to join her.

The woman asked, "What is it you see?"

Francine almost expected the woman to have concluded the question with saying, "My child," as if she were an aged nun opening eyes of innocents to see beyond their corporeal world.

Francine stared at the painting while the lady's calming voice entranced her to see with eyes closed, merging within herself into a dream. "I see a young woman with one foot in this world, but her heart elsewhere. Being moved to see beyond what others see."

"Very lovely, my dear. What else?"

"I thought I remembered Joan only being inspired by a knight-like soldier, her St. Michael. But now I see—no. Not just see, but feel two other, barely formed saints. Two women saints."

"That would be saints Margaret and Catherine."

"They are more imagined than present. Like two friends—wished for friends. Just beyond reach."

"Helpers."

"Yes. That's it. Helpers."

The two women sat in silence a moment, bathing in murmurs of polite visitors strolling in the distance.

"What are you thinking?" the lady whispered close to Francine's ear.

"So strange," Francine uttered, hardly hearing her own voice.

"Go on."

"I always viewed my father as my strong helper, ignoring my mother and oldest brother who waited in the background like the two women are waiting in this painting. Almost not there."

"This masterpiece speaks to you."

"More personal than I realized."

"And now you do. Realize."

"I never let Mom and Andrew know I appreciated them. Needed them. I shielded myself from their words, letting them bounce off me. I did not allow their words to sink through my thick skin to a place to stockpile them."

"And your father's words?"

"Harsh."

"Did his harsh words sink in?"

"Sadly. Making me feel little, insignificant."

After lengthy silence, the lady whispered, "St. Michael is our protector."

"Yes," Francine mumbled. "But not necessarily kind."

"What I adore of art," the lady said with the voice of a teacher, "is how we all see in art, what our pasts and growth commands. No two of us see the same. And yet, those varied visions of art are truths."

Francine pondered the lady's riddle. She turned to thank her, but the aged, volunteer curator was gone.

The gallery felt empty, as if life in the painting had been snatched by the art-society lady; as if the woman had bonded with the art and both evaporated into another realm.

Aaron broke the spell, arriving at Francine's side. "Sorry it took me so long."

"I'm fine," Francine mumbled. She inhaled deep breaths, returning to having her feet on the ground. "I was talking with a curious, fascinating woman. An art aficionado. Volunteers here as an unpaid, unofficial curator."

"Interesting. What is it we're trying to do?"

"See this painting?"

"It's gigantic—well, to have in a house. Taller than my ceilings. Eight-foot ceilings."

Francine smiled, keeping private her journey into art with a senior citizen, thinking that in contrast, she was now sitting with a man enamored by size.

"So?" Aaron asked. "Why are we looking at this item?"

"Item," Francine mumbled. "I think I learned what Azza—or our serial killer—may see in this particular St. Michael painting."

"We know she looks at it?"

"Speculation. But I'd bet your year's salary on it."

"My salary?"

"You're more into numbers than I. I think she'd say she sees that Joan not only has saints Joan and Michael guiding her, but has those two women saints in the background helping."

"Oh yeah," Aaron said. I see them now. Faintly."

"Our killer is wearied from being alone. And like Joan, she desires for two women friends to help."

"Azza does?"

"Uh huh," Francine uttered.

"And you know this from looking at this piece of art?"

"A hunch."

"I see. A hunch."

"And the two friends Azza desperately wants as her helpers are ..."

Aaron waited a moment. "Yes?"

"Myself and Jasmine."

"Jasmine?"

"Uh huh."

"She knows Jasmine?"

"She knows me, you, Bram, everyone with whom we associate. She stalks us. And presently, she's pissed that I—we—rejected her friendship, ignored helping her."

Aaron stood and scratched the back of his head while circling the room. He returned to the bench, stood on one foot while resting the other on the bench. He crossed his arms and leaned them on his knee, perched like a lawyer about to unleash a case-changing question. "Have you been sleeping okay?"

Francine stood. "My father used to do that to me. Question my sanity by inquiring about my health. I never had a good solution for that. Now I do."

Aaron removed his foot from the bench.

Francine wrapped her arm around Aaron's waist and escorted him toward the exit. "Dream with me, Aaron dear. See where this goes. Then you may question the sanity of my dreaming."

They exited the gallery and were almost to the Great Hall when Francine's phone rang.

"Yes?"

She stopped to listen. "I'll be right there."

"What?" Aaron asked.

"Jenetta called from Gramercy Park. There's a dead young man lying face up. No signs of trauma. I'll meet you later at the station. Wait there for me."

Aaron chose to glance at a few paintings scattered about the massive building before leaving, stopping by the information desk. Arriving, he had judged the attendant, Laura—according to her nametag—was about his age. She had appeared to enjoy their two-way flirting while she directed him to Francine and the St. Joan painting.

He waited for Laura to look up from her desk and smile before he spoke. "Thank you for your earlier help. I found my boss easily due to your superb directions."

Laura slid a dangling strand of hair over and behind her ear. "My pleasure."

"My boss was mesmerized by St. Joan with the help

from one of your volunteer curators."

"One of our what?"

"Senior citizen volunteer curators."

"We don't have volunteer curators."

"Oh." Aaron appeared bewildered.

Laura leaned forward and lowered her voice as if about to gossip with girlfriends. "The elderly lady who just left? We've caught her before, pretending to be an official employee. We tried discouraging her, even escorting her out a couple of times. Every few months she changes her appearance. She's not really old. Once she showed up dressed as a strapping young Marine."

"No shit," Aaron said. "A convincing Marine?"

"Very. And another time a nun."

"Holy crap."

"Adept at costumes and makeup."

"How do you know it's the same person?"

"I minored in theatre. I can detect even subtle makeup techniques. And she has these weird hand movements."

Laura demonstrated drumming fingers with her left hand while tapping the back of that hand with her index finger. "She does that no matter who she's imitating."

"Oh God." Aaron displayed his badge. "I need all information you can give me on her. Immediately."

JUNGLE FLOWERS FOR SOULS

Gramercy Park held a special place in Detective Francine Boult's heart. When she was a rookie cop, she had been ordered to talk on the phone with a sixteen-year-old girl who had called, saying someone had broken into their Brooklyn home. As alerted officers raced to the girl's address, Francine had tried to calm the girl, promising she would be rescued within minutes. Francine heard the girl scream and a struggle ensue as the intruder grabbed her phone.

The intoxicated man demanded ransom money. Francine attempted to negotiate but could not penetrate the man's fortress of rapid speech. His words tumbled over one another as incoherent phrases. Straying ideas sprayed out of his mouth like machine-gun fire at any and every one until the phone line went dead.

The following morning, a report came in that the girl's body had been located in a flowerbed near the Edwin Booth statue in Gramercy Park. She was lying on her back with a small slit in her carotid artery. Blood had slowly leaked out, prolonging dying. Francine had pictured the girl living her last minutes in horror.

Everyone in the station and everyone in the city had told Francine that she was not to blame. No words, no hugs, no pats on the back, no tearful eyes among others brought comfort.

Over the years, Francine had visited the park many times and sat in the flowers by the Booth statue where a nanny and her charge had stumbled upon the girl.

Madeline had been the girl's name. Sixteen-year-old Madeline.

Today, when Francine arrived in Gramercy Park,

officers from Precinct Thirteen, including Commanding Officer Inspector Ron Eredia, were waiting. Ron led Francine to the deceased young man, saying, "There's no outward evidence of foul play. He's lying there peacefully. No disturbed grass or flowers. No body trauma of any kind. He just looks asleep."

Francine took a quick look. "This was not the work of our serial killer. I'm not saying this guy didn't die from fentanyl or heroin or even carfentanil. I'm not saying he wasn't deliberately poisoned. I am saying something's missing that we never revealed to the news. There's no butt imprint in the grass around his head. All men died with our killer caressing their heads in her lap. This death was not by her."

"Wow," Ron said. "That's pretty darn specific. A detail that creeps me out."

Ron motioned for the medical crew to remove the body and transport it to forensics.

Within minutes, Francine was alone in the park.

In the past, on occasions while venturing into the jungle—as her oldest colleagues referred to their city— Francine allowed off-duty and lunch-break passion to shepherd her to Gramercy Park to the flowers where Madeline had drawn her final breath. Several times, she had even lain in the flowerbed below Edwin Booth's likeness, looking up at sky that Madeline had viewed.

Francine did not believe the dead can commune with the living, but knew for certain there exist sacred sites where vivid memories of the dead flourish, where abandoned people slip into talking to shadows.

A couple of times in Gramercy Park, she heard teenagers snicker as they spied her talking to the sky. She thought, no matter. One day, those same street rats are destined to do the same. Age has its gifts.

What she did not expect was Aaron's familiar throat-clearing-attention call. She sat up. "What the heck? I asked you to wait at the station. Are you following me?"

"You told me about this place. Especially these flowers next to Edwin Booth. Where the young girl died."

"Madeline."

"Madeline. You said this spot of ground was sacred. You were so inebriated, I bet you don't remember telling me."

"I don't."

"My God, I love discovering you're human." Aaron removed his jacket, revealing already-rolled-up shirt sleeves. "You were stuck on my grandest pedestal for the longest time. And now here you are, rolling around in a manure-enriched flowerbed like we mortals."

"I can explain."

"Sure you can. So can I."

"Okay, smarty pants." Francine smirked while brushing off clinging leaves. "You explain first."

Aaron crawled into the flowerbed beside her. "I hope park police don't ticket us."

"I'll flash my badge."

Aaron collapsed onto his back. "Shit. You just scaled back up on your pedestal."

Francine giggled at discovering a playmate had joined her in a backyard sandbox.

Aaron began his explanation as if he were reading his How-I-Spent-My-Summer paper to his fifth-grade class. "My explanation to Captain Boult by Aaron Galanis."

Francine covered her mouth, but a snort escaped.

"I had a sister. Harriet. Two years older than me. Insisted on being called, *Harry*. Mom and I complied. Dad refused. Harry used to read to me—Mom and Dad never did. I used to be burdensomely shy and mumbled.

Subhuman mumbling."

"You? Shy?"

"Unbelievable, huh? Anyway, way back then, I mumbled. Mom and Dad couldn't comprehend a word. Harry was my translator. Navigated my world. Made me feel safe."

"She sounds delightful."

"Childhood leukemia stole Harry from me. I was seven."

The following silent moment lasted longer. Memories for both drowned out city sounds. Slowly, pigeons cooing and taxis honking faded in.

Aaron sat up. "This place is sacred for you. Harry's grave is sacred for me. I miss her every day."

The two grown detectives stretched out with hands behind heads for pillows and stared at the sky. Blue except for crisscrossing jet vapor trails.

Stepping into another's shoes is comforting; stepping through another's eyes into the soul is life-changing.

Aaron first broke the silence, doing so with gentle voice. "You're not the only person missing Jasmine. She stepped into all our lives. Like Harry, she is tough but with generous heart. Daring. Excelling in sports—almost the same crewcut as Harry. She's a reason you admire that Joan-of-Arc painting."

Francine rolled on her side and picked at bordering ground ivy. "How did you find me?"

"I had the world's best orienteering teacher."

"You need a key to access this park. Or did you resort to the tacky thing of flashing your badge?"

"Worse. I dropped your name to a groundskeeper."

"Don't utter one more word that's caring, sentimental, or ass-kissing. I'll vomit in my mouth."

"That's my tough lady." Aaron sat up and from his

jacket, retrieved a folded paper wadded into an entangled mass.

Francine frowned, yanked the glob from his clutches, unraveled it, and read aloud. "Metropolitan Museum of Art." She stared and then gestured, *so?*

"Something not sentimental—possibly ass-kissing—you be the judge. A printout of the MET's various art pieces and paintings of St. Michael."

Francine rolled her eyes and huffed like one of the street rats. "You, better than anyone, know I already viewed all of those ad-nauseam."

"Yes, but this go-round, the charming, flirting library-information-desk lady, Laura, presented me with a gift."

Aaron sat still, wearing a smug smile.

"I don't play guess-what-the-gift-is games."

"Okay. Laura informed me that a woman once requested this very same St. Michael list. After I flirted with her—refusing to enjoy I had to do that—she blurted out that the woman usually signed in with differing peculiar names. Visited wearing various disguises. Speaking with various accents." Aaron frowned as if smelling something icky. "And had strange hand movements."

"No."

"Our lady Azza. Dressed as an elderly woman today."

"Holy fuck."

"One time, when signing in—out of carelessness or for whatever reason—the mystical woman used her friend's—or that was what she claimed—friend's museum membership card. I flashed my badge—which tragically ended all flirting with lovely Laura—and persuaded her to retrieve the entrance log. Does the name Elisabet Norgaard ring a bell? Heir to the super wealthy Oskar Norgaard Shipping empire? The Dakota as one of the family's many U.S. residences? Her family making the papers daily until most of them died?"

Francine remained still as an ancient temple stone.

"Evidently not," Aaron said. "Anyway, Elisabet, when not in cheap makeup, is the similar age, similar height as our suspect. And guess what else? She wasted away her teens as a two-bit actress."

"Holy shit."

"Holy shit. Nothing definite but ... There it is. Gift-wrapped."

After a moment of staring down trees and shrubs, Francine turned to Aaron. "Should we pay Elisabet Norgaard a visit?"

"Oh please. Let's do drop in."

As Aaron stood and took a step, Francine grabbed his arm. "Thank you, Aaron. Thank you for going to the trouble to deliver this gift to me in person."

"Captain Jenetta and team are on standby." Aaron pointed through the trees and shrilly whistled.

On came combinations of strobing red, blue, and white lights atop a string of cars and vans.

Francine screamed, "The entire fucking department knows I'm here wallowing in these flowers? I bet you told them why I come here, didn't you?"

Aaron shrugged. "Maybe."

She sucker-punched his shoulder.

As they began walking, Francine yelled, "Wait a minute." She knew the answer, an answer causing blood to rush from her body up into her face, but she inquired. "The volunteer curator. The elderly woman sitting with me."

Aaron whispered, "Elisabet Norgaard."

Francine's body swayed from her knees weakening. Her entire career, her entire life swirled in her head.

"How did she find me? I took the number one, then hiked to the park, then grabbed a cab to the MET. How in hell?"

"No idea."

After a moment, she took in a deep breath. "Let's get this bitch."

CASTLE IN THE SKY

Aaron and Francine climbed into the backseat of a black SUV as Captain Jenetta drove and Sergeant Ted rode shotgun.

"Where we headed?" Francine asked.

Jenetta powered the tinted windows up and flipped on air circulation before taking the lead in the line of vehicles. "220 Central Park South."

Francine nodded. "That's 59th Street. Damn ritzy neighborhood."

"Most expensive U.S. real estate ever," Ted announced. "One condo cost a quarter billion. Most purchasers are anonymous. Secretive purchasing process."

Aaron huffed. "How is it you are a walking, talking Big Apple encyclopedia, Ted?"

"My mother's a tour guide."

"God, that explains so much. Is there an off button?"

The line of vehicles turned onto 58th Street.

"Why 58th?" Francine asked.

Ted turned on his tour-guide voice. "The eighteen-floor villa opens on 59th, the seventy-floor tower on 58th."

Pressing her nose against the window to gaze upward, Francine murmured, "This tower looks new."

"Limestone. Both tower and villa opened 2019. A 1954 apartment building stood where the villa is."

Aaron laid his hand on Francine's knee, his frown and shaking head signaling, *For God's sake, don't ask this guy one more thing. Please?*

Jenetta drove their car through the porte chochere while others in their procession parked on 58th.

The manager and head of security stood waiting.

Jenetta asked, "What? Someone tipped them off?"

"I didn't," Ted quickly responded.

"Jesus," Aaron mumbled, but not soft enough.

Jenetta presented the manager with a warrant. The prepped man glanced at the document and handed it off.

While the security chief scanned the warrant, the manager poorly faked he was extemporizing. "Ms. Norgaard sold her residence last week. All arrangements were conducted through a private, overseas agent. She left no forwarding address. The new owners have yet to arrive or identify themselves. I invite you to inspect her quadruplex penthouse. Rashid here will be glad to accompany you."

"Quadruplex penthouse," Ted blurted out. "I volunteer to inspect."

"Any idea where she is?" Francine asked.

The manager removed his sunglasses for a clearer view of the commander. "Ms. Norgaard's family owns private jets. And homes in thirteen countries."

Francine spoke with a firmer tone. "Take your best guess. Where do you think she went?"

The manager turned his back to the detectives and consulted his clipboard while talking. "Ms. Norgaard is a private person. We rarely see her. I haven't laid eyes on her in years."

Aaron squinted his eyes as if he had X-ray vision to penetrate skulls. "I hope she paid you off well to guard her whereabouts. Because when we uncover that you know, you will be charged as an accessory to murder."

"As I said," the manager replied with the look of a snob talking to peasants, "Ms. Norgaard is private. Rashid is ready to escort you."

RICH PEOPLE LIVE ON DIFFERENT PLANETS
- June 2022 -

Sergeant Garfield of the tenth precinct remained lead detective with what had been dubbed: The Juliet Case. Although he had followed many dead-end leads, today, he promised new intel.

Garfield, Commander Boult, FBI Agent Jia, and various detectives gathered at the Midtown North Precinct. Everyone working on the case agreed that Azza—now identified as Elisabet Norgaard—had likely fled the United States, her whereabouts being unknown.

Ted asked, "How could she escape our all-points bulletin? Don't bulletins alert TSA agents anymore?"

"The wealthy escape because they have money," Lin said. "They have know-how and means to circumvent airport security. Plus, this particular criminal has access to a fleet of private jets and yachts."

"But somebody has to pilot those jets," Ted said. "What kind of people transport wealthy scumbags knowing their passengers are likely on the lam?"

"People who don't have money," Aaron mumbled.

Another officer added, "When I worked on the border, I saw it all day long. Mexican smugglers working for the cartel. Those guys were small potatoes compared to crooks smuggling wealthy snobs to their international playgrounds."

The mood of the gathered law officers was one of despondency. Only a week before, they had felt certain they were closing in on Elisabet, excited by the promise of arresting—or if she fought back, kill her, knowing she had taken the life of their fellow officer.

Francine began the meeting. "Sergeant Garfield, bring us up to speed."

"First thing," Garfield said, "we checked out the Norgaard's Tarrytown mansion. It's owned by the suspect's nonagenarian grandfather."

"The what grandfather?" Francine asked.

"Nonagenarian Oskar Norgaard. In his nineties."

Francine blushed. "New word for me."

Garfield nodded with pride. "The mansion was closed and vacated except for one caretaker, Carlton. I think he may be an octogenarian—meaning in his eighties."

"That word I know. Thank you."

"Carlton said Oskar Norgaard left months ago to vacation indefinitely, living on his megayacht."

While jotting a note, Francine asked, "Did the caretaker report where the yacht is located?"

"For the moment—they relocate often—they're anchored off a small Greek island." Garfield referred to his palm-size notepad. "Hydra. That one's in the Aegean Sea. Mostly Greek vacationers. Few foreigners. No cars allowed."

"Did you turn up anything helpful at the Tarrytown mansion?"

"Carlton seemed stoked to show off the castle-like residence. I think he was lonely. He explained he spent weeks draping furniture with hundreds of beige dust-covers. I've only seen furniture covered like that in movies. Rich people."

Garfield stuffed his notepad into his pocket. "I asked more about the yacht. I'm looking to buy a daysailer."

With an impatient tone, Francine asked, "Is Oskar Norgaard presently on the yacht?"

"He is. But he's disabled because of age."

"How disabled?"

"Wheelchair bound. His yacht has elevators. I'd pay to see elevators on a boat."

"Did you ask about Elisabet?"

"Certainly. Carlton told me she cut ties with her family when she was a teenager, right after her parents were killed in a plane crash in Alaska. Carlton said there was lots of complaining over the years from family, angry Elisabet only pops up when she needs money—lots of money. But Carlton claimed he hadn't seen her in years."

"Do we know if she visits her grandfather in Greece? Other places where the yacht is docked?"

"I inquired several times, but never got a solid answer. My apologies, Commander."

"We'll check it out, Sergeant. Good job."

Francine circled the seated group while talking. "In addition to our suspect being able to finance an evil life, she is as devious as I have known. Two weeks ago, she sat next to me in a museum, impersonating a museum curator. We talked. She got me to reveal personal matters of my heart. As we talked, she touched my hand and shoulder, so close she could kill me and easily get away. She had me so focused on the painting, I didn't look at her face. And then as if by magic, she was gone."

"That's freaky," Ted said. "I'll have nightmares about that."

Lin asked, "Are you doing okay, Commander Boult?"

"Besides nightmares?" Francine asked. "Besides no appetite, no sleep? Sure. Other than minor miseries, I'm proceeding ahead at full throttle."

Returning to a business deportment, Francine asked, "Agent Jia? Can we track so-called megayachts?"

"Much like aircraft," Lin said, "large yachts over three-hundred tons are required to have transponders sending out identification data. They're easy to track, unless of course, transponders have been disabled. I'll need the name of the yacht to hunt for her."

Francine looked to Garfield.

Garfield retrieved a cellphone from the jacket hanging on his chair. "Carlton showed me a photo. He told me he sailed on the yacht once. I took a phone pic of his yacht photo."

Garfield carried his phone to Francine and pointed at the name on the yacht's bow. "Gjenganger. I'm not sure if my pronunciation's accurate. In Norwegian, the name means ghost."

HYDRA

Elisabet stretched out in a lounge chair on the Gjenganger's swim platform and rubbed slick coconut oil on her legs and arms. Although in her mid-thirties, in her revealing swimsuit, she looked to be in her late twenties. She obsessed with wanting to look as if she were in her early twenties.

She knew enough Greek to order cocktails and various fish dishes, but not enough to translate insults that young Greek men were slinging at one another from their neighboring small ferry boats.

When the men nodded toward Elisabet, elbowed one another, and cackled, she assumed she was fortunate to not comprehend their local dialect. Their crude body language, however, was simple and obvious.

She checked to make sure all areas of her skin glistened, adding oil to dull areas. She remembered one of her mother's spartan teachings: *Be sure every bit of skin glistens, or your tan will be uneven.*

If she worked at it, she knew she could resurrect more obtuse sayings from her mother. Remembering her parents, however, hurt, launching avalanches of emotions about what fate had stolen from her.

The men in the water taxis must have realized Elisabet's mind had drifted elsewhere. They elevated their crude gestures by touching index finger tips to thumb tips to form circles, and then fornicating the holes with opposite index fingers, poking in and out as their bodies lurched in copulating rhythms.

Elisabet aimed a middle finger at the men, inciting them to cheer heartily enough to rock their boats. She ascertained her response had been what the men desired.

She smiled at them and they returned softer smiles than she expected. Maybe the men had sisters and daughters—certainly mothers—and her gesture reached deep into their better selves, stirring their hearts as they relished Elisabet's playfulness.

There was one man, however, different from the rowdy cluster. He sat alone at the end of the dock. While others made obscene gestures, grunted, and cat-called in Elisabet's direction, the lone man's face was void of emotion. His eyes reminded her of a tiger that had fascinated her on an Indian safari. The tiger had stared at Elisabet with a glare that signaled, *Every fiber of my body desires you for my next meal.*

When Elisabet surfaced from her safari memory and looked at the end of the dock, the lone man had vanished.

No cloud blocked the sun, but Elisabet felt chilled as if there had been a drop in temperature, raising goose bumps to protrude through the sea of glistening oil.

In the evening, Elisabet relaxed after dining with her grandfather in their covered outdoor lounge. She watched as two stewards aided the frail head of the Norgaard empire to his quarters.

Elisabet asked to be served a glass of Tsikoudia. Another steward, Maia, having anticipated wishes of the special passenger, arrived with a silver platter holding a crystal decanter of the Cretan pomace brandy and poured the colorless liquid into a crystal rocks glass. The steward was on top of her game, recalling Elisabet would desire to squeeze a drop of fresh lemon into her green-apple-fragranced liquor.

"Thank you, Maia," Elisabet said, waiting for the steward to lift the drink from the platter.

"Will Ms. Norgaard be visiting the village tonight?"

"If the night calls, Maia." Elisabet accepted the drink.

Once Maia returned inside, Elisabet reached into her hand-size evening bag and retrieved a gold pendant and necklace. She suspended the chain from the neck of the decanter so that she was face to face with a tiny version of St. Michael raising his sword to decapitate Satan.

"Michael," Elisabet whispered, as if the archangel were a friend. "How should we spend this evening?"

She continued to sip, not allowing her eyes to stray from her saint.

The following morning, Tarik, the Gjenganger's chef, prepared Chaussons aux Pommes and French radishes with butter and salt on toast.

Tatjana, politely bowed and asked, "May I have a word with you when you have time?"

"Of course," Elisabet said.

"When will be a proper time, ma'am?"

"Now is fine," Elisabet said. She leaned back in her chair, brimming with curiosity.

"I know you like to walk at night on the docks and visit the taverna for an evening quencher."

"I do."

"I do not wish to alarm you, but we were made aware of danger that spoiled last evening's festivities."

"That doesn't sound good."

"A man, who anchored his ferry beside us, was stabbed in the throat last night on this dock. He died almost instantly. You should be careful going ashore at night. Even cautious stepping onto the dock."

"Thank you, Tatjana, for your concern. Who knows? Maybe the docks are safer now that the man has departed. Can you please bring me a new coffee? A bug seems to have drowned in this cup."

Tatjana frowned, unsure if Elisabet had comprehended her concernment. "Yes ma'am. Right away."

ALL THE WORLD'S OUR STAGE
-August 2022 -

Infrequent clues surfaced from various European law-enforcement agencies, alluring Francine and Aaron, but never bearing out to be consequential. "The Norgaards own a lake villa in Geneva." "A Sorbonne art student died studying Raphael's St. Michael painting." "In Budapest, carfentanil was uncovered in padding of a lawn-mower packing crate."

Upon learning such news, detectives of the Midtown Precinct North theorized, sometimes as much as an hour, but by day's end, interest and hope withered.

The topic of Elisabet was all but shelved.

One August day, Ted approached Aaron. "You got a minute? This will interest you. I got it from our online international feed."

"Bring it on, big guy."

Ted grinned and passed his sloppy, three-sentence, handwritten note to Aaron. "It was in German, so I jotted it down for you in English."

Aaron read it out loud. "Two carfentanil deaths found by police in Hamburg." He turned to Ted. "You read German?"

Ted squirmed. "Jenetta does. She told me what to write."

"So … How did you know what the feed originally said?"

"I brought it to her attention."

"Okay. Help me envision what took place."

"I'll draw you a road map. I took a feed to Jenetta to translate—"

"Cause you couldn't read it."

"Something like that. And Jenetta translated it. But it was fully my idea to share it with you."

"Just to be clear, you had no idea what it said until Jenetta translated it."

"It was my idea to bring it to you. Here it is. A gift."

"Gosh, Ted. Fantastic job, buddy. I'll take it from here."

"Can I watch?"

"Watch what?"

"When you take it to Commander Boult."

Aaron had the scowl of an older brother not wanting a little brother to tag along. "Tell you what. Let me tell the commander all by myself—give you the piles of credit you deserve—and then invite you in. Sound fair?"

"Sounds swell. Thank you, Captain." Ted saluted, an action he performed whenever he was at a loss for what to say.

Aaron returned a half-salute, searched the Internet for pertinent articles and supporting intel, and marched his laptop to Francine's office.

As he entered, Francine grinned. "Ted told me to expect you with crucial intel he uncovered."

"Oh my God. He only … Never mind. Never mind. There were two carfentanil deaths in parks in Hamburg. Similar as here. Two young German men laid out. Hands crossed. Same card in their hands—but in German. Here are printouts of original German news articles, and the full translations."

"I'm fine with the German."

"Of course, you are."

Francine read and reread the article.

Only after she appeared finished, did Aaron speak. "This has to be Elisabet's work."

"Our lady's on the warpath. Are there any St. Michael churches nearby in Hamburg?"

"St. Michaelis Lutheran Church."

Francine sat at her computer and searched for Hamburg on her map app. "What's the address?"

Aaron examined his notes. "Engl. Planke. Guess that's a street."

"Okay. Here it is on the map. St. Michaelis. And the names of the parks?"

Aaron referred to the article. "One's Heinepark. And the other … Planten un Blomen—or however you say it."

"Damn. Both within a mile of the church." Francine took a slow victory lap around her desk. "Her DNA's all over this."

"Wish it were her actual DNA." Aaron pulled up images on his laptop and pointed. "Here's the church." He chuckled before saying, "And here's the steeple."

Francine covered her face and mumbled, "Cute."

"And get a load of this. Here's the statue in front of the church."

Aaron zoomed in on a massive green-bronze statue above the front entrance's colonnade parvis.

Francine gulped when Aaron tapped his finger on the angelic wings of Michael and then on the grotesque Wizard-Of-Oz-monkey wings of Satan. Michael had his spear aimed straight down at the back of Satan's skull while Satan strained to execute a pushup.

Francine pulled Aaron's screen closer to her face as if she had become severely myopic. "Huh," she mumbled.

"What?"

"Nothing."

"Don't do that to me. What?"

"It's embarrassing."

"Really? Now you gotta share."

"Okay, okay." Francine refused eye contact. "These figures in these museums and churches give me the willies. Like they're about to move or talk."

"Huh."

"Now I am thoroughly embarrassed. Happy?"

Aaron shrugged. "We're looking at great art. It's lifelike. These figures are posed, ready to move or speak."

Francine spoke with purposely pressured speech to redirect the topic. "Who can we contact? We need to inform someone. Share what we know."

Aaron referred to the printout. "Polizeipräsident Ralf Martin Meyer, head of the Hamburg city-state police."

Francine circled the room. "Two deaths—that they know of. You and I know there have been or will be others. If we can help prevent one—even the last one—it's worth our pulling out all stops."

Aaron spotted Ted peeping in the doorway and whispered to Francine. "There's a stray, giant-eyed puppy at your threshold starving to be told it did a good job."

Francine whispered while covering her grin. "For what?"

"Don't ask."

Francine yelled, "Great job, Sergeant."

Ted saluted, clicked his heels, and sharply executed an about face.

Aaron stepped out of the office and immediately returned. "We should notify Lin."

"I don't want the FBI snatching this case away from our lead."

"I know this case is personal, but the FBI works in parallel. They share with us. We share with them. We still lead."

Francine began thumbing through the German papers. "Uh huh." She selected a paper, put on her glasses, and began reading.

After waiting a moment, Aaron left.

GREAT PLAINS SPIRITS

Approaching her thirty-sixth week of pregnancy, Teresa developed elevated blood pressure, blurred vision, and shortness of breath.

Jasmine insisted she call her obstetrician at Bellevue Hospital. Dr. Walsh promptly arranged for an emergency evaluation.

Teresa's platelet count had dropped significantly and her liver enzymes had slightly elevated. Dr. Walsh diagnosed her as having preeclampsia and hospitalized her for blood pressure that had soared to 150 over 100.

Dr. Walsh and her assistant, rolling a mobile workstation, entered Teresa's hospital room. "How is the headache?" Dr. Walsh asked.

Teresa kept her eyes shut, having learned that light and struggling with blurred vision aggravated the pain. "The mag sulfate helped. Thank you."

"Have you thought more about delivering early?"

"Jasmine and I discussed that. I'm approaching thirty-seven weeks. We understand it's best for the child if we wait until after that."

Jasmine held her friend's hand tightly as if keeping her from falling off a cliff. "We read that if she can be treated with corticosteroids, the baby's lungs will be more mature, be stronger."

"Absolutely." Dr. Walsh smiled. "How did you two learn that?"

"Google," both women answered together.

"Of course, you did. It's wonderful working with people who inform themselves. We can wait. We must make certain your blood pressure doesn't rise higher. Bedrest here in the hospital should help."

"How high is too high?" Jasmine asked.

"Anything near 160 over 110 and we may be forced to induce delivery. We also must consider parameters like bleeding into the liver since your platelet and red-blood-cell counts are low. Are you experiencing nausea?"

"Not so much since the headache is less intense."

"Good. If we begin corticosteroids, you may get face and leg swelling, even more belly swelling."

Teresa forced a chuckle. "I'll sign up for a beauty pageant."

Dr. Walsh checked her computer. "Let's see. Your LFTs—your liver enzymes—actually have improved. Your blood pressure's down a bit. Good signs."

Dr. Walsh placed her stethoscope on Teresa's abdomen. "Got to hold on to some old traditions, old-fashioned methods." She closed her eyes and listened. "Baby's heart sounds strong. Excellent."

"It's a boy," Teresa said."

"I saw that on your sonogram."

"I didn't look until last month once I was ready to select a name."

"I helped her," Jasmine said, smiling proudly as if helping to create new life.

"How nice," Dr. Walsh said, wanting to ask if they were a couple, but not wanting to assume or intrude. "What name did you select?"

"Cheyenne," Teresa answered. My grandmother's grandmother belonged to that tribe."

Dr. Walsh smiled. "What a delightful way to honor your ancestors. Cheyenne." The physician leaned close to Teresa's abdomen and whispered, "You have fine people looking after you, Cheyenne."

EINE GLEICHGESINNTE

In the German city-state of Hamburg, Elisabet woke one morning, realizing she no longer desired input from women's groups to identify fallen souls. Over the past years, she had gained insight from multiple encounters and felt capable to observe and judge men—sometimes women—who had strayed from God's grace. And of course, her archangel-protector had her back.

Similar to finding Captain Boult in New York to be a kindred spirit, she had stumbled across Head Inspector Andreas Richter, feeling secure they would make a fruitful team.

She had first spied on Andreas leading an inspection of the sacrifice in Heinepark. She systematically tailed him around the city, learning his frequent routes, his favorite pub, and his food and drink preferences.

One evening, after Andreas had changed into civilian attire, Elisabet followed him to a food-serving pub, Zum Sibersack, located in a festive neighborhood near St. Michael's Church and the Elbe River.

Elisabet selected a seat at the bar beside Andreas and portrayed a forlorn woman. While staring at everyone in the pub except Andreas, she gently stroked her glass in a suggestive manner of pleasing a man.

Andrea heard Elisabet chatting with the barman, speaking masterful German with a strong Norwegian accent. As the bartender served Elisabet a second drink, Andreas skipped pleasantries to inquire about the woman's speech.

Elisabet had prepared a story of growing up in Norway, attending Colombia University in New York, and studying criminal psychology at the University of

Edinburgh.

She had no need to reveal more of her story, finding it effortless to encourage Andreas to reveal his past by bragging in one-word increments about facets of his embellished autobiography.

Upon their third pub rendezvous—and after a half dozen drinks—they kissed lightly at the bar, quickly escalating to kissing heavily. Andreas groped at her while Elisabet offered her expertise about identifying abusive men, confusing the inspector when she described details about the Heinepark murder, details that had never been revealed to the public.

Elisabet offered to aid Andreas with locating abusive Hamburg men. The detective, however, had become a Masai Mara lion stalking a lioness in heat, oblivious to what sounded to him to be meaningless chatter.

Elisabet shrieked and shoved the pawing creature aside, insisting she deserved to assist him. Andreas pressed his hand over her mouth and demanded she go outside with him.

Elisabet slapped Andreas. After a moment, he laughed and mumbled about the ridiculousness of her offer. "There is no way I need your or any woman's assistance."

Elisabet willed herself into a tranquil state. "You're right, Andreas. Forgive me." She took his hand and led him outside.

They kissed long and hard, progressing to rough caressing. She feigned that her hand bumping his genitals was an accident. "Let's move deeper into the alley in those shadows, out of sight of all these souses coming and going from the Quer Club."

They moved, fastened to one another, continuing to make love.

Amidst loud music and crowd noise, Elisabet retrieved

her tactical pen, extended the switchblade, and stabbed Andreas in the neck. As he slid to his knees, clinging to her waist, passersby assumed the man was another sloppy drunk being aided by a mistress, a one-night-stand lady, or a prostitute.

Elisabet strutted away, leaving deceased Andreas doubled over as if he were kneeling on the cobblestones and praying.

SAFE DISTANCE

Francine spent an hour with three detectives who had come forth with complaints about Detective Joseph Barbieri for bribing and physically threatening witnesses.

Francine ordered the accused sergeant to come to her office.

"I called you to my office twice before," Francine said. "This is a third time for the same offenses: bribing and physically threatening people to force confessions—or worse—intimidating innocent witnesses who are fearful to report information they may know."

Joseph smirked. "If it works, it works." There was no hint of apology in his voice.

"I made it clear to you that such behaviors don't work for me and don't work for the NYDP."

"Pardon me for saying so, Commander, but you know and I know that I get intel when no other officers can."

"Until otherwise notified, you are suspended with pay. Turn in your badge and your firearm."

"You're shitting me. I did nothing—"

"Now, Officer."

Joseph stood, pressed his body against the front of Francine's desk, and stared down at her like he was ready to bite a chunk from her face. He gently laid his firearm atop her reports and then flung his badge onto her side of the desk with enough force that it bounced and ricocheted off her chest. He did not stay in the room long enough to witness her facial expression.

Joseph sped past Aaron who was reading reports while waiting for Francine. "What the hell did you say to Joseph?"

"I suspended him," Francine said.

"Long time overdue."

Francine took a deep breath and relaxed. "Now, that that's done, what's up?"

"We got a demand from …" Aaron glanced at the papers and slowly attempted to properly pronounce the words. "From Polizeipräsident Rolf Meyer in Hamburg."

"That can't be good." Francine motioned for Aaron to sit.

Aaron read aloud. "It is suspected that a woman killed Head Inspector Andreas Richter, the lead detective for a serial-killer case. A bartender reported that the detective and the woman in question, a woman with a Norwegian accent, visited his pub on several evenings. The woman and detective never arrived together. Each time, the woman approached the detective at the bar. The couple had always appeared amicable until the last visit, when the bartender overheard the woman offer to assist the detective with cases. When the detective laughed at her idea, the woman slapped him, grabbed him, and began passionately kissing him. Within minutes, the couple moved their intimate maneuvering outside. People in an alley beside the pub discovered the detective was dead from a wound to his neck. The woman had disappeared."

"Well," Francine said, breathing out after practically holding her breath. "That fits Elisabet Norgaard's modus operandi to a tee."

"Meyer wants us to consult."

Francine appeared alarmed. "Phone consult?"

"In-person consult."

"Oh my God. Talk about out of our jurisdiction."

"Our FBI friend, Agent Lin Jia, highly recommended us, telling Meyer we were gifted at crawling into this killer's skin."

"And gifted crawling out of her skin."

"I agree. The last thing we need is her to haunt us

again. I lost so much sleep—and pounds—worrying how to keep Colt safe. I even thought about sicking Joseph on her."

"That's not funny."

Aaron grinned and raised his eyebrows. "Maybe they would have killed one another."

"Really not funny."

Aaron's face quickly appeared stern. "There's no way I will go to Germany."

"Nor will I. Call whatever Meyer back and tell him no for both of us."

"Me call?"

"Please close my door on the way out. I don't need more European news drifting in here today—or the rest of my life."

SKIING AIN'T WHAT IT USED TO BE

A week had passed when the receptionist, Lane, rang and interrupted Francine and Aaron preparing a precinct summary for the police commissioner.

"Is it important, Lane? Aaron and I are in the middle of—"

"It's from Switzerland. The woman refused to give her name but said she's a detective and it's important."

"Oh my God. Put her through." Francine turned to Aaron. "A Swiss detective. I'm afraid to guess what this means."

"She's on the line now, Commander."

"Thank you, Lane. Hello. This is Commander Boult of the Midtown Precinct North speaking."

"Do you miss me?" a female voice asked.

"Pardon me?"

"We had the potential to make a great team. You, me, and your handsome second-in-command."

Francine flipped the phone to speaker.

"Who is this? Please identify yourself." Francine's hand trembled as she set the handset onto its base.

"You know who this is, Commander. Why are you being distant?"

Aaron turned pale and circled the room as he listened, interlacing his fingers on top of his head to form a skullcap.

The woman's voice had a Swiss-German accent. "I really could use your help. You wouldn't believe the number of sinners this side of the pond. Mountain villages are overflowing with perverts. Too many for one crusader to handle. Think about it. You two could join me. Of course, skiing's not what it used to be with climate change roasting mountain tops, but it's still breathtaking. Picture the three of us bringing about justice while in this spectacular setting. I'll be in touch."

The phone clicked and went silent.

"Fuck," Aaron screamed.

Francine rotated her chair to stare outside at a blue-sky day. "Just when she was only intruding into my thoughts once or twice an hour."

"What do we do?" Aaron asked.

"I don't know about you, but my feet are planted on this side of the pond."

"I'll trace the call."

"Do you doubt it's from Switzerland? Or that it is a burner phone?"

"Shit."

Francine pushed aside a pile of reports on her desk. "Pray winter snows improve for her skiing and that all things Swiss continue to intrigue her." Francine lifted the end metallic ball of her physics desk toy and let it crash into the neighboring ball, setting off a chain reaction. "For the rest of our lives."

"Sounds like she'll be feasting on villagers."

"Any news on the location of her yacht?"

Aaron sat and buried his head in his hands. "No longer in Greece. Or so we think. The transponder was disabled. Let European authorities worry about that. It's no longer our business."

Francine halted the swinging metal balls. "I've never in my life wished for someone's life to be snuffed out as I am wishing for this bitch."

"Amen."

Days later, two oil paintings of the Austrian Red Devils of Kitzbühel racing the giant slalom were delivered to the precinct. One was tagged for Francine and one for Aaron.

TO ACCEPT OR NOT TO ACCEPT
- September 2022 -

Days later, Aaron approached Francine at the overworked coffee maker. "Got something for you. Promise to not fly off the handle if I show you?"

"I would never fly off the handle at you, dear Aaron."

Aaron handed her a report.

Francine skimmed through Aaron's hand-printed notes in twenty seconds. "So, the gist is, you questioned an eighty-two-year-old woman about her neighbors, two brothers whom she reported are nasty monsters, taking turns raping a severely-mentally-challenged woman whenever the woman's guardian leaves to shop. Am I understanding your summary correctly?"

"That's pretty much it."

"Uh huh." Francine read the pages more carefully. "So, how did you know to question the brothers' elderly neighbor?"

"Remember, you promised to not blow a fuse."

"I promised to not fly off the handle. Different creatures."

"I got the men's names from a list and was curious if the list had merit."

"A list?"

"This is where it gets morally tricky."

"Should we go to my office, close the door, pretend it's a confessional?"

"Elisabet."

Francine drew a blank look. "Elisabet?"

"How many Elisabets do you know?"

Francine continued appearing confused, and then frowned as if a distant idea was beginning to germinate, and then a more concerned expression as the idea popped into daylight, and then an explosion of rage as the idea detonated. "Holy fuck."

"Don't throw anything."

"Holy fuck."

Aaron motioned with his hands to stay calm. "Let's go into my office and talk about this."

"How the fuck could you have gone behind my back and followed her advice, no, no, not advice, but demands, followed the demands of that God-damn bitch who ruined all good things in our lives. How? How? Tell me how."

"I was curious."

"Fuck."

Several detectives rose up in their seats, stretching their necks for a better view.

Rolling Aaron's papers into a log and slapping the log against the coffee maker like a judge's gavel gone wild, Francine screamed, "This is crap, Detective Galanis. Unacceptable, Aaron Pavlos Galanis."

Francine had never spouted out his full name. Only his mother did that for mortal errors such as causing a loud rumpus that caused her baking cakes to collapse. "It paid off. The Bronx Police Department arrested the brothers yesterday."

"Not our jurisdiction."

"All I did was interview the neighbor and tip off the local precinct. They pulled together the case. They took action. Not me."

"But you took the word of a wanted killer to catch the two criminals."

"Are you listening to yourself? I don't think so. We get intel from prisoners left and right."

"Yes, but … but … but … Shit."

They both stood in silence, staring upward at fluorescent lights, waiting for God or someone, something divine to declare a ruling.

Finally, Aaron asked, "Aren't you going to congratulate me?"

"Hell no." Francine searched the coffee station, opening and slamming drawers. "We're out of creamers."

"I'll grab a handful from the kitchen."

As Aaron hurried away, Francine yelled, "French vanilla."

THE BAD SEED

Karol opened her phone to text Francine, but decided texting was too impersonal. She preferred being able to hear voice intonations to read between the lines.

She phoned. "Hi Francine. It's K.C."

"Good morning, K.C. What's going on?"

"I was wondering if you had a spare half hour today or tomorrow to meet with me."

"Sure hope so. I'll check." After a few seconds, she returned. "I could meet at 3:30 today. Wanna meet at the precinct?"

"What about around the corner at Bibble & Sip?"

"Great coffee. Sure."

"And chocolate tarts."

The word chocolate cued both women to immediately think of lethal danger, but neither mentioned it.

Francine was five minutes late to the coffee shop, which was a superb feat considering detectives had hounded her to review a request for vacation time, sign off on a warrant, sign a reimbursement request, and check over a high-school-program presentation.

Francine rushed into Bibble & Sip. "Sorry K.C. I finally had to yell for everyone to back off and give me space for an hour."

"A full hour? Great. Hope you don't mind that I already ordered."

Francine waved a finger at the woman behind the counter. "She knows my usual. What's up with you and Bram these days?"

"As much as it unsettles me, I have to admit his and my mind work on the same track. Our methods differ. Mine are antiquated. Bram's are super modern."

"I thought you had retreated from solving world problems. Left that for Bram to secretly plow ahead."

"That, he certainly is doing, but I must admit, I am dabbling a bit."

"I know you better than to accept you are only dabbling."

Karol brushed crust crumbs from the table into her napkin. "I'm haunted by the human who tried to poison me and my son."

"So are Aaron, myself, and all our team."

"In the old days, my friends at the state department in the Oversea Citizens Service Records and Other Overseas Records section—"

"That's a mouthful."

"Definitely. They were a giant help. They owe me— unofficially, of course. Off the record."

"Naturally. What did you learn?"

The two women paused talking while the waitress served Francine.

Karol resumed. "The section was helpful, but here's the catch—and you can never let Bram know—but I saw on his phone that—"

"You didn't."

"I did. He screen-captured messages he had received on Tik Tok."

"I know about Facebook and Twitter. I'm in the dark about Tik Tok."

"So was I. So, I googled about Tik Tok and searches for missing people. Facebook got a hundred or so hits for people liking a specific missing-person request. Tik Tok got over a million."

"My gosh."

Karol waited for Francine to quit pondering that fact and look at her. "Very few answers mind you, but a million hits. Enough subscribers responded to Bram, however, that he learned more than double the number of residences for Elisabet Norgaard and family than did my state department friends."

"Amazing. So, what do you want me to do?"

"I want to apply brakes to my kid."

"Good luck with that."

Karol handed over a list. "This contains all that I could find plus an equal number Bram added. I airdropped his list to my phone and printed it out."

Francine reviewed the list. "Penthouse on Central Park. That one's been sold—or so we were told. Wyoming ranch outside Saratoga, Wyoming; Dakota apartment here in the Big Apple; cabin in the Thousand Islands; mansion in Tarrytown. That one we checked out. Villa on Marettimo Island, Sicily; ski lodges at La Parva, Chile, at Zermatt, at Sun Valley; Penthouse in Saanich, BC, Canada; penthouse in Abu Dhabi; penthouse in Singapore; manor house in Oxfordshire, Britain; villa on Jupiter Island, Florida. And more. Shit. I'd like to vacation for just one night in any of those."

"I have another gift for you. This one is my own."

Karol retrieved a folded document from her large purse. "These are transcripts and evaluations from Cornell Medical School. Ms. Norgaard was a medical student there beginning in 2009 and a surgery resident in 2013."

"She's a doctor?"

"A physician, yes, but dropped out of surgery residency her first year—or rather, she was asked to leave."

"For what?"

"She blackmailed two women medical students, coerced them to falsely accuse an instructor she didn't like of inappropriate sexual behaviors."

"My God. She was born a psychopath."

"A bad seed. Like the movie by that name that scared the bejesus out of me as a kid."

"Surgery. No wonder she's a virtuoso with sharp objects and drugs."

"She had top scores in med school."

"Fits her cleverness. Are there more discombobulating discoveries?"

"As a resident, she married a third-year medical student. One week after their justice-of-the-peace wedding, the young man committed suicide. That was never investigated."

"Okay. Enough coffee chatter," Francine said. "I need a walk in the sunlight. Join me."

"Let me snatch another chocolate tart. I need another to soothe my nerves."

"That's all it takes?" Francine asked.

"My dad's sister got me started during her spoiling-aunt visits. It works."

Karol's smile quickly faded and she sighed as loudly as a giant yawn, her face showing wear and tear from months of despairing. "No matter how thrilling these discoveries are, we're never going to find her, are we?"

"Actually," Francine said, "I believe she'll come to us."

"Why on earth?"

"In her crazy way of thinking, she bonded with us." Francine eyed the heavens for direction as strongly as a lap dog eyeing a Thanksgiving spread for a taste. "There are more days I want someone else to take over this case than days I want to play this deranged woman's games."

"Before you abdicate—and I don't believe for a minute you will—I need a favor."

"Uh oh. I don't like the sound of that."

"This will sound cruel, unconscionably devious, but I

want you to take this list, and when Bram approaches you with his discoveries—and he will—I want you to say you already identified these places. Plus make up a couple more so that he feels he made very little contribution."

Francine leaned far back in her chair. "Oh my gosh."

"Please?"

"Shoot him down? Bram's an eager kid. His flame is barely lit and you want me to be the one to extinguish it?"

"I don't want to lose him, Francine."

"His growing up isn't losing him. You're gaining a person like people you and I admire. People like Sol."

Karol felt she had been punched in the gut. She remained speechless for a long moment. "I lost Sol."

Francine realized she had stepped over an unforgiving boundary that was too painful for her friend. "I'm sorry. I didn't mean to—"

Karol grabbed her jacket and purse. "I'm sorry. I can't. I gotta …"

"Before you rush off," Francine said, rapidly scooting her chair so that a screech caused patrons to flinch, "why are you helping Bram—even minimally—if doing so is so repulsive to you?"

Karol turned to Francine. "It's what his father would have done."

Karol darted out into the afternoon.

TIK TOK IS FOR KIDS

A week passed before Bram showed up at the precinct with his Tik-Tok-aided list. He impressed Aaron with his technique of reaching out to the world for help, but Aaron had words of warning.

"What if Elisabet uses Tik Tok? She may have intercepted your request. She already came after you and your mother once. What if this upsets her far more?"

Bram never blinked. "Detective work is always risky, right?"

"Some of it is. Not all of it. We have to pick and choose. Commander Boult asked me to share with her if you uncovered important information."

"So, you're saying this information is important?"

"Let's see what she thinks." Aaron stepped into the hall and nodded to Francine who was already on standby.

"Commander Boult," Aaron said in a highly professional tone. "This is a list our helper Bram presented to me of places the Norgaard family and corporation members reside when traveling, doing business, or entertaining at home and overseas."

Francine glanced at the list and then looked at Bram, acting surprised. "You found these locations? On your own?"

"Yes ma'am. Using Tik Tok. People scattered from around the world helped when I posted I needed to find Elisabet Norgaard or her family. These are the locations they shared."

"Tik Tok. Kind of like Facebook, right?"

"Uh … somewhat."

Francine faked carefully studying the list. "Very comprehensive. Excellent. Thank you."

Francine turned to leave when Bram stopped her. "Is my list helpful?"

She turned to him. "We already have identified these locations, but the fact that you used a different means to identify the same locations is remarkable. Great job. It will be fascinating to see what you do when you one day study intelligence, or law, or whatever calls you. Have a good day, gentlemen."

She departed, feeling guilty as if she had told a young child that he or she was ugly. As she reached her office, she mumbled beneath her breath, "Forgive me, Sol."

An hour later, Aaron entered Francine's office. "That was cold."

"It was what K.C. asked. An ugly favor she demanded."

"This boy's got spunk. He's in love with mystery. With what impacts human souls' behaviors. With what—"

"I know, I know. You're preaching to the choir. I feel used. Dirty."

"We have a bigger problem."

The sudden detour yanked Francine to her feet. "What at this moment is bigger than assaulting a child's heart?"

Aaron handed a sealed letter to Francine. "It's addressed to both of us. No return address."

The color drained from Francine's face as it had when they received previous anonymous letters. She looked at the postmark: *Bratislava, Slovakia.*

She slid on gloves and a mask as had become protocol and cautiously sliced open the top edge of the envelope. She unfolded the typed letter and read aloud. "Congratulations on apprehending Colin and Sean Jefferson for raping the disabled woman. Well done. Shame on you for not pursuing Howard Tokacs. He went on to rape and strangle an elderly grandmother on Staten Island. You could have prevented that. You did not. I am now hunting for his relatives in Slovakia."

Francine and Aaron sat in silence, each swimming in a slurry of guilt, anger, regret, and annoyance.

Aaron said, "After that, she's coming back, isn't she?"

Francine tossed the letter onto her desk. "Lucky us."

DOGGONE THOSE NOSY NELLIES
- October 2022 -

One of three Norgaard Gulfstreams—one not branded with the family name—landed at night, east of New York's border at Massachusetts's Pittsfield Municipal Airport. It would be a two-hour car trip for Elisabet to the suburban village of Briarcliff Manor.

Her family's eight-bedroom cabin sat snuggled among hills, thirty miles north of Manhattan on the east bank of the Hudson River. The residence was a well-kept secret of Elisabet's grandfather, his retreat from business and from throngs relentlessly seeking philanthropic funding.

The cabinesque building—large enough to house the entire Donner pioneer party—had been off limits and unknown to most relatives. Elisabet, however, being her grandmother's favorite, had been whisked away from her parents for frequent sojourns.

Few locals had laid eyes upon the heavily wooded, secluded, gated property.

Although the cabin's exterior was coated with an unfathomable number of hand-hewn logs, interior rooms varied in taste from Indian Maharaja trappings to asymmetric Venetian Gothic. Only one bedroom had a cabin feel in which Daniel Boone or Davy Crockett would have found themselves at home.

Elisabet's jet had been scheduled to land in White Plains, NY, but the pilot radioed that his fuel indicator was misbehaving and requested to land at Pittsfield. While a fuel truck checked fuel levels, Elisabet slipped from the airliner into the passenger seat of the fuel truck. Once the Gulfstream was refueled, the truck exited through a perimeter gate and the aircraft resumed its course to White Plains. It was a strategy Elisabet had adopted from her grandparents.

A couple of miles from the airport, the fuel-truck driver pulled into a Citgo station, allowing Elisabet to transfer to a chauffeured SUV. The Tarrytown caretaker, Carlton, approached the truck driver, slipped him an envelope of hundred-dollar bills, and without speaking, returned to the SUV.

The chauffeur, Loudon, greeted Elisabet and placed her carry-on in back.

Loudon asked his passenger, "Will you be going straight to Sleepy Hollow Cabin, ma'am?"

"Yes. Thank you, Loudon. I wish to get an early start in the morning."

"Will you be desiring a car to the city?"

"Just nearby to the Philipse Manor Station."

"Very well. Let me know if you have a change of your adventuresome heart." Loudon privately frowned, disapproving of public transportation.

As Loudon began driving, Elisabet asked, "Carlton, how is Tarrytown Manor?"

"Missing you and your grandfather both, of course."

"Poor house."

Carlton pivoted to look back at Elisabet. "Twice there were detectives nosing around, making inquiries of your grandfather's whereabouts. And about the yachts."

"The yachts? I hope Grandfather isn't in tax trouble again. His mind's unwell, deteriorating more daily."

Carlton resumed looking forward. "No worries. I know you and your grandfather cherish privacy."

"Thank you for your loyalty, Carlton. I bought the two of you special gifts. They'll be delivered to Tarrytown."

"You're much too generous, ma'am."

Thinking about recent incidents, Elisabet sighed.

"Detectives can be a great nuisance."

Carlton laughed. "You know how I absolutely adore the sport of evading nosy nellies."

Elisabet's mood brightened. "I haven't heard that term since Grandmother Linnea died."

Carlton's tone of voice revealed his fondness for the Norgaards and the good old days. "One of your grandmother's favorite phrases. She used to swear in front of all of us that your grandfather's side of the family was inundated with nosy nellies. With tones of displeasure and vehemence as if about to violently curse—but always acting the lady she was—she would say, 'Doggone those nosy nellies.'"

Elisabet had flashes of listening to family stories, sitting by roaring fires in the otherwise dark game room as mounted lion and elk heads' eyes flickered orange. "I had forgotten Grandmother's intolerance of meddlesome people. I imagine she thought that was reason enough to escape to the cabin and hang out in Briarcliff Manor. People in that village whispered when we passed, but left us alone. Grandmother would say, 'Anonymity—even when staged, my dear child—is a treasure.'"

Carlton thought, Perhaps famous and wealthy people being free to go unnoticed was the attribute that drew the Vanderbilt, Astor, and Rockefeller families to retreat to that particular garden spot.

Still looking forward, Carlton said, "I imagine it was your grandmother with her fondness for overseas shopping who taught you how to slip in and out and of the country."

Elisabet longed for the smells and touch of Grandmother Linnea. "Clever woman."

"I do believe that you of all the children and grandchildren, favor her the most."

"Thank you, Carlton. Your kind words bring me comfort."

"Yes ma'am." He thought for a moment. "Anything you ever need; you can count on me."

"Me too, ma'am," Loudon said. "For anything."

"I may be doing just that, gentlemen. Call upon you."

Elisabet settled back into the plush, heated seat, thinking of possible strategies for her return in the morning to Manhattan.

Once Elisabet was safely within the protective walls of the giant cabin, Loudon approached Carlton. "You never mentioned to Ms. Elisabet about the detectives' query of her whereabouts."

Carlton shook his head. "The missus has enough worrying her, what with her grandfather's poor health and her inability to keep friends. Lonely girl—woman actually, but in many ways a little girl taking on the world by herself. She doesn't need me adding to her woes."

Carlton recalled the first week he served the Norgaards. Five-year-old Elisabet and her mother, Emma, arrived for a visit to Tarrytown. Emma showed off her Bengal kitten, Cleopatra. Although wearing the spots of leopard cats, Cleopatra displayed the temperament of a docile Ragdoll cat.

He had observed Emma lounging Cleopatra on her lap, stroking the feline as it contently purred and became as malleable as a soft pillow.

The peaceful moment was disrupted when Elisabet charged into the room and taunted Cleopatra, pinching, thumping, and squeezing her enough to inflict pain, laughing at Cleopatra attempting to escape.

Carlton had watched Elisabet turn her back to him and her mother. He felt certain that during that moment, the girl squeezed the breath out of the struggling animal.

Carlton had been stunned but obeyed when Emma requested for him to cart the limp body to the woods. Her words still haunted him. *Allow other wild creatures to dispose of it.*

During dinner, Emma had covered for Elisabet, demystifying to family members that the kitten had been sickly and died of natural causes.

As Carlton and Loudon bid one another good night, Carlton kept the knowledge to himself that he had doled out a hefty sum of money to the fuel-truck driver; an amount established a decade earlier by Master Norgaard. Carlton thought it amazing how the Norgaard empire appeared to be functioning on autopilot with teams of trustees and unnamed overlords functioning while no single person possessed a grand overview—certainly no view of what was amiss.

And yet, the pharaoh's pyramid continued to rise above desert dust.

In the morning, Carlton would serve tea and croissants; Loudon would deliver Elisabet to Sleepy Hollow's Metro station. All actions aligned like the smooth movements of a fine Swiss watch.

THE RICH ARE INVISIBLE

Aaron was in Francine's office reading a report of a man threatening to shoot the U.S. President the moment his limo arrived at the U.N.

Oblivious that Francine answered her phone, Aaron asked, "Why did they send us this report? What's this have to do with homicides? Is our squad supposed to lead proactive policing? Not our job."

"Sssh," Francine hissed. "Sorry, Lin. Let me include Detective Galanis on speaker. You're on."

"Hi Aaron."

"Hi Lin."

"Repeating what I told Francine," Lin said, "there was no sign of Elisabet Norgaard getting on or off the White Plains jet, or boarding a jet flying from an airfield outside of London to Lima for a meeting of oil execs."

"Why do we think she was flying?" Aaron asked.

"Swiss facial recognition spotted her in Sion Airport, a Swiss jetfighter base until recently. Now it's a local airfield."

"I didn't realize we had an image of her," Francine said.

"She has a record of being camera shy, even in college and med school. She was recently photographed by a man fascinated by their yacht in Greece. Evidently, more fascinated by the woman sunning on the deck. He circulated his photo on Facebook, bragging as if he had landed a rare fish."

"Darn paparazzi always helping us," Francine said.

"My bets are on the Norgaard jet flying from Sion to White Plains. It stopped for an alleged fuel problem in Pittsfield, Mass, but there's no TSA evidence of her disembarking there."

"She's here," Francine said. "Don't know how, but she's here. I feel it in my bones."

While talking on his office phone, Lin paperclipped loose pages together. "None of the leads for the multitude of Norgaard residences throughout the world that your unnamed intelligence officer uncovered have panned out. We'll continue checking. Anything going on at your end?"

Francine nodded at her second-in-command. "Aaron here, is itching to bring the Norgaard caretaker in for questioning. The house in Tarrytown has been shut down all week, but we have eyes on it. Unusual for a mansion that size to remain abandoned so long."

Lin pounded his stapler to force it to penetrate a large report. "Rich people have electronic surveillance out the wazoo. Allows them to travel and still safeguard their valuables."

CARRIAGE HOUSES
- January 2023 -

Three months later, Francine's bone feelings proved to be more accurate than reams of investigative data.

Already speaking as he entered Francine's office, Aaron dropped a report atop a letter she was editing. "Ross Conifer Arboretum, Bronx Park. Twenty-five-year-old man who moved here from Fort Lauderdale. Opioid death. Chocolate icing on his lips. Butt print in the snow. And of course, a card in his hand."

Francine closed her eyes tightly but the world did not go away. "Shit."

"She's back touting nasty habits."

"Okay," Francine said. "You wanted to bring in the elusive caretaker. Do it. Whatever you have to do to find him or however many agents it takes."

"The man knows something," Aaron said. "I heard it in his voice on the phone. I'll bring in the fucker."

"And you'll claim probable cause based on what? Hearing his voice?"

"Aiding and abetting. Withholding. Accessory. I don't care."

Francine's tight grin revealed her mind's devilish scheming. "We'll use the man as bait."

"Should I ask for a warrant based on the premise the man will make irresistible bait?"

"Wise ass. Go get him."

"Yes ma'am."

"And take Ted with you."

Aaron stopped in his tracks. "For real? He's a podcast refusing to turn off. Can I gag him?"

"Believe it or not, his minutia-based mind sometimes

strikes gold."

"Babysitting. Reason I get paid big bucks, right? Tarrytown full speed ahead. Right away, boss."

***

On the drive, Aaron whined about his doubts that Carlton would be at the mansion.

Ted nonchalantly announced, "Even the newer mansions have two-story libraries, indoor basketball courts, home theatres, multiple kitchens, carriage houses—"

"Carriage houses? Really Ted? When's the last time you saw someone ride in a carriage?"

"Besides at royal weddings, we have fifty-five-minute carriage rides in and around Central Park."

"Central Park? Right. Probably Disney World too, huh?"

"Disney World has horse-drawn wagons, princess carriages, wild-west carriages, trolleys."

"Right. Every human should know that."

"Carriage houses usually have rooms atop them. Living quarters for staff."

"Well, I didn't see a carriage house at the Tarrytown mansion."

"Mansions used to own more property than now. But they downsized. So, some carriage houses are out in the neighborhoods, not adjoining the mansions. For instance, the old Fifth Avenue mansions like the Frick House—now a museum—once had its—"

Aaron yelled, "Quiet."

After both men sulked a moment, Aaron asked, "Do you think that could be the case with the Tarrytown mansion? Its carriage house is in the neighborhood?"

Ted sulked longer.

"Well, do you?"

"Do I have permission to talk now?"

"God almighty. I just asked you a question. So yes. You have permission to talk."

"Yes. The mansion has an off-site carriage house."

"Why didn't you lead with that?" Aaron yelled.

"You didn't give me a chance."

"Because you beat around the—never mind, never mind. Where is this carriage house?"

"Here's a satellite view from Google Maps." Ted held out his cellphone for Aaron to look.

As soon as Aaron glanced at the phone, Ted yanked it away. "Wait to look when you aren't driving."

Aaron said nothing. Well, not verbally.

***

Once in Tarrytown, Ted led Aaron to a two-story building squeezed between an ice-cream parlor and a barbershop with a rotating pole of red, blue, and white stripes.

The desired structure had a road-level floor repurposed to be a two-car garage and a small antique fabric shop with hand-sewn couch pillows in the window.

"There she blows," Ted said.

"It's a garage and a shop," Aaron mumbled. "Not a whale."

Ted took a first step up the side-alley staircase.

Aaron grabbed his shoulder. "Wait. I'll do the talking. I met Carlton. He's polite, but evasive. I know the zigzag courses his kind take. Slippery fishes. I have experience balancing kindness with authority to win recalcitrant suspects over to cooperating."

"I was just going to ask him," Ted said.

"See why I should do the talking?"

"You want me to just watch?"

"Exactly."

Ted nodded, but appeared as baffled as if his partner had advised him to approach the suspect with unlaced shoes.

Aaron appeared equally flummoxed that even after his demand, Ted proceeded upward first, blocking Aaron's climb.

Ted knocked.

Carlton opened the door, having returned home for a few hours to check mail and acquire a change of clothes. "Good day. May I help you gentlemen?"

The formal and warm greeting pleased Ted enough that he forgot Aaron's dictum. "Good day. I'm Sergeant Mateo and this is Captain Galanis from the Midtown Precinct North in Manhattan. We were wondering if you would so kind as to accompany us to the precinct and help us with questions about a case."

"One moment please," Carlton said. "Let me fetch my jacket and hat." He approached a wooden coat rack that had occupied the quarters for two centuries, and collected his two wool items.

"Apologies," Ted said to Aaron. "I got caught up in the minute. The question popped out of me. The man's quite civil, don't you think?"

Aaron followed the two men down the staircase, listening to them chat about weather and the historical transformation of the old carriage house.

***

At the station, Francine asked Aaron, "Was Carlton difficult to persuade?"

"Don't ask," Aaron said.

Ted served tea to Carlton instead of coffee, having learned the man's preference during their nonstop discourse while Aaron silently steered.

Francine looked at the name on the warrant. "Pardon me, but is your name Carlton James or James Carlton?"

"James is my surname, ma'am."

"Thank you, Mr. James. Have the officers explained why we asked you to come in?"

"Questions, I believe. About a case."

Francine looked quizzically at her detectives and then at Carlton. "And what case would that be?"

"I am expecting you to tell me, ma'am."

Francine looked to Aaron who said, "Mr. James and Sergeant Mateo seem to be of a similar mindset. Both enjoyed discussing the history of the Hudson River while I chauffeured."

Francine, although amused as she attempted to picture Aaron's hour-long torment, bit her lip and regained composure. "Mr. James, we asked you here to discuss your employer, Elisabet Norgaard. She is your employer, correct?"

With no disturbance in his congenial mood, Carlton answered, "Mr. Oskar Norgaard is my employer. Ms. Norgaard is his granddaughter."

"And where at the moment is Mr. Oskar Norgaard?"

"On his yacht, I believe. Somewhere in the vicinity of the Aegean or Ionian seas likely. I have not had correspondence from him in some time."

"Some time being days, weeks, months?"

"Or goodness no. Not months. Weeks, I imagine."

"And do you know the whereabouts of Ms. Elisabet Norgaard?"

"Our last radio contact with the Gjenganger, the family

yacht, was several months or so ago. Ms. Elisabet was aboard at that time."

"And since then?"

"I can attempt to contact Ms. Norgaard and inquire if you wish."

"Let me be more specific. Have you personally seen or heard from Ms. Norgaard since her time on the yacht months ago?"

"That lady is quite a free spirit, a mind of her own, if you know what I mean. A honeybee flitting flower to flower with no home hive. But I wouldn't be surprised to hear from her within a fortnight—should she need something."

"Let me be very clear. We are pursuing Ms. Norgaard for multiple felonies, including murder. She is not just a possible suspect; she is an indisputable criminal. Should you have knowledge of her whereabouts and withhold that knowledge from us, you can be charged with accessory to murder. Have I made myself clear?"

"Oh dear. Murder." Carlton paused to reflect upon three decades of memories of Elisabet, his mind returning to her as a child torturing her mother's cat. But murder? "No. That I cannot believe. She is a lady. Always has been. Always will be."

Francine rose and leaned over the desk, supporting herself with arms pressing into the desk top. "Let me ask again. And be very careful how you answer. Do you know the whereabouts of Elisabet Asta Norgaard?"

Carlton paused, his face remaining emotionless and his voice firm. "I will contact you the moment I see her. I can promise that."

"And if you hear from her?" Aaron asked.

"And the moment I hear from her," Carlton answered. "That I also can promise."

Francine desired to play staring into one another's eyes, but Carlton's stare was at her chest and appeared to be unfocused.

While Carlton listened, Francine peered at Aaron and Ted. "Detectives? What do you think?"

Aaron responded first. "He knows."

"Agent Mateo?" Francine asked.

Ted stared at the aged man a moment. "Mr. James is a polite and gracious man, much like my mother's brother, Uncle Sylvester, who goes by the nickname: Sly. Which fits. He almost answers, but never quite fully. That has brought disasters upon our family."

Aaron's surprised expression showed he was caught off guard by Ted's answer.

Ted continued. "Like Professor Moriarty in Sherlock Holmes, my uncle is a mastermind at being *aloof from suspicion*. Maybe it's just an irrational gut feeling of mine after listening to Mr. James. But there it is."

Ted lapsed into his podcast voice. "Did you know that Sir Conan Doyle included Moriarty in five short stories including—"

"Focus, Ted," Francine said.

The three detectives stared long and hard at the statuesque elder before them.

Francine walked to the door. "I agree, Ted—Sergeant Mateo. This man is slippery. Present him with the evidence from the FBI questioning the fuel-truck driver at Pittsfield Airport. Read him his rights, gentlemen. Make sure to ask him if he desires a lawyer. I'll personally obtain the arrest warrant if this man continues to evade answering truthfully or insists on leaving. In any event, Mr. James, I assure you, you will be staying overnight in Manhattan."

CALL FROM THE WILD

Lane rang Francine's office. "There's a woman on the line for you. She refused to give her name, but said you would definitely want to speak with her. I asked for her name again, and asked what she wanted, but she cursed at me, called me a bitch, and ordered me to put her through."

Chills ran up Francine's spine and along her shoulders. "I'll take it." She waited for the click. "This is Commander Boult."

An angry but controlled woman's voice replied. "How dare you mistreat a gentle man who has been like a loving uncle to me all my life."

Francine spotted Lane summoning Aaron to the hall and directing him toward Francine's office. Francine scribbled a note saying, *trace this call*, and handed it to Aaron. He nodded and jogged toward the tech room.

"Are you still there?" The woman's voice asked.

"Yes. Still here ... Is this Elisabet?"

"Who the fuck else would you think this is, bitch?"

"What man are you referring to?"

"Don't play stalling games with me. I'm on a burner phone and far from home. I want you to release Carlton immediately."

"And if I don't?" Francine asked.

Elisabet yelled, "My grandmother proudly swore we were descended from the Norwegian Viking ruler, Eric Bloodaxe."

"First time I've heard your voice. I had pictured someone composed, in control, not someone falling apart. Guess I miscalculated."

"Guess I must be more Norwegian Viking than human. Especially when people I care about are unjustly treated."

"We're treating him well."

"The fuck you are."

Francine maintained a calm, even tone. "He broke the law. Was acting as an accessory to your crimes."

"Carlton has never been involved in a crime in his life."

"Paying off a truck drive to illegally smuggle a passenger out of airport security to evade customs and passport control qualifies as a crime."

"He told you that?"

"And much more."

"You're lying."

"Why? Do you believe he's your loyal pawn, minion, servant, underling? Or is he something more? You said he's like a loving uncle. But you placed him in this position. I wouldn't call that loving on your part."

Elisabet caught herself escalating with anger. She brought her deportment under control to match Francine's measured presence. "You know nothing of our relationship."

"I call it exploitation."

"You're far off base."

"Why don't you come in and let's debate that?"

"Does the academy teach officers to humiliate people by treating them like they're mentally deficient?"

"Mentally deficient? Very politically correct."

"And treat people like they're uneducated?"

"That's right. You attended medical school."

"And you lived on an Indiana farm with your grandparents while your parents were separated for a year."

Francine felt electricity course throughout her body. She could not remember ever revealing that fact to anyone but her best friend in third grade.

The air felt heavy during many seconds of silence.

"Cat got your tongue?" Elisabet asked. "I know all about you. All about the people in your life. We could have been a team—we should be a team. Unfortunate for both of us. But what's life without disappointments, right?"

Francine heard a click and the call ended.

Aaron approached. "We traced it. Probably a burner phone. Richmond, Massachusetts. Little town near the Pittsfield Airport. She must be partial to that area."

Francine stuttered. "Yeah … uh … have someone check it out."

"Are you okay?"

"This psychotic vigilante knows personal things about us. Intimately personal."

"Should we double security details?"

"I wouldn't feel at ease if we tripled them. Have you any cause to believe she stalked you and your family?"

"Every day I feel stalked. Every vender. Every car slowing for people to look at street signs. Women squeezing produce at outdoor market stands."

"I looked in our station's DSM, the psychiatric diagnosis book. I now qualify for paranoid personality disorder."

"Is there medication for that?"

"A chilled-glass neat martini."

"Gin or vodka?"

"After the first one, does it matter?"

MORNING COCKTAILS

Aaron entered Francine's office and was immediately perplexed upon seeing a glass half-filled with golden-brown liquid that could be Bourbon or a similar-colored whiskey or liquor.

"In all my years," Aaron said, "I have never seen a glass of spirits grace your desk. What gives?"

"I partake of late-night office drinks now and then." Francine motioned for Aaron to sit.

Aaron held out his watch and tapped its face. "It's top of the morning."

Francine extracted a second glass from her bottom drawer and set it before Aaron. She retrieved a crystal liquor decanter from a cabinet below her window.

Aaron studied his commander's face. "From your expression, I detect we are not celebrating, but are descending into gloom."

Francine held up her glass as if toasting the air. The slanted manner she held it made Aaron uneasy. He deduced she had already imbibed a glass or two.

Francine slurred. "We released Carlton James."

"We what?"

"Released Carlton James on bond—more money than I'll ever see."

"How did that happen?" Aaron asked, his voice ending on a high pitch.

Francine swirled her drink. "Orders from above."

"Orders?"

"An ultimatum masquerading as a request or suggestion. On the phone, I heard our mayor and police commissioner arguing. Something to do with essential funding of our drug programs."

"Norgaard funding," Aaron said, surveying Francine to see if she flinched after he accused their leaders of rakish rationalizing. She did not.

"Fuck," Aaron yelled, placing his hand over his glass to prevent Francine from pouring him a drink.

Francine nodded like a bobbing-head toy. "You and I are assuming the same backstory. We're on target."

Aaron paced the worry-circle path worn into Francine's dark blue carpet. "Such bullshit."

He circled one more time and stopped. "We'll still have eyes on Carlton, right?"

"He was released at six this morning. The commissioner's officers lost track of him."

"How in hell is that possible?"

"Carlton was allowed his one phone call last night. This morning, he taxied to Grand Central. A homeless man or woman—impossible to discern gender beneath innumerous layers of clothing—followed Carlton inside and into the men's room. Carrying a bundle. The morning rush happened. Thousands of New Yorkers in and out. The officers lost him."

"Was there video?"

"Cameras caught a homeless couple—both with excessive layers of clothing—exiting the men's room. They crossed the Main Course, passed the famed opal-glass clock for shits and giggles, and disappeared onto the street."

"Fuck. But we can go after him again, right?"

"Although it was not clearly stated, pervasive innuendos screamed: *hands off.*

"Fuck," Aaron whispered. "Feels great to know command has our six, huh?"

Aaron held out his glass for a pour.

EAT AND DRINK LIKE A GREEK

Jasmine strolled into Taverna Santorini and scanned faces for her tattooed friend, pouting when she failed to find her. She declined an offer from a trio of women gesturing for her to join them, preferring to sit alone in a dark corner booth and order a plate of Tomatokeftedes.

Instead of a waitperson, a woman stranger approached with lulling body language as if they knew one another.

"Dining alone, Luv?" the stranger asked with a British accent.

Jasmine scooted the neighboring chair from beneath the table. The woman required no gesture or verbal invitation to sit.

Jasmine eyed the woman's elegant full-length silk-and-lace dress. "Lora Jean?"

The woman smiled. "Absolutely. Sustainable, green clothing. Attempting to do my part to combat the garment industry's child slavery."

"Your Brit dialect is disarming, calming."

"Urban Yorkshire. I adopted my mother's speech rather than my father's Cornwall pirate gibberish. I adore your short cut. Brilliant. I've been considering such a hair style. Conserving morning grooming time is deliciously appealing."

"I'm Jasmine."

"A pleasure to meet you, Jasmine. And I am Joan. Joan Arche. Come here often?"

"Now and then. And you?"

"Actually, I'm new to the New York scene."

"In that case, welcome."

"There's a bobby over—pardon me—a police officer by the entrance staring at you. Friend of yours?"

"Hardly. I heard there's been trouble here recently. He must be watching over this place."

"Do all American police carry guns?"

"Wow. You are new to New York. Yes. Well, maybe not security-guard types. But police? Yes."

After a plate of cheeses and olives and two shot glasses each of room-temperature raki, the two women's fingers snaked across the table until gently resting upon one another.

The question had been answered. Fingers can indeed kiss.

***

The second time Jasmine saw Elisabet—alias Joan Arche—at Taverna Santorini, they immediately approached one another smiling. They were cautious to not smile too big and look like goofballs to an assemblage exhibiting a laidback presence for the moment.

Elisabet spoke first. "Missed seeing you the past three days."

"Really? I got tied up helping a friend with medical problems."

"That's kind. Good on you, girl. Your friend is lucky. What kind of medical problems?"

"She's postpartum," Jasmine said.

"Depression?"

"She had eclampsia. Still has problems with blood pressure, headaches, some liver problems—nothing fatal. Her baby boy's colicky, crying for excruciating hours at a time—or so it seems."

"Your poor friend," Elisabet said.

"Thank you."

"Does she ever come here with you?"

"She's not a party type. More into symphonies and musicals—at least when she's well. Detests loud music."

"You come alive when the music revs up."

"You bet I do."

Elisabet extended her hand. "You want to dance?"

"I thought you'd never ask."

They laughed and moved to the dance floor where stars of silver light bounced on them, the floors, the walls, the ceiling, and even the food.

Elisabet nodded toward the police officer appearing preoccupied with Jasmine. "Your bobby buddy must fancy you."

"Jasmine shrugged ignorance. "Are you certain that's the same guy?"

"Positively."

"I don't remember him being that cute. Do you think he has any hint I'm queer?"

"He's a bobby. He's clueless."

Jasmine laughed hard enough that she snorted. "Here, here."

After tame music ended and a techno-and-Greek-blended song began, Elisabet tongue kissed Jasmine and then whispered in her ear, "Let's get away from that peeper eyeing us and go somewhere private."

Jasmine laughed. "He looks harmless. I'm fine."

"No. Really. Let's go somewhere else."

"Thanks, but I can't stay much longer."

"We could go back to my place," Elisabet said. "It's just around the corner."

"Thank you. But I can't."

"We could go to the ladies room and slip out the back exit. Avoid that bobby making fun of us."

"I really can't."

Elisabet stopped dancing and appeared as stern as a

scolding parent. "Do you have somebody you're hooking up with?"

"I need to get back to my friend I told you about. Postpartum with the colicky baby. Remember?"

"Do you check on her every night?"

"I live with her. I have for six months."

"What? You live with a woman who has a baby?"

"Is that a problem?" Jasmine asked.

"No ... Not a problem. I just thought that ... Nothing. Forget it."

Jasmine placed her hands on Elisabet's shoulders and peered into her eyes. "What?"

"I thought you lived with someone else. It doesn't matter. Let's dance."

"I'm confused. You thought I lived with someone else? Why would you think that?"

"You're sexy. Beautiful. Fascinating. It makes sense that you would not be alone in this world."

"I'm not alone. I'm with Teresa. We're sharing raising her son."

Elisabet stepped back. "You're with who?"

"Teresa. My friend who has a baby."

"I thought you were with—"

Seeing Elisabet censor herself, Jasmine's voice rose in pitch. "Who? Who did you think I was with?"

As tempers surged, Elisabet lost her British accent. "I made an assumption. Forget it."

"Why did your accent change?"

"What?"

"Your accent was British. Now it's American."

Elisabet's accent returned to being Urban Yorkshire. "I pick up accents fast from wherever I'm visiting. A month in New York and I'm ruined."

Jasmine looked down at Elisabet's hands crossed on

her abdomen. Anxiety had launched Elisabet to drum her left fingers while tapping the back of her hand with her right index finger.

Jasmine recognized the idiosyncrasy Francine had described, realized who was propositioning her.

Panic danced throughout Jasmine's insides as she forced a calm demeanor to hide her fear. She scanned for the officer, but could not locate him. Her panic intensified. Where was Sergeant Hudson? He was assigned to keep her in sight. "I gotta make a call."

Elisabet emitted a chilling stare with her eyes narrowing into hyper-focused slits. "Why?"

Jasmine stuttered. "My friend. Her baby. I should check on them."

"What about your lover?"

"Who?"

Elisabet overly enunciated. "Your lover Commander Boult."

"How do you know about her?"

Elisabet grabbed Jasmine's wrist and twisted it. "Is she no longer good enough for you?"

"You're hurting me."

"You unfaithful tart."

"Let go."

"The three of us could have worked together. Stood for something, but you ruined that."

Jasmine shrieked, invoking several patrons to stare. While scouring for Sergeant Hudson, she attempted to jerk free.

Elisabet yelled inches from her face. "You're less than worthless." She darted to and out the metal backdoor.

"Oh my God." Jasmine stood frozen and then screamed loud enough to supplant pulsating music and bring everyone on the dance floor to a halt.

UPS AND DOWNS

When Francine arrived at the precinct, Lane pointed toward the waiting room and mouthed, *Jasmine.*

Francine immediately detoured to the waiting room where Jasmine sat alone, still dressed for a short night out on the town. "It's great to see you, but I must say you look ragged. Rough night on the town or crying baby issues?"

"I met her," Jasmine muttered.

Francine frowned.

Jasmine looked about to assure no one else could hear. "Your serial killer lady. I met her."

Francine sat in the neighboring chair, clasped her friend's hand, and whispered, "Where?"

"The Greek bar, pub, club."

"Santorini?"

While staring at the floor, Jasmine nodded like a little kid confessing to a parent.

"How do you know it was her?"

"The hand movements. Her being forceful to get me to go with her. Her knowing you and I used to be together."

The last phrase broke Francine's heart. Even though she knew that truth, neither of them had ever spoken it.

"Did she follow you home?"

"I came straight here. I needed a safe place. I told them not to wake you."

"Oh my God, Jasmine."

"She became enraged the three of us aren't a team—whatever that means. She's crazy, Francine."

"I'm relieved you're safe."

Jasmine buried her head in her hands. "She dressed up and talked like she was British, but lost her accent when she got pissed—pissed as in angry, not drunk—although she was both."

Francine placed her arm around Jasmine's shoulder. "I'm sorry you were pulled into this nightmare."

Jasmine embraced her friend.

Francine whispered, "Was Sergeant Hudson there?"

"He had been guarding every move I made. But when I panicked, I couldn't find him. Maybe she drugged one of his endless Diet Dr. Peppers."

"Possibly with a laxative. His name's on the sick-call list. Before he gave in, he called for a replacement."

"I didn't hang around to see."

"You're lucky she didn't drug you."

"I hope Sergeant Hudson's okay. Is this woman really that clever?"

"I'll fortify your security detail. Teresa and her baby are now at risk."

Jasmine openly wept. "This is wrong."

"This woman is causing many good people to suffer."

Jasmine kissed Francine on the cheek. "Thank you." She gathered her belongings. "I should get back to Teresa. Reassure her in person I'm okay."

Jasmine walked toward the open door, and then stopped. "I should tell you. I talked to the women's group, offered to be a go-between them and your squad."

Francine paused breathing. "Wow. That would be fantastic."

"I've been thinking about it ever since you told me your squad passed along info about the two brothers taking advantage of the mentally-challenged woman."

"That was Aaron's idea. Did the group agree?"

"After much discussion. Trust issues."

"Thank you. I would like to meet the women."

"They don't want to meet you. Sorry. They insisted you

talk to me and I relay messages and vice versa."

"Oh … That will be fine. Thank you."

After discussing further precautions, Jasmine left the station. Francine continued sitting alone in the waiting room. She not only was alone; she felt alone.

She heard Aaron's boisterous voice greeting Lane. That helped. He was one of the few people she knew who was talented at disrupting loneliness. She tried to recall other people who had been able to disrupt her fidelity to feeling lonely. It was a short list. How silly I am, she thought. She walked toward the cheerful voices, open to the idea of allowing cheerful people into her life for the moment, much like not fighting off a puppy determined to lick her face or cuddle on her lap. "Morning Detective. You sound chipper."

Aaron whisked a cardboard box from Lane's desk. "See what I brought?"

Francine frowned. "Donuts? Really?"

"Not just any donuts. Cole and I made these."

"Nobody makes donuts."

"Cole wanted to. So, we did."

Although a stereotypical offering for police, this specific box of donuts was wrapped in joy.

No one cared that they tasted terrible.

***

Hours later, Aaron entered Francine's domain, surprised to find her resting her chin on her desk and staring at her Newton-Cradle-Pendulum-Ball toy, an item that had sat frozen on her bookshelf past months collecting dust. He watched as she swung a ball, a second, and then a third, her unfocused eyes oblivious to collisions of metal balls as if she were a cat dizzy on catnip.

"Francine?"

She continued thumping balls. "Yeah?"

"What's going on?"

"I'm swinging pendulum balls."

"I see that."

Still occupied with her toy, Francine asked, "Where do you think we get our wisdom? From books or grandmothers?"

Aaron watched a round of balls run out of energy. "I take it you've been at this game a while."

"Which? Books or grandmothers?"

"What wisdom did your grandmother pass along?"

"Many things." Francine grabbed a center ball to interrupt the action. "She informed me that all people chase people who chase other people."

Aaron watched a new round of ball swinging. "Do you think she was talking about love?"

Francine again interrupted the chain reaction. "I used to think that." She lifted a ball farther out. "Each time, however many balls I release on the front end, that same number swings away on the back end. Predictable. No surprises. That's comforting." She thumped metal balls several more times in varying combinations. "Preferable to waiting for the other shoe to drop."

"What other shoe?"

"That's the problem. We don't know if it will be a dainty bedroom slipper or a heavy Kevlar combat boot. My desk is stacked with reports of DNA testing, tire-track confirmations, blood types, stolen gun reports, 3-D-printed-gun discoveries, confessions of prisoners to other murders or squealing on other murderers. But all I can think about is what this one woman could be up to."

"How is—"

"And don't ask if I'm getting enough sleep."

"I wouldn't dare. I was about to ask how Jasmine is doing. Lane told me about Jasmine's ordeal with Elisabet."

"She's not planning to tell Teresa. Teresa's already in a compromised state. Jasmine thanked me for placing officers outside their building and in the hallway. She actually arranged to be a go-between to interact between that Daughters of whatever group of women and our squad. Can you imagine that?"

"That's a turn around. A win-win."

Francine thumped another metal ball. "Yeah."

"I would think that would feel good."

"Nothing feels good." Francine pointed at a stack of papers at the far end of her desk. "Typical homicides involving jealous, revengeful, abused spouses; two atypical parricides; extermination of a neighbor who banged out late-night-early-morning drum and cymbal clangor—who wouldn't have broken that guys fingers and then shot him, right?"

Aaron could not remember ever seeing his superior officer this dispirited. "That's a heavy load."

Francine mumbled into the crook of her elbow. "The usual crap. What isn't usual is ... I'm not bothered by those cases. I can only obsess about one single, notorious, cunning, brain-damaged witch."

"Witch?"

"I demoted her from bitch status. Witches are more aligned with the unholy."

Although his companion was wallowing in homicides, Aaron felt relieved she retained an inkling of her typical wit.

"No matter where I go," Aaron said, "what I see, hear, the witch is over my shoulder too."

Francine crossed her arms on her desk, slumped over,

and rested her forehead on her arm pillow.

Aaron's face lit up. "You'll never believe what gossip I overheard yesterday at our coffee maker."

Francine raised one hand and let it flop back, gesturing, *what?*

"Ted told Jenetta that he considered you and me to be his two best friends."

Francine raised her head. "Ted said that?"

"I could tell he had been crying."

"Crying? Ted?"

"Crazy, huh? He's always podcast flat. So later, I heard Ted sniffling and blowing his nose. I asked if he was okay. Not a big deal, right? You and I ask each other that. But for the first time, I asked Ted, and he told me that he and his wife—I don't even know her name—that he—"

"Laura. His wife's name's Laura."

"That he and Laura miscarried. They had been struggling with infertility and undergone in-vitro fertilization. After a bunch of attempts, they were finally pregnant. But in the tenth week, Laura miscarried."

"Poor Laura—poor Ted."

"Yeah."

Both detectives silently relived memories of family births and losses.

"So," Aaron said. "Ted ended by telling me he looked forward to you and me inviting him to tag along, get his mind off his loss long enough to feel hope."

"Hope? Ted said that?"

"He did. But reminded me assignments are in your purview. I didn't know what else to say."

Francine looked as perplexed as the time Aaron informed her that a gang member shoved a rival off the Manhattan Bridge. The falling man's belt had caught on a bridge painters' platform. When the killer leaned over to shoot the guy, the killer slipped and plunged to his death.

Aaron gently tapped his fist on the desk. "Even though Ted said that, I will not desist from whining every time he launches into one of his interminable orations."

"That's what Ted expects from you. What works for him."

Aaron left and Francine had no clue why she felt better, but she did. She put away her swinging-metal-balls toy and slid the pile of reports to where she could review them.

VAPING GIRLS KNOW
- June 2023 -

For Elisabet, having money made most life tasks easier, tasks such as staking out the Whaanga household. Elisabet rented a neighborhood house. Even though she probably would use it for only a few weeks, she paid cash upfront for six months. The attic had a small window aimed directly at the Whaanga's front door. She could also see a kitchen or backroom's side door.

She additionally had an unobstructed view of the police car parked along the street. Was its true purpose to intimidate would-be intruders or stalkers? If so, they were failing.

Watching Ms. Whaanga got under her skin. Every afternoon, the woman carried a picnic basket covered with a red-checkered-cloth-napkin to the officers. Home baked cookies? Petit cakes? Finger sandwiches? Did she know the officers or was she generous with everyone?

While spying through her military binoculars, Elisabet occasionally saw a teenage boy trailing behind Ms. Whaanga, reinforcing her earlier belief that the boy was her son. Today, he followed his mother, appearing to be pitching a mild tantrum. Did he oppose his mother feeding the neighborhood patrol?

Elisabet zoomed in on the officers' faces. They appeared tickled pink—one of her grandmother's favorite phrases—tickled pink that the day's treats were being carried their direction. Must be delicious, she thought. She wished she could offer them her chocolate-icing treats. Maybe it wasn't the baked treats tickling them pink, but the officers enjoying the woman's pleasantness and generosity. Elisabet pondered for a moment. She could not recall her family members modeling such attributes of kindness toward strangers. Although Elisabet had demonstrated kindness when she impersonated a country-western singer, it was a trait she had imitated based on studying characters on *Grand Ole Opry* reruns.

The following morning, Elisabet emerged from her rental, dressed as an elderly woman carrying a cloth shopping bag, appearing to be weekly shopping for a person living alone. Her modest black dress was innocuously simple. Her unadorned white sneakers were fashionable for senior citizens proving to the world they could function independently.

She waited at a street corner half-way to the school. She had studied what time the officer and boy passed daily.

The boy and the youthful officer were laughing and chatting energetically as if emerging from a baseball game won by their favorite team.

Elisabet waited for them to pass and then stalked them, observing from the opposite side of the street. She timed crossing the street to arrive at the school the moment her subjects arrived, counting on there being the usual cluster of girls in the front yard—some of them vaping.

Elisabet spilled her groceries at the girls' feet. "Oh no," she screamed. "I hope nothing broke."

"Here, let me help," one girl said as others remained too cool to react. Another girl cursed as she checked her pastel-color sneakers for food splatter.

The helpful girl stooped, lifted light-weight cartons and cans, and placed them in Elisabet's bag.

As the officer and the boy approached the school's door, Elisabet pointed and asked, "That boy? I see him every morning with an escort. Is he important?"

"Oh him," the sneaker-checker girl whined. "He thinks he's like so cool cause his parents must be like somebody important."

Another girl said, "Over-protective, smothering syndrome. Probably from a rich, paranoid family. He looks like he's from Hawaii. Probably tech money."

Another girl with hands on hips, said, "He can't be all that rich. He walks for gosh sakes. He must live nearby in one of these boring condos or houses. Not where anybody who's like anybody lives."

Another girl said, "I searched for him on Facebook. No social presence. Maybe his parents or somebody made him delete everything. When I asked, the jerk laughed at me. Like really?"

"Maybe he did something creepy and got kicked off," another girl said.

"Is he from a famous family?" Elisabet asked. "What's his name?"

"Bram's all I know," the helpful girl answered. "I think he's cute."

"Like be real," the shoe-checker said.

Elisabet accepted the last carton from the helpful girl. "Thank you for helping me with my groceries. I think the boy may be my neighbor. From the Whaanga family."

"Right. That's Bram's last name," one of the vaping girls said and laughed. "Like such a vampire sounding name." She conjured up a Boris Karloff vampire voice. "Let me drink your blood with my fangas."

Her allies remained too cool to respond.

The sneaker-checking girl said, "I never noticed him until a week ago. It's not like he's on the football or basketball team or hangs out with anybody who's anybody."

"He's in my math class," the helpful girl said. "He's

super smart."

The other girls rolled their eyes, huffing and mumbling, "Whatever."

Elisabet wished the cluster of girls a pleasant day and crossed the street, mumbling, "Bram. Whaanga. Bram Whaanga." She paused to watch the school, noting that after a minute, the officer left the building and returned toward his partner and car.

Elisabet focused thinking about Bram, no longer fretting about Jasmine. Like members of her family, she was adept at putting the past behind and moving forward, not dwelling on what-ifs, guilt, or anger as did lesser families.

Before she directly dealt with Bram, she wished to occupy the busy-body police. Such a plan was outside her routine province. She would seek St. Michael to bless her circuitous design.

THE LITTLE GIRL WHO CRIED WOLF

Elisabet never considered herself to be a mastermind, but accepted she had a talent. Instead of wasting hours pondering what to do, she was skilled at having a spontaneous idea and forthwith launching into implementing.

She initiated a diversion, resting assured, should she stray off base, St. Michael would redirect her.

Her strategy was straightforward: frighten a crowd of citizens, publish a breaking-news article about the event, and deflect blame upon the police. She would create chaos, annoyance, humiliation, and more importantly, preoccupation of authorities.

Her achievement would inflict pain upon people who betrayed her, people who deserved God's wrath.

Elisabet sat by the Peace Fountain on Amsterdam, sensing that the looming St. Michael statue held greater power than her small pendent. She opened her Bible to the Old Testament and read aloud. "Nahum One. The Lord is a jealous and avenging God; the Lord takes vengeance and is filled with wrath. The Lord takes vengeance on his foes and maintains his wrath against his enemies."

She closed her eyes and waited for St. Michael's blessing. Within seconds, she heard massive car horn beeping and looked to where 11th Street and Amsterdam intersected.

She beheld a blind man tapping his cane while walking toward a point where traffic crisscrossed from four directions. Cars, taxis, and trucks slammed on brakes and smashed into one another with sickening thuds as dust and radiator spray clouded the scene. Once substances settled, Elisabet spotted the unscathed blind man standing amidst the vehicle corpses.

"Thank you, my archangel."

Elisabet purchased a cannister of potassium table salt. Once home, she poured the white crystals onto a napkin and googled a photo of hydrogen cyanide crystals. They resembled enough. She returned to the store and bought salt cannisters and boxes of small plastic baggies.

She printed and adhered cyanide-poison-warning labels to baggies with information about the poison being a chemical asphyxiant. She sprinkled a few salt crystals into each baggie and crumpled bags so they appeared used.

She printed coupons claiming to be exchangeable for tickets to the musical: *The Lion King*. She placed fake coupons in envelopes marked: *Free Coupons for Broadway Plays*, sprinkled salt crystals into the envelopes, and sealed them.

She sought out well-advertised events in Central Park and selected a family-oriented run, a fundraiser to replace band uniforms and instruments destroyed by a three-alarm fire at a Harlem middle school.

When Elisabet arrived, hundreds had gathered for the sunny-day outing. On the registration tables were donation forms, numbered stickers to place on runners' outfits, handouts about school projects, raffle tickets, and advertising leaflets from nearby restaurants donating the day's profits to the cause.

Elisabet slipped her envelopes among table items and dropped her cyanide-warning baggies into open trash bins at the feet of the busy organizers, assuring labels faced upward.

Parents and older children snatched the envelopes and swooned over the *Lion-King* coupons, ignoring the presence of white crystals transferring from coupons to their hands. A few parents complained to sponsors, but no alarmed protests ensued until an eighth-grade science teacher spotted a disposed baggie with a cyanide warning label.

She screamed, "Cyanide."

Panic erupted.

People became dizzy and complained of feeling nauseated. Some induced vomiting in themselves as well as in their children. Many became flushed and sweated as profusely as juice being squeezed out of lemons. One man shouted that he lost vision in both eyes.

Ambulances raced to the scene.

If anyone had doubts about the size of New York's police and fire departments, those doubts were quenched by the onslaught of uniformed and plain-clothes officers descending upon the park.

The eight-grade science teacher notified the NYC Poison Center. The Hazardous Materials Response Team arrived to mitigate the incident. Dogs trained in odor detection failed to signal presence of poisons, leading one officer to remove his gas mask and sniff the powder as people around him gasped at his cavalier attitude. "No almond smell. These crystals are the wrong size."

The nearest emergency departments became inundated with scores of screaming families reminiscent of persons shoving one another on sinking ocean-liners.

Elisabet photographed the chaos with a disposable cellphone and sent photos and a pre-prepared news flash to the city's least ethical tabloid: *The Big Apple Bulletin.*

Her fiction described that the police ruled the mass-poisoning event to be a hoax. She included a police-artist sketch of a possible suspect.

The *Big Apple Bulletin's* special edition hit the streets

even before the last victims of the ruse were medically evaluated.

One midtown officer personally delivered a copy of the tabloid to Francine, saying, "I think you better look at this, Commander."

Francine read the 48-font headline: *Hundreds of New Yorkers Fooled into Believing They were Poisoned with Cyanide.*

At the bottom of the page was a rough sketch of a man, labeled: *Artist sketch of the prime suspect wearing a police uniform.*

Aaron rushed into Francine's office waving his copy of the tabloid. "What the fuck? Did you see this?"

"I just saw it this minute."

"That's me."

"No. That resembles you. It's a rough sketch."

"It's a computer-altered graphic of me." Aaron held it inches from another officer's face. "Is that me, or not me?"

The officer pulled the graphic close to his face, and then held it at a distance. "Looks kind of like you. Younger. More muscular."

Aaron circled the room several times and force-dunked his copy into the trash. "She did this. And you know it."

"She's trying to throw us off. We need to keep our cool."

Aaron screamed, "I don't want to keep my cool. I want her head. I want it this minute."

I'LL PICK UP THE KIDS

It took less than a day for Elisabet to assemble a NYPD officer's uniform and paraphernalia. She arrived at Bram's school and asked the receptionist to send the principal to meet with her in front of the building.

Elisabet explained, "I don't want to cause a school disturbance. Kids see our uniforms and immediately ask to see our guns and ask if we ever shot anyone. Afterwards, they don't settle back down in class. I want to spare your school that drama."

Principal Breitenstein met Elisabet at the Bedford Avenue entrance.

"Thank you, Principal Breitenstein. I am Sergeant Gomez of the 70th precinct. I need to ask one of your students to go with me to the station. The student called us from school, reporting—"

"Students aren't allowed to have phones," the principal said.

Elisabet ignored the intrusion. "He reported his estranged father, who has a history of physically abusing him, called him at school and threatened to kill him tonight. The boy said he feels safe at school but is terrified to return home. Even though an assigned officer accompanies the boy to and from school, the father has a history of hitting the bars and then late at night forcing his way into the house. We need to take the boy to a supervised shelter while my team interviews his mother. We have her at the station, but we don't want the boy to know until we get there."

"So much chaos these days," the principal said. "Last week we had a cherry bomb explode in a urinal and now this. At least the school is not being threatened—for the sake of the other children. Who is the boy?"

Elisabet pulled out professionally-looking child-custody and pickup orders.

"Bram Whaanga?" the principal asked. "Oh my gosh. I only recently met his mother. Shy, polite lady. But the boy is a handful. He skipped second grade, so he is young, an immature showoff challenging my teachers. They'll be more than happy for you to take him for the rest of the day—even the rest of the month. I never suspected a problematic home life. Poor boy."

"We may have to keep him at the shelter for a few days while we investigate."

The principal peered over his reading glasses. "I hope Bram made up that story. That child has a vivid imagination." He glanced over his shoulder to assure no one was listening. "Generally, I am required to call parents before we release children."

Elisabet pointed at the second page. "The judge approved and signed this."

"Well ... I suppose this is above board."

Elisabet reordered her papers. "Thank you. Let's hope the boy's report is exaggerated. I didn't have time to change into plain clothes. At least I was able to grab an unmarked car."

Elisabet pointed across the street. "I'm driving that sedan behind the end school bus. We're short staff since COVID, but if I need backup, I'll radio for assistance before we drive away."

"Seems most unusual. But then again, what hasn't been unusual since COVID turned our world upside down."

Principal Breitenstein entered the school while Elisabet waited halfway between the entrance and her car.

Minutes later, the principal walked Bram to Elisabet.

"Bram? This is Sergeant Gomez," the principal said. "She has questions she wants to ask you down at the precinct station."

The principal was puzzled when Bram grinned as if he had won the lottery. He was even more confused by the enthusiasm in the child's voice.

"This is so cool," Bram said. "Where's your car?"

Elisabet pointed and Bram practically towed her to the vehicle.

Principal Breitenstein watched the pair drive away, thinking there was an excellent chance Bram was pulling the wool over everyone's eyes to escape English class. He felt a duty to call his student's mother, but feared that could be misconstrued as impeding a police investigation.

Pulling away from the school, Bram said, "I was worried Captain Boult would never want to see me again."

"Captain Boult, huh?" Elisabet asked. "Guess she must value your ideas. That lady's hard to get to see."

"Something must have happened."

"Guess so."

"Do you know what's going on?"

"I'm just playing chauffeur today. Low woman on the totem pole. Take up whatever you and Captain Boult talk about with her."

They drove a dozen blocks before Elisabet spoke again. "Listen. This is my third run of the morning. Didn't get to grab coffee. Okay if we run into the coffee shop at that light?"

Bram grinned. "And a donut?"

Elisabet frowned. "Really kid? I don't eat donuts. Like as in never ever."

Bram stifled the sound of his giggle into his clinched fist. "There goes another one of my stereotypes down the drain. Just when I think I have the world figured out? Wham."

"Let me know if that happens. You figuring it out."

They pulled into a metered parking spot and walked toward the shop.

Bram pointed at the meter. "Now that fits my stereotyping perfectly. Cops don't pay meters. Even if in an unmarked car."

Once inside, Elisabet order an espresso and turned to Bram. "You want anything? Or do you fit into my stereotyping? Too young to drink coffee."

"If you're offering, I'll have one of those bottles of chilled, non-caffeinated green tea—oh yeah. Please."

"Wow. Now you shattered my preconceptions."

After a few minutes of sitting and sipping, Elisabet asked, "Can you grab me a creamer? This is really strong."

Without answering, Bram nodded and walked to the counter.

Elisabet slipped one of the original types of white flunitrazepam tablets into his drink and watched it dissolve as a colorless addition.

She waited until Bram appeared slightly dizzy. "Let's get back to the car. I should get you to the captain."

Slowly becoming intoxicated, Bram stood and asked, "Why didn't Stuart—I mean Sergeant Caldwell—staking out our house come get me?"

"I learned to not ask. Just follow orders."

Bram complied.

MAMA BEAR

With no fanfare, Lane redirected the call from Bram's protective detail to Francine. On the other end of the line, Sergeant Stuart Caldwell sounded rushed. "When I got there, he wasn't at his school. The principal said a woman police officer picked him up mid-morning and took him to the precinct for questioning."

Francine shoved her roller chair back hard enough it hit the wall. She had to pace a moment before she could speak. "Do we have a description?"

"She fits the size of our killer," Stuart said. "The principal said she had a Brooklyn accent, wore a uniform, and had pickup orders."

"Did the school make copies?"

"No ma'am."

"Shit. Do we have security video?"

"We have it with us."

Stuart waited for follow-up questions but heard nothing. "Are you still there, Commander?"

After additional silence, Francine spoke with a lifeless, monotone voice. "I'll call his mother. Don't stop by your station, Sergeant. Come directly here and check in with me the second you get here."

Francine ended the call and speed-dialed Karol.

Karol finished their panicked phone call while walking out the front door as a Brooklyn police car arrived to transport her.

Waiting for Karol, Francine and Aaron reviewed the school security footage several times.

"Not much to her," Aaron said. "In my head she grew to become a mammoth beast." He borrowed Francine's behavior of pacing in a circle while speaking. "I bet Bram's taller than her. Maybe outweighs her."

"Assuming he's alive," Francine said, "she likely drugged him to control him."

"Oh, he's alive. I know he's alive. I don't know what it is she wants, but that boy's alive."

"She wants us to suffer," Francine said. "She already threatened that."

"And that means keeping him alive, right?"

"Like you," Francine said, crossing herself, "I am praying for that."

There was only one new officer in the station, a man who did not know of the famous K.C. Whaanga, and he was the first person to see Karol charge into the station. He body-blocked her mid-hall.

Francine had never heard Karol raise her voice or curse, but the entire detective squad heard every word as Karol shoved the officer. "Get out of my way, you fucking twerp. Your commander is expecting me, asshole."

When the confronting officer lifted an arm to strike Karol, another officer grabbed the fledgling's shoulder and threw him to the floor, yelling, "She's fine, moron. We know her."

While watching the school videos, Karol sat as paralyzed as if she had been wounded with curare-tipped arrows.

"Want to see them again?" Francine asked.

Karol shook her head and mumbled, "What about her car?"

Francine nodded to Aaron to speak. "We traced the car to a coffee shop. A camera across the street captured the two of them entering the shop. As they exited, she was propping up Bram. Elisabet must have drugged him inside the shop. They climbed into an Uber. We located the driver. He dropped them off at Grand Central."

Karol forced herself into being the calm, calculating, non-mother intelligence case officer she had been in another life. "I'm trying to wrap my mind around this. A woman police officer drags a falling-down boy through New York, and no one stops to ask what is wrong with this scene."

Aaron spoke up. "She ditched her police shirt before climbing into the Uber. Pulled a loose black dress overtop—right there in the parking lot."

Karol talked with eyes closed. "And again, a grown woman drags a severely stumbling boy through Grand Central, and no one questioned that. Is everyone in this city blind?"

"I see wacky situations every time I take the train," Aaron said. "It's New York."

Karol walked to Francine's window and stared at a pigeon sitting on the sill. "This is the nightmare I have fought for fourteen years to prevent. It's like it was inevitable. God's cruel joke."

Aaron did not dare say it, but he found himself worrying about Cole. Would his family be next? Elisabet attempted to ensnare Jasmine. Now, she had kidnapped Bram. "I'll be right back." He hurried out of the office, falsely signaling he had an urgent call from nature, but was on a mission to phone his wife to take Cole and hide out at her sister's.

Francine passed a list to Karol. "I've already put out calls for inspections of every residence that you and Bram and others helped identify. A vast, multi-continent stakeout."

"She has other places," Karol mumbled. "We can count on that."

"We included photos with our national and international alerts," Francine said. "Requested the TSA and all authorities be on the lookout for a mid-thirties woman with a fourteen-year-old boy, informing them the boy may appear drugged. If she attempts to leave the country with him, we'll nab her."

After a long pause, Karol asked, "Do you believe my boy's alive?"

"Yes," Francine answered. "This creature wants to extend our worrying, our fright. If she were to kill him, we'd suffer, but that would bring closure. The last thing she wants is for us to have an ounce of closure. She wants to inflict eternal pain. And don't forget, your son is a force to deal with."

Karol nodded. "Like his father." Her mind visited better days of traveling the world with the love of her life. "I never have a day without wondering if Sol is dead or alive." Karol looked around the room, having no idea where she tossed her purse as she entered. "I will track this woman down."

"We're leaving no stone unturned," Francine said.

Karol stared deep into her friend. "Have you located the Gjenganger?"

"We're trying."

"That family is addicted to expensive real estate," Karol said. "As Russian oligarchs know, megayachts are expensive and evasive real estate. I'll locate the Gjenganger. Be certain of that."

Without another word, Karol left.

Aaron arrived. "Where's K.C.?"

For the first time since the unsettling day's news, Francine sat back in her chair and inhaled a relaxed breath. "I have the feeling that our serial killer stirred the wrong mama bear."

WINE CELLAR

Bram woke with a headache. Spotting hundreds of wine bottles, he felt confused. Nothing looked familiar. He could not remember how he got there or where he came from. The last thing he remembered was being at school and Principal Breitenstein signaling him to follow.

He thought he must be dreaming when an unfamiliar female voice jarred him. "You were out a long time. Guess a ruffie chased with Ativan reacts different in children. Do you want some water?"

Bram squinted, flummoxed by seeing a muzzy image of a woman in a lengthy black dress standing on the other side of metal bars. "Where am I? Who are you?"

"I picked you up from school. Brought you here. This is a wine cellar."

Bram struggled to scrutinize his surroundings. "Duh. No joke."

"You're still slurring. But obviously, the drugs didn't dull your smart mouth."

"Are these bars locked?"

"A few of those bottles are worth thousands of dollars. Steel bars prevent the help, burglars, other riffraff from stealing our wine."

"I wasn't stealing your fucking thousand-dollar wine. I don't drink alcohol. Except sip a beer on special occasions. Where the hell are we?"

"A cabin. Deep in a cellar where no can hear you."

"Fuck. So, I'm locked in here? Why?"

"This is my grandfather's retreat. One of his many wine cellars. He's wintering in Greece. I check on this place time to time."

"You didn't answer my question."

"You were threatening my plans, kid."

"What fucking plans?"

"Do you always curse this much?"

"What fucking plans?"

"Plans you should have kept your nose out of. Issues that don't concern you. But you made yourself my concern."

"Let me go and I swear I won't tell anyone you have expensive wine imprisoned in your basement—pardon me—your grandfather's cabin basement."

"He's too old to drink these heirlooms. He shows them off to impress people."

"How did you get me here?"

"A little white pill in your green-tea drink."

"I don't remember a green-tea drink. I don't fucking remember you."

"That's how ruffies work. The date-rape drug. People could do anything to you or with you and you wouldn't remember."

"Shit. You didn't mess with me, did you?"

"Really?"

"Sex. Nude photos. Dress me in women's clothes. Whatever perversity lights your fire."

"I have principles. I let you sleep in the car. I walked you through the cabin to here. I dragged that mattress in here for you to lie on. That's it."

"You swear?"

"Were you hoping for more?"

Bram scowled. "You're sick."

"Just an ordinary kidnapping."

"Kidnapping isn't ordinary."

"For me, kid, kidnapping is ordinary."

"What are you? A Russian agent? A mob boss?"

"Here are the parameters. You are here to talk about

you and what you know. No questions about me."

"I don't know anything."

"What did you talk with Captain Boult about?"

Bram paused a long moment, connecting past and present situations. "Shit. You're that serial park killer."

"What did the two of you talk about?"

Bram paused to gather his wits, feeling more alert. "If I tell you, will you let me go?"

"Would you believe me if I said yes?"

"No."

"Good grasp on reality. Better chance you'll get through this and survive, kid."

"Quit calling me kid."

"You are a kid."

"I haven't been calling you a fucking bitch. Which you are."

For the first time in their conversation, Elisabet smiled. "Okay. I'll stop calling you kid. Mutual respect. What did you talk about with Captain Boult?"

"You're not going to stretch me on a torture rack?"

"I don't have a torture rack. No James Bond laser beam. No dentist drill or whatever American movies dream up."

"You're not American?"

"Mostly I am. I told you; we will talk about you. Not me. Get on with it."

"Or what? You'll starve me to death?"

"I will feed you."

"Gruel?"

"Gruel? You know what gruel is?"

"*A Christmas Carol.*"

Elisabet appeared perplexed.

"Charles Dickens?"

"I know about Charles Dickens, thank you very much.

My grandmother read *The Christmas Carol* and *Great Expectations* to me."

"I thought we weren't talking about you."

"I'll leave you to your own thoughts for a bit, allow the gravity of your situation to sink in."

Elisabet switched off the lights. There were no windows and no lights on the cooling cabinets to provide an inkling of light.

"No," Bram screamed. "Don't leave me here. Please, please, please."

Elisabet switched on the lights. "Afraid of the dark? Interesting."

Bram's words were rushed. "I don't like dark. I don't like being in strange places with no one to talk with."

"You mean argue with."

"Arguing's in my nature. Just the way I am."

Elisabet moved closer to Bram. "You act tough, but I guess you really are a little kid."

"You're being nice to me—somewhat. But I guess you really are a bitch."

Elisabet laughed out loud. "You can't help yourself. You're a piece of art. You know that?"

"I like art," Bram said in a meek voice.

"You like art?"

Bram nodded.

"Huh. A tough guy who likes art." Elisabet paced, studying her captive, thinking that on his knees and begging, he looked like a street urchin in a 17th century painting. "What kind of art?"

Bram shrugged. "I sketch, draw. Paint a little."

"What do you draw, paint?"

Bram stared at the floor, fearing his answer would be dismissed. "Super-hero crap mostly. Once in a while, I create something my mom frames and hangs in our house.

It's no fancy cabin with a jail wine cellar, but it's home. It's nice."

"Your home is nice. I've seen it."

Bram thought about the cupcakes with carfentanil-laced icing. This was the woman who tried to poison his mother—poison him. Now the woman had control over his life. "I need to go to the bathroom."

"Believe it or not, like most sections of Grandfather's grand estates, even his cabin wine cellar has facilities. Can you imagine? Turn left past the third row. And Bram? There's no window. Two-feet-thick stone walls. No way to escape."

"You know they're likely already searching for me."

"Who? Captain Boult? I hope so. That's my plan."

"Why would you want her—"

"I thought you needed to use the toilet."

Bram stepped toward the toilet, but then stopped, turned, and stared into Elisabet. "No cupcakes with chocolate icing?"

Elisabet gave him a cold stare, her eyes seething enough that Bram thought to himself, that was a mistake. I'll die in this hell hole.

Elisabet rattled her keys, ascended the stairs, secured the bolt lock, and switched off the lights. The door was thick enough she could barely hear the boy's screams.

She stood listening for a couple of minutes. When the screaming abruptly ceased, she thought, He discovered the toilet has a light.

BREAKFAST AND STORIES

Bram had cried himself to sleep. When the cellar lights switched on, he hurriedly wiped his face, embarrassed there may be telltale signs revealing his weakness.

"I brought you breakfast," Elisabet said. "Go stand near the back row of wine. I'll leave this food tray for you."

Bram complied, assessing how she unlocked the door with one of many keys hooked to a stretch wristband. No chance of dropping them.

"Bon appétit," she said, exiting and locking the metal gate. "No gruel."

Bram's face brightened as he marveled at the presentation of eggs benedict, various melon slices, croissants, jams, and orange juice.

"That's like fancy meals I've seen in that restaurant near the Museum of Modern Art."

"La Grande Boucherie?" Elisabet asked. She sat on the floor and properly tucked her legs beneath her. "You know that place?"

Bram thought about the restaurant for a moment and shrugged he was uncertain. "Lots of palm trees and chandeliers."

"That's the place. I promise this will taste better than their prétentieuse fare."

Although sitting on the floor, Bram endeavored to display proper manners, waiting until his last bite was swallowed—as his mother insisted at the table—before speaking. "Is your name really Azza?"

"Why would you think that's my name?"

"My mom sells your condos."

Elisabet had a mind-flash review of her life. Many names. Many stories. "Azza. A name I used off and on a few times."

"But not when you pick up men."

"Wow. To the point."

"Mom says even simple moments of life are too long to beat around the bush."

"Wise woman."

"She's just a real estate agent."

"Just? Perhaps she's wiser than you credit her."

"Do you live in a mansion?" Bram asked.

"A high-rise. Top floors. Rather like a mansion in the sky. Actually, one of several places I live."

"So, you're wealthy?"

"Not from money I earned on my own."

"Spoiled?"

Elisabet chuckled. "Am I a super-wealthy spoiled brat? Absolutely I am."

Elisabet spotted an upright bottle of wine on the floor beside the gate. Its cork and neck were absent. She could see the bottle was almost full. "Did you break that?"

"Might as well taste one."

She squinted to read the label. "That's a Leroy Domaine d'Auvenay Meursault."

"So?"

"That bottle's probably worth eight or nine thousand dollars."

"Then it should taste good."

"Don't touch another bottle."

"It sucked. I spit it out. Why do you wear that long black dress?"

Elisabet shook her head with dissatisfaction. "Uh ... A silly way of sometimes dressing like my grandmother."

"Cause you love her?"

"What?"

"If you dress like her, you must love her.

"Do you have favorite clothes?"

"My Steph Curry jersey."

"Do you love Steph Curry?"

"I admire him."

"Does your jersey comfort you?"

"Yeah." Bram swallowed another bite. "Is this your real accent? The one you're talking with now. Mom says you sound different every time."

Elisabet paced. She thought of scolding her captive for inquiring about her, but quickly realized that by listening to him, she was learning about the world that was searching for her. "Do they call me Elisabet at the precinct?"

"Some call you the Juliet Killer."

"The what?"

"The Juliet Killer. Cause the men die with their heads on your lap."

"What the …?"

"Like Romeo dying, his head on Juliet's lap. The person she loved—even if only for a few days—died as she held him."

"How do detectives know that?"

"Your butt print on the grass and snow under their heads."

"Shit."

"It's not like DNA. Butt prints are just butt prints. But they know you did that with each of them. At least they think they know all of them. They didn't know about the first guy in New Haven. I figured that out."

"New Haven?"

"Beaverdale Park."

"He wasn't the first."

"Oh." Bram gently pushed his meal aside and waited.

Elisabet leaned against a pillar. She wanted so bad to

tell someone. But confide to a fourteen-year-old punk kid? She thought, he'll be dead soon, so no worries he'll tell anyone. The truth ached in her belly and brain, like it was a creature determined to claw its way out of her.

Peering into Bram, she said, "My brother was first."

Bram's face cried out, oh my God, fuck, shit, and all expletives at once. Abruptly, he was fearing more for his life than any moment so far.

Elisabet recognized and enjoyed the fear in her captive, the emotion she expected the outside world to display if they knew her truth. There was a strange comfort in the exterior world matching her internal turmoil. "Aren't you going to ask? You've been interrogating me non-stop."

Bram shook his head, remembering his mother saying, "There exist truths none of us should learn."

"Your face is screaming you want to ask."

Bram froze in place as Elisabet moved closer to the bars, talking low as if the hundreds of wine bottles were perched to spy and gossip. Her voice was breathy as if the two of them were sitting by a campfire relating ghost stories.

"My brother and I were in our parents' backyard near the sound. Pitch black. Quiet except small waves breaking on the shore. I mixed him a drink. He drank it. Laid his head in my lap."

After silence, Bram realized Elisabet was not going to tell more of her horror story until he showed willingness by prompting her with questions. "How old were you?"

"Fourteen. My brother was fifteen. He had an older college friend, Jake, who had talked him into trying cocaine and heroin. Jake promised it would relieve my brother's pain."

Again, it was clear Elisabet would not continue without him questioning. "What pain?"

"My brother had a rare type of trachea cancer. His windpipe. Progresses rapidly. Always fatal. Difficulty breathing. Breathing hurts. It was torment seeing him like that. Listen to him gasp."

Bram thought it best to sit in silence a moment, allow her to decide when she felt a need to continue.

"My brother brought some of the drugs home. One vial, he said, was a hundred times stronger. Would kill someone. He hid that vial in his closet—or thought it was hidden. Later that night, he couldn't catch his breath. The worst I had seen him suffer. Tears running down ... So, yeah. When he was finally able to catch a breath, I helped him inhale Jake's powder. But I switched vials. So yeah, I ... I—"

They both sat silent a long while.

Elisabet talked first. "I didn't help him until I had first asked for guidance, for permission."

Bram looked around with wishful thinking there would be someone else to be the one to inquire: *from whom*?

After a long moment, Elisabet appeared to ask herself that question. "My grandmother taught me that St. Michael is always there for me, like he was for Joan of Arc."

"How is he there for you?"

"Whispers."

"Like the wind whispers?"

"Wind whispers. Soft bells. Nature singing."

Bram knew that if a character in his comics or superhero movies had said that, he and his friends would race one another to sing, *psycho*, and then laugh, doubting real people could be that crazy.

They both sat in silence for minutes, the only sound being the hum of wine cooling cabinets.

Elisabet broke the silence. "Our parents knew he had

been using drugs with his college friend. The coroner reported my brother's death as accidental. Police charged Jake."

Bram sat open mouthed, being cautious his breathing made no sound.

Elisabet stared at her lap as if her brother were there. "His breathing became peaceful. There he is. His head resting on my lap. Star gazing. He knows every constellation."

Elisabet turned and watched Bram. He was staring at his shoes, twisting a shoe lace as if that and nothing else in the world mattered.

"I've never told anyone that," Elisabet said.

Bram could not bring himself to look at his frightening storyteller. "You loved him."

"The year before, one of Jake's roommates tried to molest me in our boathouse. My brother beat the shit out of him. That jerk was twice my brother's size, but that didn't matter. He was protecting me."

Bram glanced a micro-second at Elisabet and turned away.

"Don't," Elisabet said in the tone of a pitiless parent.

"Don't what?" Bram uttered into the back of his hand.

"Don't give me a look that signals you think you understand me."

"I didn't—"

"It's written all over your face. I don't need you or other assholes sympathizing. I am fine on my own, thank you."

Bram slid his food tray away and resumed interest in picking at his shoe laces.

Without looking back, Elisabet rocketed out of the room, leaving the lights on, not bolting the stairwell door.

Bram took note, but also noted that his prison-like door remained impenetrable.

HEAT SENSING VIPERS

Unlike past visits, Jasmine phoned ahead that she wanted to meet and share big news with Francine at the station. They agreed on two o'clock after Francine returned from lunch discussing TSA protocols with Lin.

"Well," Francine said, during their quick opening hug. "It's good to see you."

"Good to see you too." Jasmine took a seat.

Francine recognized that Jasmine was growing her hair out and no longer wore piercings. She chose to not comment. "You doing okay?"

Jasmine bit her lip, nodding but breaking eye contact. "Less nightmares. Not every night now."

"Good—if that's an improvement."

"I don't know how you do this job and not have nightmares."

"I do have nightmares." Francine took her seat behind her desk. "My nightmares don't usually make sense. Perhaps they echo my life, but if so, I can't figure them out. What's the big news you wanted to share?"

Jasmine cleared her throat. "You once told me that like you, I couldn't commit. And you were one-hundred-fifty-percent correct, even though I couldn't see it."

Expecting what was coming, Francine asked, "And now?"

"And now ..." Jasmine paused, wondering if her timing was wrong. Maybe there never would be a good time. "Teresa and I are getting married."

During quiet hours while driving alone, Francine had anticipated one day hearing such news and had rehearsed graceful responses. "Wonderful for the two of you—three of you. I wish the three of you the best."

After Francine presented her prepared response, Jasmine's eyes teared. The words were what she had yearned to hear, but had discounted the possibility of a compassionate response. "Thank you, Francine."

"What do you think changed, opened you to commitment?"

"Having a lover who was near death, who was highly dependent upon me, who emerged with great strength to be an equal or more. Having a lovely child, who will take years and forever to grow into taking care of himself. Those things I guess."

"This is magnificent, Jasmine."

"You're not angry?"

"Jealous as hell, of course. But I'm finding out about myself as well. I'm still committed to my love: my job."

"Of course."

They sat in silence for a moment.

"Can we still be friends?" Jasmine asked.

"Forever and a day," Francine answered.

Despite Francine's acceptance, Jasmine continued to look on edge, look haunted. "You've had near-death experiences, right?"

Francine sneered. "You nailed my job description. More near-death events than I let myself admit. I superbly pretend to be invincible, an essential tool for this job."

"Did those times change you?"

Francine took time to dig deep for an answer. "I used to hide from the fact that evil and sickening sights changed me. Now, I'm more open to what I learn from bad times. Embrace the changes."

"You sound almost human."

Francine laughed. "I am human, thank you very much. If you are up for it, I would enjoy always getting together to celebrate changes as they arrive for us."

"Deal," Jasmine said. "Are you still helping to raise that young detective?"

"Aaron?"

Jasmine burst out laughing. "No, no. Not Aaron. The boy who thinks he's a detective."

"Bram."

"Yes. Bram." Jasmine did not understand Francine's sudden dive into a melancholy state. "What's wrong?"

"The woman who stalked you kidnapped Bram."

"Oh my God." After a moment to reorient, Jasmine asked, "Is there anything I can do?"

"You being here is doing more than you know. It's comforting to have you by my side."

"I'll always be here for you, Francine." After another moment of both women staring within themselves, Jasmine added, "Between changing diapers."

They both laughed and then slid into a morose mood.

Jasmine asked, "Do you think she'll kill him?"

"She'll keep him alive to use as a bargaining chip."

"For what?"

"I don't know—I don't even think she knows."

"Did you take Bram underwing?"

The question caught Francine off guard. "Uh … Aaron did. Mostly. But Bram's parents were my friends, colleagues. We go way back. So, I feel … ownership, attached—I don't know what to call it."

"Committed."

"Uh … Why not? Committed."

"How close are you to his family?"

"Although Sol, his father, and K.C., his mother, were both former intelligence case officers only seven or eight years older than us, they were leaders, like parents for us, guiding us through hard times, being stunning role models, being kind beyond belief. Sol disappeared in Iran.

K.C. disappeared into her shell. Bram has no idea of their former lives. It's not my place to tell him."

"So … it makes sense you are committed to this kid."

"Uh … I guess it does—know it does."

"I hope you succeed finding and put away or kill this twisted viper."

"For Bram's sake. For your sake. For me—all of us."

"Where do you think she is?"

"Like your viper analogy, she has keen heat-sensing pits. She detects all of us warm-blooded pursuers. Keeps one step ahead. We've staked out every residence we identified—places scattered across the country. The FBI is all over this."

"And out of the country?"

"Out of the country makes for a worse nightmare."

ART AND BEHOLDERS

After skipping breakfast, Elisabet arrived with a take-out lunch for Bram: garlic shrimp, crab-stuffed mushrooms, and roasted broccolini with lemon and Parmesan.

Bram was sketching with colored pencils on an art pad she had provided.

"What are you creating—in the light I left on for you?"

Bram knew the lights being on was accidental. He answered without looking up as he would have done when his mother was snooping. "A surprise."

"Mysterious. A good surprise or a bad surprise?"

"Not sure." He slid pencils back into the box, closed the cover of his pad, and stepped back for Elisabet to enter. "It's an artistic surprise. Will have differing meanings for different beholders."

"Must be good art then. What's your favorite painting?"

Bram waited for Elisabet to step out and lock the door before assessing his lunch. "I never saw the actual painting, just a photo of it in my mother's art book. *The Tiger Hunt.* Peter Paul Rubens. My favorite since I was four. I wore down the edges of the page."

"You liked that as a four-year old? I know that gruesome painting." Elisabet grimaced, remembering the vivid war of men and beasts. "I saw it once."

"Saw it? Like really in the flesh saw it?"

"One way to put it. In the flesh."

"Shit—I mean wow. Where?"

"Musée des Beaux-Arts de Rennes."

"Huh?"

"Museum of fine arts in Rennes, France."

Bram lost interest in lunch. "How did you get to see it?"

"One of many excursions with my grandmother. Others

in our family were attending a football game. That's soccer to Americans."

"Please. I'm not totally retarded," Bram said.

"What did you like about that brutal painting?"

"Hunters and great cats battling to the death." Bram shrugged. "What's to not like?"

"I don't like it. But what did you like?"

"Nothing matters to the hunters or the tigers except to not give in. Both sides. Dedicated to accomplish goals that drive them no matter the price."

"Do you go all out to accomplish your goals?"

"Like you, I imagine. I go all out."

"Huh." Elisabet sat on the floor, being curious enough to remain and talk while her prisoner ate. "Which side do you think is good? The warriors or the great cats?"

"As my mom says, life is complex." Bram pinched the tail off a shrimp. "I imagine both sides think they are justified." Bram assessed that his captor's face had softened enough to ask a more personal question. "We're not discussing the painting anymore, are we?"

"We're all jungle creatures," Elisabet answered. "Driven. Hoping for divine inspiration."

"I don't know what that is: divine inspiration."

"Do you pray?"

"Mom works overtime to get me to pray. Do you pray?"

"In a roundabout way. I wait for divine answers to come."

"From?" Bram whispered.

"From saints. From paintings. From nature. From music speaking to me. Unexpected places. Where do your answers come from, Bram J. Whaanga?"

"You'll make fun of me."

"I'm in no position to be the one making fun."

"Movie and comic-book heroes."

"Ah. Heroes created by authors and artists tapping into their own souls," Francine said, remembering her grandmother's lessons. "But what matters, Bram—as it sounds like you already know—is how observers interact with those creations that rise from the hearts of those with driven souls."

"I wish you taught my music and art classes."

"Wow. You are a surprise." Elisabet rearranged her position on the floor for more comfort. "What is it your teachers teach?"

"Symbolism. Metaphors. Influences of artists upon other artists. Nothing about inspiration or guidance from within, nothing about searching for truths."

"I bet you are a brilliant student, and at the same time a pain in the ass."

"What my teachers say. What Mom says." Bram felt reluctant to share, but then said, "I skipped second grade."

Elisabet raised an eyebrow. "So, you are smart."

"I think second-grade teachers didn't want to deal with me. Palmed me off on third-grade teachers."

Elisabet laughed. "I can picture that. Okay. You have procrastinated and distracted me long enough." Elisabet stood. "Open that sketch book and let me see your art."

Bram retrieved his sketch pad and approached Elisabet at the metal-bar divide. "You ready?"

"What drama," Elisabet whispered.

Bram opened the pad and held his sketch near her face.

Elisabet's body jerked as if a roller coaster she was riding accelerated from zero to sixty in one second. "Oh wow." She studied the sketch, squinting and turning her head side to side. "Moderately abstract." She started to speak, but then paused to examine the art closer. "Describe exactly what I'm seeing."

"More important, what do you see?"

Elisabet pressed her forehead against a metal bar for a closer look. "I see a woman from the back—I think—staring out a window—no. She's staring into an heirloom-looking mirror. Wearing a long black robe or dress—like I sometimes wear—no jewelry. Brown, short, simple hair."

Bram eased back a step so that light focused squarely on the sketch. "I know it's only a rough draft, but can you make out what she sees in the mirror?'

"Well … in her mirror, everything's dark. Like being underwater. Yeah. Underwater, cause there are fish swimming at the top. Swimming around a rock."

Elisabet gripped the bars on either side of her face and squinted. "I think that rock has a face. Yeah. It does. It's a sculpture. Now I see. There's a shield and … and uh … Fuck. And a sword. Am I seeing this right?"

She glared at Bram. "That's Saint Michael in the mirror. Under the sea."

"I'm sketching it for you."

"Fuck you." Elisabet backed away, trembling. She about-faced and fled the room.

Bram yelled, "I didn't mean to offend you. I wanted you to like it. Don't be upset with me. I'm sorry."

He waited but heard no answer. He screamed louder. "I said I'm sorry."

OLD FRIENDS

Karol no longer had access to mainframe or super computers. She began her yacht search on simple apps that Bram had once shown her: Ship-Tracker and Marine-Traffic. Bram had been fascinated that the apps showed locations of greater numbers of ships than the Department of Defense's Maritime Automatic Identification System. The DOD system could not locate ships when their transponders were damaged or disabled.

Karol identified many ships tagged around Greece and various Greek islands. She tapped the colorful ship tags one at a time, but none of the appearing names or photos matched vessels of the Norgaard fleet.

Karol contemplated for a few minutes whether or not to ask a friend in intelligence to break protocol and help her locate possible sites where her son might be imprisoned.

She called an unlisted number at the Department of Defense. "Bharti? This is K.C."

"Oh my gosh," the woman answered. "Where are you—what are you up to—is everything okay?"

"Everything is not okay. My fourteen-year-old son was kidnapped by a serial killer."

"Oh, my God, K.C. Someone took Bram?"

"He's fourteen now and has the curiosity and drive of Sol. Now, he's fallen into a grave position. I have reason to believe he is or will be held captive on a super-wealthy kidnapper's yacht. Can you help me? Please?"

"To locate the yacht?"

"Exactly. Please, Bharti?"

Karol heard noises of busy Pentagon people in the background, and then heard Bharti speak in a whisper.

"Is this your cell phone?"

"Yes."

"I'll call you from another phone. Give me ten to fifteen."

"Thanks, Bharti."

Fifteen minutes felt like half a day to Karol, but her phone rang and displayed: *No Caller ID.* "Hello."

"This is better," Bharti said without explaining. "Why do you think Bram is being held on a stranger's yacht?"

"We know Elisabet Norgaard often hides out—"

"Of the Norgaard empire?"

"Exactly."

"Jesus, K.C. That family has been on our radar for decades for everything from—"

"I know. I know. Their yacht, the Gjenganger, was in the Greek Islands in recent months and then disappeared. Greek police lost track of it. Evidently, its transponder was—"

"Turned off. Not the first time they pulled that stunt."

"Do you have other means to locate it?" Karol asked.

"You know what you're asking isn't above board, right?"

"It's my son."

"Of course." Bharti paused to consider how to approach a truth. "We both will be taking risks of—"

"I wouldn't ask you, but I didn't know who else to—"

"I can possibly get permission if you send me info. Who's working this case?"

"The Manhattan midtown homicide squad, FBI Agent Lin Jia, other crime—"

"FBI. Good. I know Lin. Let me call you back."

"What's possible?" Karol asked.

"We have databases of satellite images of three-foot segments of ships, large yachts, including the oligarch megayachts. The EAS, European Space Agency, works with us using satellites, smallsats, Sentinel missions. Plus PNT, the Positioning Navigation and Timing Systems, collect bathymetric data. We can monitor RF emissions, VHF channel radio transmissions, radar signals, satellite phones, and more. It's difficult to hide from us."

"You lost me," Karol said. "I've been out of the loop too long."

"You have, K.C. Welcome back. Let me run this up the ladder. I have faith I can get permission. We still love you and Sol. I'll call you back in an hour or so."

Karol breathed a sigh of relief. She and Sol had not been forgotten. It appeared old friends would be there for her as if no time had passed.

BALD TRAVEL
- July 2023 -

Elisabet called her older first cousin Amalie in village-like Somerville, New Jersey. Growing up, Elisabet and Amalie had often been mistaken for being sisters. Elisabet knew that Amalie had three children. One was Todd, her sixteen-year-old son.

"I need a favor," Elisabet said on the phone, applying the demanding tone her grandfather often used. "I need to borrow your and Todd's passports."

Amalie paused to consider a lesson from her lifetime education: it is less painful to give into Norgaard relatives and not question demands.

"I suppose we can," Amalie said. "We haven't traveled since COVID hit. Todd's recovering. Somerville is a safe haven for us."

Elisabet sensed her cousin's comment as simple and pleasant, but with judgmental overtones snaking beneath. "Thank you, Amalie. I trust life is good for you."

"It's getting better," Amalie said.

"I'll send someone for the passports. Same address?"

"Same for twenty years."

"Good." Elisabet ended the call and walked to the kitchen. "Carlton? I need you to send Loudon on an errand."

***

Elisabet fed a ruffie and a mild sedative to Bram via his standard green-tea drink. Once the teen was silly and malleable, she began shaving his head. Bram giggled like a young kid at the barber. "Why do I need a haircut?"

"So, we can travel, be travel buddies."

Elisabet removed the attachment guard from the hair clippers for a closer shave. "Let's go very short. Make you look bald."

Bram giggled as if he were a five-year-old hearing a dirty joke. "Why will I be bald?"

"It's what happens with chemotherapy."

"What's that?"

"Cancer medicine that causes hair loss."

"Do I take cancer medicine?"

"Yes."

It took thirty seconds for Bram's curly locks to be sliced at the roots, drop, and carpet the floor.

"Who's my doctor?" Bram asked.

"I am."

"You're not a doctor," Bram said with a child's teasing voice.

"I am—was. Almost became a surgeon."

"Will I have to go to the hospital?"

"An overseas hospital."

Bram looked at himself in the mirror. "I want to wear a cap."

"Some of the time you can, but I want people to see the top of your beautiful bald head. Know you're on treatment."

"That's sad." Bram appeared on the verge of crying as he stared at himself.

"You know what will help?" Elisabet asked.

Bram shook his head.

"I'll insert an IV into your arm and give you other medicine to make you feel better."

"Is that medicine good?"

"Very good." Elisabet opened a small suitcase, allowing Bram to study IV saline bags and plastic tubing.

When Carlton and Loudon returned from errands, Elisabet met them on the cabin's side veranda. They were surprised to see Cawthorn, an attendant from the Wyoming ranch. The two men only knew Cawthorn through zoom planning meetings.

"Gentlemen," Francine said, "I believe you know Cawthorn. And Cawthorn, this is Loudon and Carlton. Carlton? I want you to swap positions with Cawthorn for a week. I need Loudon and Cawthorn to accompany me out of the country."

"Did I offend you, Ms. Elisabet?" Carlton asked.

"Goodness no. Very much the opposite. Your current status, however, would complicate our leaving the country."

Carlton had almost forgotten his legal standing. He appeared downcast, guilty that he had failed.

"Chin up, Carlton. It's not of your own doing. You are a treasure. Don't forget that."

"Yes ma'am."

"You should attend to packing. Alessandro will drive you to the airport. We have a plane on standby." She nodded toward a limo parked in the drive.

With head bowed, Carlton walked toward his quarters above the garages, recalling Elisabet's mother's words: *Allow other wild creatures to dispose of it.*

"Now, gentlemen," Elisabet said, "accompany me to the game room."

Elisabet had Bram asleep on the game-room couch with a slow IV drip.

Elisabet whispered as if Bram were a sleeping infant. "This is my cousin's son, Todd. My cousin dropped him off here. The poor child has a brain tumor that causes delirium. A bout of COVID intensified his symptoms. At times, he doesn't even know his name."

Both men sympathized with anguished grimaces.

"My cousin has a dysfunctional family," Elisabet said. "Her husband is abusive, refusing medical aid for Todd. I vowed to my cousin I would seek the best medical care for her poor boy. That will require a trip to Abu Dhabi or Italy. Same British surgeon, but one who alters practicing in two locales."

Cawthorn moved closer to Bram. "Poor lad. Is there nothing closer?"

"Tragically no. I must ask both of you to be devious. I'll pose as Todd's mother, Amalie, to transport him overseas. Illegal, but something I must do. Some planning I will keep from you—for your protection. I can't force you to help, of course, I can only appeal to your better angels."

Cawthorn knelt by the teen, staring into the boy's sleeping face. "Yes ma'am. I'm on board."

"Loudon?"

"Yes ma'am. For family."

***

One of Norgaard's Bell 429 helicopters landed in the meadow near the Norgaard cabin. Elisabet, wearing surgical blue scrubs beneath a fashionable jacket, accompanied Cawthorn and Loudon as they led Bram from their SUV to the aircraft.

With IV sedating medications clouding his sensorium, Bram staggered. Cawthorn aided the compromised boy into the helicopter and wrapped him in a blanket while Loudon loaded a wheelchair on board.

Sunny, windless weather provided for a smooth ninety-minute flight to a grassy apron beside a private hangar at Portsmouth International Airport in New Hampshire.

Bram drifted in and out of sleep as Elisabet held his

hand, much in the manner she had observed Amalie hold Todd's hand when they had video-chatted and the teen was struggling with COVID symptoms.

Using Amalie and Todd's names and information, Elisabet had filled out electronic advance passenger information online to obtain preliminary clearance for the Norgaard Gulfstream flight from Portsmouth to Venice, Italy, continuing onward to Abu Dhabi.

The Portsmouth airport at Pease was a joint military and civilian airport with a recently reconstructed eleven-thousand-foot runway to accommodate massive refueling tankers. The non-hub facility, however, heavily catered to general aviation flights, operating only five or six daily commercial flights.

A TSA agent and an agent with a drug-sniffing German shepherd approached the hangar harboring the readying Norgaard jet. Cawthorn and Loudon both tensed, but Elisabet's ability to disengage from emotions as easily as people blacking out sight by shutting eyes, served her purpose. The TSA agent examined the passports of the four passengers and two crew members, and then questioned Elisabet. "I'm confused. Are you this boy's physician or mother?"

"Both," Elisabet answered. "Until we reach our final destination. Once we're in safe hands, I'll resume being a devastated mother seeking the help of top specialists."

The agent examined and read aloud from the flight manifest. "Portsmouth to Venice, refuel, continue to Abu Dhabi." He turned to Elisabet. "Correct?"

"Yes," Elisabet answered. "The Sheikh Shakhbout Medical City is partnered with our world-renowned Mayo Clinic. The lead clinician for my son's rare illness is there."

The agent paused a moment, appearing morbid, and

mumbled, "I guess Middle-East oil money buys the best of anything they desire." Speaking up, he said, "God be with you all."

He patted Bram's shoulder and departed the hangar.

***

The Gulfstream required seven-and-one-half hours from takeoff to touchdown, landing at Venice Marco Polo Airport. While the jet prepared for departure for the second leg to Abu Dhabi, Loudon and Cawthorn aided Elisabet and Bram across the tarmac to a nearby helicopter.

Bram appeared less sedated and able to walk, but was still dazed enough to depend upon being led.

Loudon and Cawthorn bid farewell to Elisabet and the boy, and returned to the jet to continue to Abu Dhabi.

After an eighty-minute helicopter flight from Venice to the village of Torraccia in the small republic of San Marino, the helicopter landed at a small grassy helipad.

The so-called mother and sick child spent one night at Grand Hotel San Marino, ordered meals via room service, and departed at sunrise in an SUV taxi, unencumbered by further formalities and deceptions since San Marino and Italy have an open-border policy. It was a simple thirty-minute taxi ride to the marina in Rimini where the Gjenganger was moored.

Elisabet's grandfather watched from his wheelchair in the yacht's outdoor lounge as his stewards aided the woman and boy. "Elisabet?" her grandfather yelled. "Who is that child? Why are you bringing him onto my yacht? I don't want a child on board."

Elisabet approached and patted her grandfather's shoulder, having withheld hugging him decades before.

She spoke loudly enough for the stewards to hear. "That is your great-grandson, Todd. Amalie's son. I promised him this trip as a middle-school-graduation gift. Todd became severely airsick. He'll be fine by tomorrow. Just needs a bit of IV fluids like you need on occasion."

"Oh," her grandfather mumbled and appeared to immediately forget the boy the moment a steward aided Bram below deck.

"I believe dinner is prepared," her grandfather said. "Have a seat."

"Grandfather Oskar? I believe it is likely breakfast or brunch."

"Oh. Still morning, huh?" He shook his head. "Time moves at a snail's crawl."

Oskar Norgaard searched for something in his clothing and the wheel chair even though he did not appear to know what.

DEPUTY OF A DEPUTY OF A DEPUTY

Lin video-conferenced with Francine and Aaron to present updates. "Bharti Patel in Intelligence, notified me that as per K.C. Whaanga's request, they located the Gjenganger moored at Darsena di Rimini on the Italian east coast."

"Did she notify K.C.?" Aaron asked.

"K.C.'s no longer an intelligence case officer. Bharti wished to honor her request, but adhere to proper channels. She said it will be your choice to notify K.C."

"That works," Francine said. "Any way to know whether or not Elisabet is aboard the Gjenganger?"

"I'm working to get Italian eyes on the ground. There's much red tape, but we're getting there."

"This woman keeps giving us the slip."

"We're still working to confirm she actually fled the U.S.," Lin said. "TSA notified us that a Norgaard jet flew Carlton James from White Plains to Shively Field in Wyoming. We placed eyes on the Norgaard ranch near there. We also know that in the past week, Norgaard aircraft left for South America, the Middle East, and Japan. My money's on the flight to Abu Dhabi. It stopped to fuel in Venice. I don't have to tell you; she previously gave us the slip while refueling."

"How far's their yacht from Venice?" Francine asked.

Aaron googled the distance. "It is … one-hundred-seventy miles."

"Any chance there's a St. Michael Church nearby?"

"Already searching that," Aaron murmured.

"Wow," Lin said. "You two are squarely on the same page."

Aaron displayed a grin shouting cleverness. "Found it.

Sixteen miles southwest of Rimini. Mondaino. Eighteenth Century. Chieso di San Michele Arcangelo—or however you say it."

"Excellent," Francine shouted. "She's either in Rimini or going there. Can the FBI go there? Can you go there, Lin?"

"If Italian authorities invite me to assist investigating." Lin checked addresses in his contacts. "We have international operation agents on the ground through our Rome embassy. With this woman's history of crimes in multiple countries and our good standing with Italy, we should be able to assist."

"What about me? Can I go?" Aaron asked, like a kid burning to have a turn riding a pony. "Liam Neeson and his kinds of characters do it."

"Oh my God," Francine mumbled.

Lin laughed. "If we can bestow special federal officer status for you, deputize you, there's a possibility you can assist an FBI investigation. I'll inform them that your team knows the intricacies of this woman's warped mind."

"I'm in," Aaron said, slamming both hands atop the desk as if showing off a trumping royal flush.

"Inquire if you can deputize me too," Francine said.

"Who would run your shop back here?" Lin asked.

Francine and Aaron simultaneously yelled, "Not Ted."

"Okay," Lin said with a tone indicating he was clueless of what history lay behind their dual outburst.

Francine said, "I'll ask someone from Midtown South."

"What about K.C. going with us?" Aaron asked. "It's her son. She hatched the idea to search for the yacht and knew who to ask to zero in on it."

Francine shook her head with an attack of doubt. "I wish, but so far, we have failed to confirm that Italy's actually the hotspot. We're poor at guessing this woman's moves."

"Even if we do confirm Italy," Lin said, "I'm not sure Italy's ready for a Manhattan entourage to infiltrate. Let's see what's possible and build from there."

THE BRIG

Like Dracula waking after a century's sleep and finding himself in unfamiliar surroundings, Bram woke. He was rendered even more disoriented by the slow swaying of the room. He soon realized his hands and feet were fastened to a bedframe and yelled. "Hey. Is anyone there? I can't sit up."

No one responded. He wanted to rub matter from his eyes, but could not.

An hour passed before he heard the metal door of the cabin being unlocked. Elisabet appeared.

"Where am I?" Bram screamed.

"I brought you food. I had Chef Tarik prepare a meal according to your strict preference: lemon and garlic poached shrimp."

"I don't want your fucking shrimp. I want to know where I am and why I'm tied down like a fucking dog on a vet stretcher."

"I didn't want you to hurt yourself. You were sick and delirious, hitting yourself."

"Why's this room moving?"

"You're on my yacht."

"A boat?"

"A yacht."

"Shit. How'd I get here?"

"Two helicopter rides and a jet."

Bram squinted. "I don't remember that."

"I didn't intend for you to remember."

"You drugged me again."

"I did," Elisabet said, displaying pride of her success.

"Bitch. Where the fuck is this boat—excuse me— yacht?"

"Italy."

"Fuck." Bram looked at his hospital gown. "Who changed my clothes? You?"

Elisabet stared at him a moment. "You wake on a luxury yacht on the other side of the planet, and your pressing question is who changed your clothes?"

"Fuck."

"At least when you're sedated, you don't vomit strings of distasteful words. A male steward changed your clothes."

"What's a steward?"

"A yacht crewperson. Male. We have male and female stewards aboard."

"Why did you bring me here?"

Elisabet examined Bram's hands. "Your hands are turning purple. The cotton lining is supposed to prevent blood flow from restricting." She loosened the straps. "That should help."

"I'm waiting for your answer. Why?"

"Your mother, Captain Boult, and Sergeant Galanis refuse to play friendly with me. I thought I'd turn up the heat, inspire their motivation."

"By drugging and dragging me like a corpse to Italy, tying me up? This is your screwed-up idea of how to motivate people?"

"We'll find out if it works."

"Did you first ask them nicely to play? Or in your usual bitch manner?"

"Give me a hint of credit, kid. I asked several times."

"What is this room?"

"A yacht cabin. Modified to be a brig."

"What's a brig?"

"A ship jail."

"You have a ship jail?"

"Grandfather's yachts were attacked three times by pirates. He had a cabin on each vessel retrofitted to be a brig."

"Does your luxury yacht have guards?"

"Our stewards are militarily trained."

Bram raised his head. "With guns?"

"Automatic pistols and rifles large enough to overcome pirates' outdated weapons."

"Shit."

"Do you want your poached shrimp or not?"

As numbness began to abate, Bram wiggled his hands. "Will I have to suffer you feeding me?"

"I'll release your hands to eat."

"And my feet?"

"Maybe later."

"Depending on what?"

"God. So many questions." Elisabet huffed like the teen school girls she had tricked. "Okay. If you go along with my plans, I will release your feet. How's that?"

"What plan?"

"I lied to my crew and Grandfather Oskar that your name is Todd. That's the name of Grandfather's great-grandson—my something or other cousin. Grandfather Oskar hasn't seen Todd forever. I passed you off as Todd." She muttered beneath her breath, "Guess that would make you and me relatives—God forbid."

"Why in hell would I pretend I like you, much less be related to you?"

"So, I don't harm your mother."

Bram paused to take a deep breath. "Why would you harm her?"

Bram abruptly became despondent, remembering the poisoned cupcakes.

Elisabet's expression hardened. "She tracked my

family."

Bram's face revealed that he found such an idea to be preposterous. "My mother tracked your family? Have you ever talked with my mother? She couldn't track a horse in a small, fenced-in pasture."

Elisabet stared at her captive for a lengthy period, trying to solve a riddle. "What? You don't know who your mother is?"

When Bram did not answer, her face reflected that her confusion had resolved. "Oh my God. You don't."

Bram yanked on his cuffs to no avail. "What idiotic fairy tales have you been telling yourself?"

"You clearly don't know your mother."

Bram screamed, "She's a realtor for Christ's sake. Sells houses and condos. Loves numbers. A person scared of her own shadow. I know my mother."

"You don't have a clue."

"Fuck. Who do you—who lives in a fantasy-bubble-psycho world—who do you think my mother is?"

"A retired intelligence case officer."

Bram was stunned for a moment. He then broke into laughter. "Oh my God. Fuck. What color is the sky on your planet?"

"K.C. Whaanga. Married formerly to Sol Whaanga. Admired intelligence case officers."

Hearing her say Sol was the name of his father, rattled Bram. He unsuccessfully worked to disguise his emotion with forced smart remarks, but sudden sweating exposed his doubt. "Your tall tale is getting better. Keep spinning."

"It's truth," Elisabet said. "Evidently, never shared with you."

"Uh huh."

"I swear."

"Spit on it. Cross your heart and hope to die. Slice your

wrists. Swear on your first born—God help him or her."

"This isn't a boy's club, Bram Whaanga. It's the real, big, bad world. Act like it."

Bram watched his captor move near a porthole and text on her overly large phone, guessing she had a satellite phone. "I don't know what happened to me while you had me drugged, or happened to you while I was drugged, but you're more insane than people say. And believe me, there are heaps of people saying that."

Elisabet disengaged from texting. "Heaps, huh? Kiwi slang. Like your Māori father, maybe?"

Elisabet sat on the floor near Bram's head. "I sought to learn about your parents because they tracked my parents."

"You're making up lies. That's what you're good at. Lying."

"I have my sources too."

"I don't believe your crap."

"My parents got mixed up doing something I never understood for Russia. Your parents led authorities to them. They were fleeing by flying to Alaska to catch a fishing boat when their Piper Cub from Anchorage to Kotzebue crashed. They were killed."

Until that story, nothing in their previous bickering had cleared Bram's drug daze. Suddenly, he felt overwhelmed by a rush of clarity. He envisioned home and multiple locked metal boxes in the closet beneath their staircase. His mother had always answered his endless inquiries by saying, "When your father ran off, he took the keys with him. I hope nothing important's in them, honey."

Bram mumbled to himself, "They weren't intelligence case officers. I would have figured that out." He thought about how his mother had worked overtime to stifle his curiosity about criminal news stories and more recently squelch his curiosity about Elisabet.

Bram glared at his interrogator. "And you just happened in this giant world with thousands or millions of realtors, happened to choose my mother."

"We selected your mother on purpose. To keep an eye on her, study her, save her for a rainy day. We like to keep something on the back burner. I thought I disguised my tracks well enough to not raise her suspicions. Guess not. And then one day, there you were. The apple of her eye. The pathway to her heart. I grabbed you. A more substantial prize."

Bram appeared even more confused. "Who is we?"

"What?"

"You said, 'we selected.' Who is we?"

Elisabet's face reddened. "I meant to say, 'I selected.'"

Bram wanted to rub his agitated stomach. "I feel rotten."

"I'll save your shrimp. Heat it up when you feel better." Elisabet stared at the youth grimacing and trembling. "I don't feel bad for enlightening you. It's shameful your mother kept you in the dark. That's not love. That's cruelty."

She left and Bram listened to the door being bolted.

He mumbled to the blank ceiling. "Nobody in my life is who I think they are." He tried to partially roll onto his side, but restraints held him back. He surrendered and confided in the ceiling again. "I don't even know who I am."

He cried himself to sleep.

SMART MOUTH

As the Gjenganger was too large for a berth, the crew had docked her at the end of Rimini's wharf. Elisabet requested for the crew to relocate a hundred yards out in the bay and tie to a mooring buoy.

Once Elisabet was satisfied with that arrangement, she approached Bram in the brig and demanded he learn about Todd, Amelia, and other family members in New Jersey.

Bram asked, "How do I explain why I was scalped?"

Elisabet dragged a finger across Bram's head. "You're no longer bald; you're fuzzy. Tell the stewards and Grandfather Oskar what you want. I didn't mention your hair. I merely said you had airsickness."

"I'll tell them fuzzy's in with skateboarder dudes."

"Do you skateboard?"

"Duh. Are you a—"

"Say bitch one more time, and I'll tell Mathias I changed my mind about allowing you on deck."

Bram bit his lip. "Thanks for making my point."

"You must be a chess player," Elisabet said.

"Duh. Are you a … one of those truths I'm not allowed to speak?"

"Oh my God, you're annoying."

"What should I say to your grandfather when I meet him?

"Simple things I taught you about family. He won't remember five seconds later anyway."

"Should I address him as Grandfather Oskar or Great-grandfather Oskar?"

"Oh my God." Elisabet threw up her hands. "Sure. Grandfather Oskar. That's simpler."

Elisabet was not alarmed about Bram's ability to quickly learn; it was Bram's enthusiasm to commit to a fraudulent role that gnawed small bites at her usual complacency. Why would he so easily help her?

Bram grinned at his own idea. "I'll remind Grandfather Oskar of the time we skied in Zermatt, and I broke a ski."

"You've been to Zermatt?"

"Googling."

"You're going to torture me with this charade, aren't you?"

"Every chance I get."

Elisabet circled Bram's room-centered bed. "Okay. Ground rule. Go tame talking with the stewards. They're not only sharp-shooters, their sharp thinkers. They see, hear, and analyze everything."

"Bet they have fun figuring you out."

"They're discreet. Which you have no clue how to be."

"I have superb table manners—when called for. And when I'm sworn to secrecy, I honor those requests."

Elisabet leaned over her prisoner. "Can I swear you to secrecy about me?"

"While on this megayacht? Sure."

"This yacht is big, maybe huge, but not mega. Can I trust you after you're on shore?"

"Sounds like there's a chance I get to live."

"That remains on the table." Elisabet turned her back to Bram.

"You know," Bram said, "I could easily have eaten one of your chocolate baked goods. Killing me has long been on your table."

"You spill out truth like you swallowed too much water in a pool and it keeps pouring out of you. You're pesky like … like—"

"Like a brother?"

Elisabet quickly shut down. She had felt comfortable with the tit for tat until Bram stepped over the line.

"I'm sorry," Bram said with a true expression of regret. "That just slipped out."

Elisabet looked out a porthole toward the harbor, relishing being away from docks where snooping tourists eye vessels and peep in portholes with faces begging to be invited aboard.

Bram asked, "Wouldn't it be easier to keep me locked down here in my brig?"

"That would raise greater suspicion. The staff know airsickness should have resolved by now. And then again, maybe I have a big heart. Don't cherish seeing you confined."

"But killing me's fine?"

Elisabet thought about how killing Bram would be up to St. Michael, but kept that thought to herself.

"You sure are salty for being fifty-five."

"Thirty-five, fuck head."

Bram laughed. "Got you."

"Whatever," Elisabet said. "I don't want you talking with the crew except in my presence. Is that clear?"

Bram nodded, saving a plethora of smart remarks for future opportunities.

Elisabet asked, "Do you swim?"

"Like a dolphin."

"Don't try it. I'm a competition-level sharpshooter."

Bram asked, "Do you swim as well as you shoot?"

"I was a blue-ribbon winner at the breast stroke. I can swim a pool length with one breath."

After Elisabet left, Bram analyzed how his captor had been playful at times, but also talked about killing with no change in voice or affect. He concluded that trait was evidence of a psychopath or cold-blooded killer. Whether he walked on eggshells or was smart-mouthed, he was doomed.

If he ever escaped, ever saw Francine and Aaron again, he felt certain they would be proud of his analytic abilities. But he knew he would never tell his mother. She had kept important secrets from him. He would keep important secrets from her.

BY INVITATION ONLY
- August 2023 -

After a flight to London and a second flight to Venice, Lin, Francine, Aaron, and Karol's jet circled over the Adriatic Sea to land at Venice Marco Polo Airport. A state police van transported the U.S. visitors to Rimini.

Elisabet Norgaard was accustomed to being pampered at the century-old Grand Hotel Rimini, a beachside purlieu flanking the port where the Gjenganger was docked. The U.S. consulting team, however, was put up at modest Hotel Royal Plaza, two blocks inland and six blocks from the port.

After negotiations with the Italian Ministry of Defense, the Policio di Stato, and the provincial Rimini Carabinieri overseeing domestic and foreign affairs, Lin gained permission for the two Manhattanites and one Brooklynite to observe Interpol facilitating operations for pursuing Elisabet Norgaard.

Francine had spent previous time in Italy, unlike Aaron who pointed and laughed at an officer donning an Alpine hat, proclaiming loudly the man looked like he was about to yodel.

Moments later, Aaron stared at provincial officers dressed in camo fatigues and ballistic vests. He was stunned to see them bearing Beretta pistols in low-flap holsters and carrying Beretta ARX-160 automatic rifles.

The U.S. team's initial briefing took place at the Carabinieri offices at Piazza Alessandro Bornaccini in the heart of Rimini.

The Deputy Chief of Police, Inspector Luca Giordano, stressed that only Lin—since he was FBI—was allowed to carry a weapon, a restriction that galled Aaron.

SUNLIGHT

Elisabet asked Bram, "Ready to test going up on deck?"

"Will I be in handcuffs and leg irons?" Bram asked.

"Oh my God." She led Bram into the hallway. "I want you to listen, not talk—except to say yes, no, uh-huh, thank you, and such. Got that?"

"Monosyllables. Got that."

Once on deck, Bram squinted as if he had been living in a cave for years and had suddenly been thrust onto a torture rack frying in bright sun.

Elisabet introduced the boy. "Grandfather, this is Todd—grown up since you last saw him as a little boy."

Oskar Norgaard peered and frowned at the boy as if examining a mounted insect collection. "Huh," Oskar sounded.

"And Todd, these are two of our stewards, Mathias and Tatjana. I'll introduce you later to Tryon, Maia, and Chef Tarik."

Shading his eyes, Bram said, "Nice to make your acquaintances."

Mathias was surprised but said nothing about the boy's darker complexion, a sharp contrast to most family members' Norwegian paleness. "Nice to meet you, Todd."

Tatjana smiled and curtsied.

Bram acknowledged them both with a nod.

Elisabet spoke with a tone of ordering. "Mathias and Tatjana will take superb care of you. Ask them for anything you need." She turned to Tatjana. "Todd likes special green tea drinks. He's unbearably particular. I'll personally attend to making those."

She turned to Bram. "Let me show you more of the yacht."

While Mathias observed Elisabet leading the boy about the deck, he noticed a stiffness in their interactions. When Elisabet laid a hand on the teen's shoulder, the boy shrugged just enough that her hand fell away.

Even after an hour on deck, Mathias had not heard the boy speak more than a handful of words.

Once out of earshot of the crew, Bram spoke freely with his micromanaging tour guide. Gazing at shore, he asked, "So, is that Italy?"

"Most certainly," Elisabet said, relaxing her breathing once she had seen how well Bram conducted himself. "Spectacular, isn't it?"

"I never dreamed I would first see another country while standing on a big, huge, but not megayacht."

Elisabet would never admit it, but she was comforted knowing that beneath the quiet, well-mannered boy's façade, a smart-mouthed creature continued to thrive.

DARSENA DI RIMINI

Once the U.S. travelers napped and showered, Luca escorted them for a walking tour of the port. He asked them to wear typical tourist clothing. Francine tried to suppress a smile upon scrutinizing Aaron's light-blue cotton sport shirt, stylish pink shorts, and sandals.

Aaron asked, "Are you grinning at my pale legs?"

Francine shook her head. "I haven't even made it to checking out your legs yet."

"Oh, this getup," Aaron said, tugging at his white cloth belt. "For your information, my mother-in-law ordered this outfit for me online. Anyway, I like your floppy sunhat."

"What's that?" Aaron asked, pointing to the end of the wharf at a white rock jetty with a blue-green bronze monument.

Luca smiled with pride. "Those two green women are wives of sailors gazing at the horizon, longing to see their husbands return from the sea."

"I could live here," Aaron said. "Most definitely."

Luca whistled to gain the group's attention. "Everyone stare and admire the statue. Use only peripheral vision to view the Gjenganger moored to its left."

As the so-called tourists pointed and admired the statue, they listened attentively to Luca. "We've spotted a thirtyish woman sunbathing. One of the officers claimed to briefly sight a boy with short hair, fitting the age of your son, Ms. Whaanga. So far, no one else has seen him."

"My son has long curly hair," Karol said, heartbreak clearly entrenched in her voice.

Francine asked, "Was the boy restrained?"

"Not according to my officer," Luca said. "In fact,

Inspector Moretti said the boy appeared to be chatting with the elderly owner."

"That doesn't fit," Karol said.

"Maybe it does," Aaron said. "Your boy has keen survival skills that likely kicked in." He turned to Luca. "Do the passengers ever come ashore?"

"The yacht was at the docks until four days ago," Luca answered. "They moved eighty to ninety meters out and tied to that buoy."

"What's the plan?" Francine asked.

"We have no doubt this is a Norgaard yacht and that the elderly gentleman on board is the owner, Oskar Norgaard. Facial recognition checked out. He appears to be confined to a wheelchair. The woman, if she is our target, rarely appears, obscuring her face with a sunhat larger than yours, Commander Boult."

"Francine, please."

"Larger than yours, Francine."

"So, do we just wait?" Aaron asked, slapping at a bug on his bare leg.

"Yesterday, a small boat approached the yacht. Two crew members immediately appeared with Beretta automatics. Same as our standard police issue."

"Weapons more suitable for army than police," Aaron mumbled.

"Many Americans are disturbed by our choice of weapons," Luca said. "The last thing we need is a firefight. We have no reason to suspect the crew intend to harm anyone. More likely they are deterring pirates and uninvited guests as do other large yachts and ships. These days, being armed like that is standard."

Aaron asked, "If you approach announcing you are officially inspecting or something, get on board, would that work?"

"We think alike, Detective Galanis."

"Aaron, please."

"Aaron. We don't want to appear threatening to the crew and they hurt the boy. The woman's killed enough people; we believe she's easily triggered. What's your son's name again, Ms. Whaanga?"

Karol answered, "Bram. Did your officer notice if the boy was dark complexioned like Polynesian dark? Bram's father was New Zealand Māori."

"He didn't say, but I'll ask. That would be helpful."

"Thank you."

"Let's head to shore," Luca said, already turning from the sea. "We don't want to linger on the dock long enough to alert them."

Aaron mumbled beneath his breath, "I hate waiting."

INTROSPECTION

Aboard the Gjenganger, secured in his brig, Bram woke in the middle of the night. He had always been excellent at shoving worries aside and falling asleep before completing the prayer his mother used to sing to him at bedtime. But if there happened to be grave difficulty left over from the day, or general unresolved thorny issues, he would wake in early morning hours and mull over details and possibilities, rehearsing corrective interventions for atoning.

He blamed waking on the full moon that was spotlighting his face through the porthole. His immediate thought following the blame game was to ponder the preposterous idea Elisabet had slung at him, a conception that opposed his understanding of his own life, a threat to his identity. She had said both of his parents had been intelligence case officers.

He entertained the idea that enemies often present truths that friends conceal. Not out of warm-heartedness, but as weapons to incite doubts about worlds we think we know. Weapons to destabilize our foundations.

He recalled Aaron mentioning he had a detective gene. Did Aaron know the secrets of his parents but concealed that truth from him? A betrayal if he did.

Had his mother been so traumatized that she concocted a dull fantasy life for the two of them? Had his mother been Elisabet's target all along? Did his own similarities with Elisabet's brother draw her to him as much as lanterns pluck mosquitos from cold, dark skies?

He wished Francine and Aaron were close by to answer his questions, accepting that his mother was too fearful or incapable to share her past with him. He had never met his grandparents—maternal or paternal. What stories would they have shared? Even if he had spent an hour with any of them, he would have grown up with a hint of who he really was. But without knowing what had transpired in his family, his identity had been stolen, shelved, locked in a vault.

And now he might die, never having had a glimpse of who he was if it had not been for his adversary blurting out truth.

An hour would pass before Bram returned to sleep. His early-hour ruminations would dive underground and remain hidden during his waking hours. Such is the manner truth plays hide-and-seek.

***

Francine had attempted days earlier to call Jasmine. After failing to make contact, she spied at Jasmine's Facebook pages. Jasmine, Teresa, and Cheyenne appeared to be a happy threesome. Jasmine's hair had continued to grow out.

Sitting on her hotel's porch, Francine used Luca's satellite phone. After four unsuccessful attempts to get an answer, she assumed Jasmine mistook the incoming call to be a robocall.

Francine left a voicemail. "Hi. It's me. Sorry I didn't call sooner. I'm in Italy. Can't say where. I know that irritates you but … that's how it is. We found your stalker. She's on a yacht anchored nearby. We're pretty sure she has Bram with her. How in God's name she swung that, we don't know. I can only pray he's safe, that he will come out of this nightmare intact. I promise for his sake and for your sake, I'll do everything possible to bring this woman to justice. It's frustrating knowing my hands are tied by being in another country."

Francine paused to gather her thoughts before changing topics.

"You're now using the cellphone carrier's standard message for missed calls. That's a wise precaution, but I miss hearing the lively, smartass remarks you used to create and update every few weeks. My favorite was: 'Hello. This is crewcut-with-glitter-in-her-hair's phone. Leave a message if you have anything smutty to add. Otherwise, don't.'"

She paused to think.

"I hope your and Teresa's baby boy is doing fine. I've lost track of how old Cheyenne must be. I saw his photo on Facebook. Eight months? Nine months? Handsome boy. Give your family my best. I hope to put this ordeal behind me soon. Maybe we can grab coffee or a drink when I get home. Miss you. Love you."

She ended the call, questioning if she should have used the word love or not. Oh well. Too late.

Even the act of trying to contact Jasmine helped, making her more determined than ever to capture the woman who had threatened her former lover. She realized she felt comfortable using the phrase *former lover* in the privacy of her own thinking, but could not use that phrase when talking to others. Not even when speaking aloud to herself.

***

Aaron was two minutes into his call with his wife, Kendra, when he asked, "Where are you right now?"

Kendra answered, "In the kitchen. Why?"

"You know what I would do with you right now in the kitchen? Remember Christmas when you walked in wearing that—"

"Aaron," Kendra said with a firm voice. "You're on speaker. Cole? Say hi to your dad."

"Hi Daddy," a little voice from across the kitchen yelled.

"Hi buddy. What are you doing?"

"Pancakes."

"Eating pancakes. Great. Yum yum yum."

"And orange."

"That's grapefruit, honey," Kendra said.

Aaron forced a chuckle even though hearing the normalcy of home voices brought him to tears. "Pancakes and grapefruit. Wonderful." His relaxed muscles informed him that his anger about feeling powerless in a foreign country was melting away.

"Any idea when you'll be home?" Kendra asked.

"Things are moving slow. You know me."

"Fit to be tied, I'm sure."

"Send me pics of you and Colt."

"I did," Kendra said.

"I can't get my cellphone to work over here, so email them. I'll go into an internet cafe or somewhere."

"You never really told me what you're doing other than it's related to Manhattan murders."

"Sorry. Uh … The basic thing is … at the moment, we're trying to save a kidnapped kid."

"Colt? Don't pour the syrup on your own. You can hold it while I help. Thank you. Seems like the Italian police could handle that."

"The kid's American. I know the kid. I can't explain it, but when I see him, I see Colt years from now. And then I feel I gotta help. And it's important to watch and cheer Francine and the locals on."

"Sounds complicated. When we have more time, you'll have to explain it. Be careful. I gotta get Colt to daycare."

"Love you."

"You too."

As the call ended, Aaron heard static and then silence. He wanted so badly to rush in with guns blazing and rescue Bram as his boyhood movie heroes did, making it look easy.

He questioned whether or not he measured up. Whether or not the world permitted him and other officers to measure up.

Watching American news shows while in Italy, he felt he was seeing home clearer. There was excessive violence on the streets. There were crooks in suits running big businesses and government. There were kids sexting graphic photos and videos of themselves. Groups of people hating other groups. How was he supposed to be a hero in that world? Evil was behind every rock, building, and electronic gizmo.

Maybe he required a clear-cut villain like Elisabet Norgaard. Someone to give him a purpose with the only debate being about the how.

Problem solved.

FAMILIAR ANNOYANCE

Bram, sitting on the edge of his bed lacing his shoes, asked, "Can you tell Chef Tarik I prefer red caviar. The black caviar sucks."

"Oh my God," Elisabet said, standing in the cabin doorway. "How do people put up with you?"

Bram stretched out on his back in the bed and stared at the ceiling. "What was your brother's name?"

"What?" Elisabet shook her head as if she could shake off the question. "What the hell did you just ask me?"

"You told me growing up you had a brother, but not his name."

"When?"

"In your cabin cellar. The wine prison."

Elisabet strained to pull up the memory but failed. Her voice became soft and shaky. "I never talk about him."

"Well, you did. How he laid his head on—"

"Why are you hell bent on figuring me out? I don't want you understanding me. Can you get that?"

"It's not for you." Bram rolled on his side and looked at her. "It's for me."

Elisabet stepped farther into the room, still holding onto the door handle. "What can you get out of knowing?"

"Learning about other people comforts me. Guides me to examine myself."

Elisabet walked to Bram's bed and looked down at him like he was a specimen under her microscope, seeing him for the first time. "You know? You're a real nut case."

"That's what my teachers say. What Mom says."

"No surprise there."

They both held their positions in silence, each reflecting about people from years past.

With her throat tightening, Elisabet sounded as if she were whispering within herself. "Lars."

Bram sat up. "What?"

Elisabet cleared her throat. "My brother's name. Lars."

"Lars … So … Lars was about my age, right?"

"Your age when what?"

"When he got sick. Throat cancer."

Elisabet sat on the edge of a chair with only her toes touching the floor as if she were about to run. "Tracheal cancer."

They both resumed silence, swaying when a passing cruise ship's wake rocked the yacht.

Bram waited a moment to muster bravery to speak. "I wonder if we would have been friends."

Elisabet wrinkled her face with incredibility. "You and my brother?"

"Yeah. Me and Lars. Friends."

Elisabet started to dismiss the idea, but thought a minute. "You both annoy me." She pulled up memories of her brother. "Lars lived to annoy me."

"I figured that."

"Why did you figure that?"

"You're clever at dealing with me when I'm annoying. Like you're familiar with someone annoying you. And when you get upset with me, you have this tiny little grin."

"I do not."

"Most people wouldn't notice it. I do."

"Even if I did, that would make you think what?"

"You would never admit it," Bram said. "In fact, you'll blow a gasket when I tell you."

"Tell me or I won't let you on deck again."

"Okay … You like me."

Elisabet opened her mouth overly wide and huffed. "I

absolutely do not."

"You have that little grin again."

"You are wishing I'm grinning. I guarantee you there's no grin."

"You're grinning now."

"No grin."

"You need an acting coach."

"A what?"

"Okay. Try this. Show me your most serious face."

Elisabet crossed her arms over her chest and flattened her expression. "How's this, Mr. Acting Coach?"

"The ends of your mouth are still pulling up a little bit—not as bad." Bram scooted on his knees to Elisabet, reached toward her face, and stopped. "Okay if I touch your face? Real gently?"

Elisabet frowned and leaned back. "Very gently."

Using the tips of his index fingers, Bram lightly touched the two edges of her mouth. "Okay. Touch where I'm touching with your fingers and hold them there."

Bram slowly removed his fingers as Elisabet imitated his light touch to her mouth.

"Good," Bram said. "Feel how the edges are turned up just a hair?"

"Not sure."

"Pull your fingertips down lower, pulling your skin down with them."

Elisabet tugged downward. "Like this?"

"That good. Now say, 'Bram, I absolutely do not like you.'"

"Keeping my fingers there?"

"Lightly, but with just enough pressure to keep the edges from sliding up. Okay. Do that and speak."

"Bram, I absolutely do not—"

Elisabet broke into laughing.

"That's worse," Bram said with a serious face. "The edges rose to your eyes."

"I'm not laughing because I like you, you idiot. I'm laughing because this is ludicrous."

"Okay. Practice that in the mirror."

"Saying what?"

Bram put on his most serious face. "Bram? I absolutely loathe you."

Again, Elisabet laughed. "You're crazy. Fucking goofy."

"You'll see. You'll improve. Swear to God."

"I took college theatre classes, wise guy. I attest we never did anything this ridiculous."

"I used to come home from movies and wonder how actors delivered lines—cause the lines were not true to their real lives—and I'd look in my mirror and try to make the expressions they did in the movies. Of course, I'm talking about only the really great actors."

"Certifiably insane. Come to think of it, you and Lars would have made a goofy pair. Gotten along splendidly."

"I wish I had known him."

Elisabet turned her head away, not wanting her acting coach to see her eyes beginning to water. "I'll be back in a minute. I need to … to go to the head."

She hurried into the hallway.

The teak door was thin enough Bram could hear her softly crying.

He thought, there's a heart beneath the layers of monster. Maybe there's a chance I'll survive this ordeal. But I was wise to not tell her deeper truth. That the young men dying in her lap were Lars.

THE ANSWER IS BLOWING IN THE WIND

Elisabet was peering through binoculars out a tinted salon window when a steward entered the room with mid-morning snacks.

Elisabet asked, "Mathias? Have you seen the men on the docks who have been watching us?"

"I noticed." Mathias set napkins and cutlery on the table. "Too well dressed to be pirates. Too calm to be paparazzi."

Elisabet took her seat. "So, who then?"

"Plain-clothes detectives or inspectors? There are always people trying to sue or defame your grandfather and his businesses, you know."

"I don't like them watching us. I need to go into town. I don't want them hounding me."

"Hold your head high and dismiss them. I've observed you do that a hundred times."

"You make me sound horrid."

Mathias laughed. "You instructed me once that you enjoyed portraying a snob for intruding landlubbers."

"I'm getting older," Elisabet said. "They irritate me now more than I can stand."

"You and I are both thirty-five. We're hardly aged."

"I have crow's feet. Your face is smooth like a teenager. Makes me jealous."

"I detect no crow's feet on your lovely face, but with such a compliment aimed my direction, what is it you are about to ask me to do?"

Elisabet grinned. "You know me well. I want you to sneak me past those voyeurs."

"Stuff you in my duffle bag and sling you over my shoulder?"

Elisabet grinned as if wanting to seduce him. "You are strong enough. But I want you to jet ski into this port and bring out our cabin cruiser. Anchor it a hundred yards or so away from the Gjenganger. I'll swim underwater, sneak breaths as needed, and climb aboard. Then drop me off at Portoverde. I'll take a taxi from there. Shop."

"Why not have me take you in the powerboat?"

"It's what I prefer."

"Very well, madame. I believe you've done this before. Jonathan told me about coming to your aid."

"So much for staff keeping my confidence. It works well for escaping paparazzi."

"And what shall we do with young Todd while you are away modeling Italian fashions?"

"You do know my yearnings. But this time, I need women's products and a respite from the teenage world."

Mathias' face reddened and his nod indicated an apology.

"Pass the word to restrict Todd to his cabin while I'm gone. Given the chance, he will run off for adventure—or swim off. He is the product of overly indulgent parenting of a highly impulsive child."

"Will do."

***

Once aboard the cabin cruiser, Elisabet instructed Mathias to coast near enough to spy on dock voyeurs who obviously were focused on the Gjenganger.

"Nothing of their clothing confirms who they are," Mathias said. He focused binoculars toward the yacht club and dry dock. "There are two police vans parked farther inland."

Elisabet had no doubt someone was overly interested

in her activities.

Mathias asked, "Any reason to believe the authorities would be interested in you or the boy?"

Elisabet felt imperiled by Mathias entertaining such a notion. "Not the police, Mathias. Some very bad people have been tailing us. I hope the police are after them."

"We'll look out for you and Todd."

Mathias increased speed toward the alternate port.

Once ashore, Elisabet hailed a taxi to ferry her inland to Chieso di San Michele Arcangelo in Mondaino.

The eighteenth-century church was simple with wooden benches and three marble mosaics. Nowhere could she find a stature or painting of her beloved Michael. The church, however, was named to honor him, providing her with hope he might come to her.

Alone inside, she sat midway along the aisle. She noted the church was more silent than Manhattan cathedrals. Perhaps because the only illumination was from sunlight radiating throughout. No electric bulbs buzzing. No heating units or air-conditioners droning. No traffic honking and screeching in the bordering narrow alley. Although she could not see it, she could hear the buzzing of a single fly in a distant window well.

She knelt and assumed a prayer position. "St. Michael, please hear me. I am far from home, far from sacred places where you and I commune. I once had clear missions, but I strayed. I allowed emotions to consume me. I beseech you, guide me back to our mission."

She glanced around the small structure, concerned the few statues were judging. She closed her eyes and turned inward, hoping St. Michael would find her there. "I have a boy—kidnapped a boy. His parents took my parents from me. I have been plotting some time for no better reason than to seek revenge. Revenge that has nothing to do with worthy missions for which you guide me. This strange, annoying boy helped me to see I am wrong. Perhaps you sent him to test me, to teach me. Accept me into your embrace like you did for Joan of Arc. I will not fail you again."

She returned to sitting on the hard bench, staring ahead but not seeing. "My erroneous actions led people to follow. Their goal is to destroy me. I seek your protection. What must I do in return? Sacrifice myself? Sacrifice the boy? Someone else?"

Elisabet walked to the front of the church and stared upward at multiple religious figures in a painting dangling above a statue of Jesus tortured and dying on the cross.

She addressed the painting. "Must I sacrifice myself?"

She breathed deeply, pivoting slowly as she studied each door, window, cornice, statue, painting, searching for a sign. There was stillness.

She returned to the painting above the pulpit. "Must I sacrifice the boy?"

Again, she breathed heavily. As she began pivoting, a violent summer gust blew open the entrance door, sending a whirlwind of leaves circling along the aisle toward her. Her heart skipped beats and her throat tightened such that she could not swallow or speak.

She waited for the whirlwind to slow and flutter to its death. She walked along the aisle and out into sunlight. The warmth on her face felt good, but her heart felt heavy. The deed before her was too familiar. In her mind the faces of Lars and Bram melted together in a way that made her tremble.

She ran the hundred feet along the alley to the waiting taxi as if church ghosts of two centuries were chasing her.

PET PREDICTORS

Atop the nine floors of condos and Ristorante Prua overlooking the harbor, Lin and Francine alternated spying upon the Gjenganger through a mounted telescope.

They could clearly identify Oskar Norgaard, but only faintly discern the back of the fuzzy head of a boy with whom the elderly yachtsman appeared to be conversing.

Lin asked, "Do you think that's Bram?"

Francine took a turn. "That's not his hairstyle. This boy's hair looks blonder. Maybe bleached from sun. He's the right height. Moves similarly. I wish he would face this direction."

Lin and Francine, of course, could hear nothing of what appeared to be congenial dialogue.

Although three generations apart, Bram delighted at the empire mogul's intelligence and experiences.

After hearing the man's complaints about the poorly designed wheelchair and stories of how his geologists had located oil deposits, Bram asked, "What's the best thing about being your age?"

Without hesitating to think, Oskar answered, "Survival. Every year adds new infirmities with challenges. Every victory over any one of those is cause to celebrate. Take a lap, even if that lap is a roll across a room and back."

Bram joined Oskar in chuckling.

"I remember one time," Oskar said, with a tone earned from decades of presenting stories, "I was alone in the upstairs of our Tarrytown home. I stumped my toe. I lifted my foot to squeeze my toe—as if that could possibly rid me of pain—and fell flat on my face, striking my chin on our blasted footstool. God did that hurt. But embarrassment, the ruling emotion of emotions, took over. I felt compelled to get up before anyone discovered my stupidity."

Bram said, "I felt that way after my bike accident."

"Exactly. How stupid are we humans, my grandson?"

"Great-grandson."

"As you say. But there I was, being highly stupid, and although I had often boasted throughout life of my keen upper-body strength, I could not get up."

"That must have been scary."

"I didn't notice if it was scary. I was too humiliated. Even though only I had witnessed my misfortune."

"What did you do?" Bram asked.

"I looked around. The closest piece of furniture that was low enough to be of help, your deceased grandmother's dressing bench, was a good fifty feet away. I crawled. Like a bug that had lost its hind four legs and was left with only two front legs to pull it forward. I used my elbows as if they were knobby feet. Elbowed my way across the cold marble."

"Why didn't you pull with your entire arms and hands?"

"Confusion? Because I had lost feeling in them? Stupidity? Who knows? But that's what I did. Elbowed my way. Created giant abrasions on each elbow."

"And when you got to the dressing bench?"

"I pulled myself up and sat there until my manservant, Hobson, like what's his face in that movie what's it called, arrived."

"Did you tell him?"

"I did tell him. I told him to bring me a damn glass and a damn bottle of champagne."

Bram laughed and clapped.

"He probably saw my bloody elbows but was too polite to inquire. He asked what I was celebrating. I was a bit forceful with the poor soul. I yelled at him. 'It's time to celebrate victory over the curses of living.' He fetched my champagne."

Peering through the telescope, Lin said to Francine, "If I didn't know better, I would think the old gentleman and the boy are having fun."

Bram asked, "What was Aunt Elisabet like?"

"Oh goodness," Oskar said, appearing stupefied. "What a question, Todd."

"Sorry. I shouldn't be nosy."

"Hells bells, my boy. Nosy is the best attribute a man can have. I hope our Elisabet's not mistreating you."

"Why would she?"

"Elisabet—and never tell her I said this—but Elisabet's never been the mothering type or even the kind-aunt type. I am shocked she went all out to assure you have a solid vacation. Let's just say she's never been the warm, cuddly, polite type. Self-centered. Now that's between you and me. Understand?"

"I do, sir."

"This may be an old man's silliness—although I swear it to be true—but one can tell how children will grow up by observing how they treat pets. How do you treat your pets?"

"I have a Labradoodle, Betsy. I leave her with my soccer coach's family down the street when we're away. Mom's allergic to other dog breeds, but I still play with neighbors' dogs. When I do, I place my clothes in a special hamper and take them to the laundromat to wash. Protect Mom."

"Look at you. Surviving adversity as if you were a wise old man. Well done, son. Well done."

"Do I get champagne?"

They enjoyed a shared hearty laugh.

Bram asked, "So, how did Aunt Elisabet treat pets?"

Oskar leaned forward and whispered. "You can't breathe a word I told you so."

"Promise. Cross my heart but don't hope to die."

"Good." Oskar looked around to see if he was alone with the boy and spotted Mathias at a distance keeping a close eye on them. "Elisabet's brother had a hamster."

"Lars?"

"Yes. Lars had a hamster. Lucy. Loved Lucy dearly. When Lars was absent, Elisabet would act like she was petting Lucy, but was roughing up the poor fur ball, rubbing her violently, squeezing her, pinching her. I worried about Elisabet growing up." Oskar returned to talking in a normal-volume voice. "I am glad to see Elisabet has a tender side, reached out to you. Sometimes life surprises us. Life works out."

"Did Lars have other pets?"

"Unequivocally. That boy loved a myriad of animals. Back then, I invested in race horses. On our home farm, we had a thoroughbred, a stallion with a chestnut coat, same lineage as Secretariat. Sixteen hands tall. And for whatever reason, that animal would only run if Lars rode him. He followed Lars around the farm like a loyal Labrador. Many the night, Lars slept in the stall beside Johnny Glass."

"That was the horse's name? Johnny Glass?"

"A Tennessee breeder named him."

"What happened to Johnny Glass?"

"After Lars ..." The elderly man choked up enough for his voice to become hoarse. "After my grandson was ... no longer with us, Johnny Glass gave up ... A heart-broken horse has no value for racing. He hung around more like a pet, until one night, still at a youthful age, he lay down in his stall … went to sleep."

Bram hesitated before asking with a reverent voice, "You mean he died?"

The old man held still a long time, appearing as if he had just gone to sleep.

Mathias approached. "Can I get you two gentlemen anything?"

Bram spoke up. "A round of champagne for us survivors, please Mathias."

Oskar came to life and chuckled. "An unsweetened iced tea for me, please, Mathias, and my great-grandson will have a … have a … What is your choice, son?"

"Green tea, please sir."

"Very well, gentlemen," Mathias said, enjoying performing as if serving royalty. With head held high and wearing a controlled smile, he strolled inside.

"Did you know," Oskar asked, "and don't dare breathe to Mathias that I told you, but that very fellow there is a world-class fencer."

"No," Bram said with his mouth agape and his eyes as big and round as his mouth.

"Competed in the Olympics, he did."

"No way. Did he win?"

"Let's just say, Mathias survived. And in life, that is winning."

When Mathias arrived with the drinks, they toasted to survival, and Bram winked at Mathias.

Mathias returned the wink.

SOMETHING FAMILIAR

In the morning shade of the upper deck lounge's canopy roof, Elisabet watched a helicopter fly over the yacht for a third time. She went below and obtained one of the crew's automatic rifles, wrapped it in a rainbow-striped beach towel, carried it to the deck, and slid it beneath the yellow-cushioned wicker couch. She sat on the couch, pretending to be engrossed in a novel Mathias had suggested.

Tatjana refreshed Elisabet's glass with sparkling water and asked, "Will Master Todd be joining you on deck for breakfast or taking breakfast in his cabin?"

"Who knows?" Elisabet asked. "He is in one of his moods. Let him pout for a bit. Can you bring me a simple tropical fruit salad? Later, I'll go to the galley and prepare Todd's green-tea drink. He's painfully particular how it's made, but this time I prefer if you deliver it to him."

"Yes ma'am."

"I need Mathias to ferry Todd and me down the coast at dusk to go star gazing. Please ask Mathias to ready the powerboat for an evening trip."

"Yes ma'am."

"Oh. And fetch the empty, long purple duffle bag from the lockers. There's a pair of water-skis in town I've been admiring."

"Yes ma'am."

"And tell Mathias to arrange a car ashore for us to travel to Mondaino. There's a glorious two-hundred-year-old church with nearby sports fields and an arboretum perfect for star gazing. Perhaps it would be a good idea if you pack an evening picnic. It may be a lengthy adventure."

"Yes ma'am. Any special requests?"

"Surprise us. If Todd chooses to be his picky self and refuses what you select, it will be his loss—oh. But tell Tarik that Bram—I mean Todd—prefers red over black caviar."

"Yes ma'am. Right away."

Tatjana retrieved a stray glass she spotted beneath a matching wicker chair and disappeared into the yacht.

Elisabet watched the helicopter circle again, desiring to yank out the Beretta and test her sharpshooter skills on something larger than typical clay pigeons.

Inside one of two police vans parked in the shadows of the carport at Darsena Sunset Bar, Francine, Aaron, and Karol waited for Lin to return from meeting with the Italian force in the second van.

"So," Francine asked, "are they going to approach the yacht? By now, everyone aboard has been forewarned by that loud machine dive-bombing every twenty minutes."

"Luca plans to approach them by boat," Lin said. "Keep a healthy distance and use a bullhorn to demand peaceful surrender of the boy."

Aaron shook his head. "Just ask them politely to turn over their kidnap victim?"

Lin answered, "We can't assume the crew is fully informed or in agreement with the misdeeds of Ms. Norgaard."

Aaron clapped his hands against his scalp. "Well, the crew sure as hell can't be thinking Elisabet and Bram are dating. The crew has to be in on this kidnapping to some degree."

"I agree with Inspector Giordano's plan," Lin said. "We don't understand what we're up against. An initial request or interaction may help us clarify. That will be a wise start."

Lin looked to Karol. "K.C.? You look exhausted. Are you sleeping at night?"

"A moment here and there," Karol said. "Not enough."

"I didn't sleep at all," Aaron said. "All this waiting. If I had a mini-torpedo, I'd sink that vessel and rescue Bram."

"And here come the Americans blazing with gunfire," Francine said. "Good thing the Italians are in charge."

"I wasn't serious, boss. Just wishing."

"I think I need some air," Karol said, sliding open the van door. "Take a walk to the water's edge."

"I could use a walk," Aaron said, leaning forward to step out.

"Wait," Lin said. "One at a time. We need as little presence as possible until we comprehend what's going on."

Aaron flopped back into his seat. "Fine."

"I won't be long," Karol said. She trudged between drydocked, car-sized boats and sat on a boardwalk bench, admiring how the gray, wooden plank walk weaved with the curvature of the shore.

Karol kept her back to a golden-sand beach that was dotted with several thousand turquoise beach umbrellas lined in rows as if they were audience members, the main event being hundreds of parents and children splashing in gentle surf.

Karol listened to the music of laughter and little-kid squeals of delight. She could not help but daydream about the fun she would have if Sol and Bram were there within touching distance.

She shook her head and the daydream vanished.

Her eyes followed the boardwalk around to a brick, fortress-like structure at the tip of the harbor. It enticed her. If she were to stroll there, she would be able to watch families on boats entering and exiting the port waterway, view the giant Ferris wheel on the opposite side of the channel. Surely, families were there celebrating varieties of birthdays and holidays.

If she were out on the tip, she would better be able to view the yacht. A piece of beautiful art that oil-and-shipping-tanker wealth coupled with airline-and-real-estate wealth purchased. And now, that yacht was a piece of beautiful art standing in for a prison, holding the one person Karol called family. What damage would it really be if she strolled nearer? Waved at the yacht? Yelled? Swam to the yacht? Simply stood there, knowing her boy was close—even if beyond reach.

She had been ordered not to look directly at the captivating vessel. But she knew if she got closer, she would not be able to resist staring at the Gjenganger. Glaring at it and devising a plan. And that plan would not include sitting in the back of an Italian police van hour after hour, tapping her fingers until they were raw.

Karol shifted to thinking about the creature that stole her boy. There was mystery surrounding that woman. Why had Elisabet Norgaard selected Karol to be her real estate agent? Ms. Norgaard had used different agents each time she purchased a condo, but always stuck to using Karol for selling them. And Elisabet had used the same alias each time with Karol. Left her condos decorated as if showing them off to Karol. It seemed Ms. Norgaard was almost begging for Karol to know her. And then there was the unexpected tragic turn. Ms. Norgaard trying to kill Karol—and her son. Killing someone is an intimate act, she thought. It delivers a personal message. But what message did Elisabet intend to send to Karol? And now Elisabet had taken her son. A deeper, miserable intimacy and message.

Their lives were slowly intertwining, colliding,

cementing.

Karol thought back to files she had gathered on Elisabet Norgaard. Granddaughter of Oskar Norgaard. Raised by her mother, Emma, who remarried when Elisabet was two. And then when Elisabet was a teenager, both her mother and stepfather died, leaving her to be raised by her Norgaard grandparents.

Karol closed her eyes and pressed her fingers against her forehead as if that would carry her deeper into her mind's files, searching for the stepfather's name. Frederik something. But Frederik what? … Frederik Calkin—no, no. Not Calkin … Frederik Galkin. That was it. Brain file found. Frederik Galkin.

Suddenly, Karol felt an electric current race throughout her body, eliciting immediate chills followed by a drenching sweat. Her stomach became an empty, devouring hole sucking all her senses into it.

Galkin. A name from her past. There had been a Galkin couple. Timur and Emma Galkin from Sands Point, New York, a wealthy neighborhood on Long Island Sound.

Was Timur a middle name? Or Frederik a middle name? Could it be one in the same? She and Sol had uncovered enough data on a Galkin couple for the state department to bring espionage charges. The couple had fled. Reports stated that the couple died in route—not to be trusted since that was a typical Russian deception. Could they possibly have been Ms. Norgaard's mother and stepfather?

Karol felt an urgency to return to the van. Confirm names. Share her discovery that Elisabet Norgaard may be carrying a personal vendetta against her.

She felt accelerating concern for Bram's safety and blamed herself. She had been rocketing toward an unimaginable trap for months or years and blind to it.

If Sol had been at her side, the two of them talking into the morning hours, they would not have been blindsided. She heard Sol's voice whispering in her ear, "Get on track, K.C. Get on track."

Rushing to the van, she played chess with herself. Which moves would win and which would lose? Could there be a checkmate? Could there be a stalemate?

She almost tripped in her hurrying.

STAR GAZING

Upon hearing Karol's reminiscences, the New York team agreed; Bram's life was in even more danger than they had assessed.

"For previous murders," Francine said, "we could only establish psychotic motives. Now, we know this woman also has diseased motives."

"I hope helicopter surveillance doesn't freak her out," Aaron said. "Doesn't accelerate her time table."

Lin selected a calming voice. "If she does try to make a break, Luca has air, land, and water units on standby."

The sun was barely touching the horizon when Mathias aided his passengers to board the powerboat.

"You already look seasick," Mathias said to Bram as he steadied the wobbly boy. "Worse than the day you arrived. You sure you're up for this?"

"The sea's tilting back and forth," Bram mumbled, clutching the gunwale. He cackled like a two-year-old. "I can crawl using my elbows."

"He's a bit goofy," Elisabet said, insisting on lugging her purple duffle bag aboard. "I believe his motion-sickness medicine backfired, threw him off kilter."

Mathias helped Bram to a seat like a parent trying to secure a toddler into a high chair. "Here's a sick bag if you need it."

When Bram tried to blow the bag up like a balloon, Elisabet threw up her hands and walked away as if saying the child was now Mathias's problem.

Bram winked at Mathias, slipped a note into his hand, and placed a finger over his lips, indicating to keep the note a secret.

Mathias appeared bewildered and checked to assure

Elisabet was not watching before tucking the note into his shirt pocket.

Elisabet scowled at the docks and yelled, "Avoid that paparazzi crow's nest."

"Absolutely," Mathias said, watching Elisabet place her bag near a bench.

While Elisabet preoccupied herself surveying the docks, Bram watched Matthias store various picnic and safety items in cockpit lockers, and then cram a cooler, small boxes, and Elisabet's purple bag beneath the bench.

While on his knees arranging items, Mathias peeked at Bram's note: *I faked taking Elisabet's medicine. My actual name is Bram Whaanga and she drugged and kidnapped me. She threatened to kill my mother if I did not play along. She is wanted for being a serial killer in New York. PS: I know you are an excellent fencer.*

Mathias reread the note and then stared at Bram, confounded the boy was looking at him with a calm, sensible expression. Bram nodded, conveying that the note was the truth.

Having spent excessive time reordering items beneath the bench, Mathias caught Elisabet glaring at him. He thrust a bottle of water toward her. "You need a drink?"

Elisabet shook her head and looked away.

Mathias approached the console, revved the inboard diesel engines, and headed directly out to sea. As he completed the turn to the south, he thought how he often felt distrustful of Elisabet, bothered by her stories and emotions mismatching. Now, Bram was making fantastical accusations that eclipsed Mathias's more ordinary suspicions.

He wondered why the note ended with a comment about his fencing? Was that the boy's way of proving he could pass a reality check? Smart kid if true.

During their days aboard the Gjenganger, Mathias had been wary of Elisabet's zeal to be the only person to prepare Bram's drinks. Had she been drugging him? Various suspicions from present and past were lining up to lure him toward believing Bram's claims.

Elisabet yelled at him. "Can we go faster?"

Why would she need to go faster? Star gazing is best after dark. And why from the land? Stars are more visible from open water.

Mathias glanced behind. Despite being daylight, a boat with bright headlights sped out of the port and turned their direction. That had happened previously when pirates pursued them, believing Oskar had fled his yacht with money and jewels. Mathias still wore shrapnel in his shoulder from that encounter.

He pushed the dual levers forward and the boat's nose rose, exposing its beveled underside pounding waves, creating an up and down rhythm, shooting water out the sides, slinging passengers about as if they were strapped to bucking rodeo horses.

Mathias watched Elisabet tug her purple duffle bag from beneath the bench, retrieve an automatic rifle, and rest the butt against her shoulder, staring at the pursuing boat gaining on them.

"Jesus Christ," Mathias yelled. "Why would you bring that aboard?"

Elisabet turned the Barretta on Mathias and yelled, "faster."

Mathias looked at Bram. The boy's face was paler than last evening's supermoon.

As Mathias sped the boat toward Portoverde Marina, he glimpsed a helicopter approaching from the coastline.

Pointing with the tip of her weapon toward the shore, Elisabet yelled, "Head into port."

Hoping Francine had correctly picked the port nearest St. Michael's Church, three police vans arrived on the Piazza Ischia where all boats entering the marina had to pass through a narrow waterway.

Five sharpshooters slid doors open on their vans and snatched automatic rifles. One officer, however, could not locate his weapon. He yelled in Italian, "I know I placed it in this van." He ran to a matching van, but his weapon was not there. He cursed in English. "Shit."

As disco dance music blasted from Night Club Ora Blu, the remaining four police sharpshooters, along with Lin and Luca, stationed themselves on the boardwalk. The officers knelt with weapons ready.

Boat slips were occupied by an assortment of powerboats, sailboats, and small yachts crowding the wooden docks and boardwalks where hundreds of tourists took advantage of clear skies and Venus as a star-like heavenly body slipping into twilight.

The red sun was halfway behind the horizon when Mathias piloted into the waterway.

The helicopter flew low enough Bram could make out the word *Polizia* on the side. He watched Elisabet point her automatic rifle at the aircraft.

"Oh my God," Bram screamed, forgetting he had been feigning being drugged. "You're going to take on the Italian Air Force? They'll blast us to pieces."

"St. Michael believes," Elisabet said, "as I believe. We should die a good death. As good as he provided for Joan."

Bram and Mathias looked at one another and with no words exchanged, understood their fellow passenger was not sharing their reality.

"There's no reason any of us to die," Bram yelled. "Let me and Mathias help you. Please, Elisabet."

"I don't need help," Elisabet screamed. "This world

does.”

Again, Bram and Mathias exchanged looks of knowing.

Although the evening was not yet completely dark, a bright searchlight on the helicopter lit up the boat’s cockpit as if anticipating an emcee of ceremonies to appear.

Elisabet fired a three-round burst at the aircraft, driving it away from the narrow channel.

“You’ll get us all killed,” Bram screamed.

“Just you,” Elisabet said, swiftly reaching into her duffle bag and exchanging the rifle for a snub nose revolver. She grabbed Bram and held the revolver to his head. “Just you.”

Mathias slowed the boat to idle in the channel and left the controls to approach Elisabet. “Jesus Christ, Elisabet. Let go of this boy.”

Elisabet aimed the revolver at Mathias, back at Bram, and then several hasty times back and forth. “Which one of you, huh? I already know which. I’ve been instructed.”

Bram saw flashing lights on police cars on shore and nodded to Mathias to look.

Mathias glanced at the scene of police positioned close to the edges of the harbor, aiming automatic rifles in their direction.

“This isn’t what I wanted, kid,” Elisabet said, still pointing the revolver only inches from Bram’s temple. “I have no choice.” She closed her eyes. “As you instructed, Michael.” She pulled the trigger.

The weapon clicked and Bram recoiled. He knew he was thinking, but was not breathing and could not feel his body. He peeped toward the horizon to affirm he was still present on earth.

“Fuck,” Elisabet screamed, leaning her back against the gunwale while pulling Bram in front of her as a shield.

"Fucking useless gun."

When Bram looked to Mathias, his eyes pleading for help, Mathias calmly extended his closed hand. He slowly rolled open his hand, careful to not spill its contents. In his palm were six revolver cartridges.

Bram stared into the tranquil eyes of the Olympic fencer who had just saved his life.

Mathias motioned with a flat hand for Bram to remain still, knowing if Bram moved, a sharpshooter may accidentally hit him.

As Mathias kicked the rifle out of Elisabet's reach, Elisabet jammed the revolver against Bram's forehead, hoping snipers would assume the weapon was functional and refrain from targeting her.

The three speedboat occupants scanned the shore, espying a half-dozen marksmen yards away, training weapons their direction.

Elisabet screamed, "I'm coming, Michael. Bless me."

She pulled Bram to her chest and began a SCUBA-style-backward somersault into the water just as Bram turned his head to the side.

In a split-second, Bram witnessed a flash on shore, heard an echoing shot, and felt Elisabet go limp.

As Elisabet tumbled backwards, a volley of shots from varying directions pierced the air, overpowering any possible sound of a body hitting water.

Bram and Mathias ducked with arms crossed over their heads.

Once combat blasts ceased, Bram peeped through his fingers toward the locus of the muzzle flash he had witnessed. Amidst parked vacationers' and partiers' cars, was his mother pushing herself up from where she had been lying face down across the hood of a car. She was holding an automatic rifle. He saw her quickly hand it off to an animated and angry police officer, pull out a handkerchief, and wipe her hands.

Bram quickly hid behind the console, hoping his mother could not see him watching.

Still partially ducking, Mathias half-crawled to Bram. "You okay?"

"What?" Bram asked, stunned from the pandemonium. "I mean yes. I guess so. Are you?"

"Yes," Mathias said. "That was close. She was going to pull you under with her."

Mathias stared at his young friend for a long moment. "How did you know I fence?"

"Oskar."

"That was clever you added that to your note, you rascal. I knew to believe you."

Bram began crying and although Mathias gently embraced him, Bram clung to the man tighter, enough to feel both their hearts pounding.

Bram mumbled, but even amidst his sobbing, Mathias could comprehend the boy's utterances. "I know who I am. I know who my parents are."

Mathias whispered, "You're safe now."

Bram pulled back. "I was thanking God you and I are alive."

Mathias knew that was not what Bram had mumbled. "I too am grateful to God, my friend."

They hugged again and were still hugging when the police boat arrived and officers boarded.

An English-speaking officer asked. "Where is she?"

"She fell into the water," Mathias answered. He pointed.

"I don't see blood," the officer said.

"She's a superb swimmer," Bram said.

"Did we get her?"

"I felt her go limp. Let go of me. I think that was because a shot hit her."

Another officer yelled, "Bring the spots over here and search." But it was said in Italian and neither Bram nor Mathias understood.

The officers, the helicopter team, and the land team radioed back and forth with so many voices talking and interrupting that Bram disbelieved they could possibly be comprehending one another.

CHAMPAGNE

Bram and Mathias were guided onto a police boat, rushed a few yards to shore, loaded into the back of a tall-van ambulance, and wrapped in blankets.

Bram thought, Neither of us is cold, but like in every photograph I've seen of rescued victims, we're wrapped in blankets. Perhaps the purpose is to swaddle victims like mothers do for crying infants, wrapping them so tight it's like giant hugs promising they'll be fine.

Music from the night club had halted with the onset of gunfire. Voyeurs crowded a roped-off area of the boardwalk while Bram studied boats spotlighting the water and trolling among docks and bobbing vessels.

"They should have found her by now," Mathias whispered to Bram. "She's a good swimmer."

Bram chewed on a knuckle. "She told me she can swim a pool length with one breath."

"I've seen her swim. Slip up for a quick breath and then back under. Are you certain they shot her?"

Bram buried his head in his hands. "I just know she went limp and let go of me."

"I don't curse often," Mathias said. "But I hope they got the bitch."

Bram thought about the roller-coaster of emotions he had experienced during his time with Elisabet. He had felt sorry for her, wishing there had been a medicine to break St. Michael's hold on her.

He recalled the sketch he had produced for Elisabet: St. Michael beneath the sea, fishes swimming above and around the archangel's stone face.

Karol was searching the docks and various vans for her son when she sighted him. She screamed his name, raced to him, and enswathed him and his rescue blanket.

Bram had never before felt his mother's body quivering as fast and as hard.

"Are you hurt?" Karol asked, kissing his cheeks and forehead with a dozen wet licks.

"How did you get here, Mom?"

"Thank God you're safe," Karol muttered and stepped back for a better view, her face startling as if discovering she had been kissing a short-haired stranger.

"She was so evil, Mom, but not like I thought evil was."

Confusion rendered Karol incapable of speaking, but her furrowed brow demanded an explanation.

Bram spoke with a voice sounding deeper than Karol remembered.

"Elisabet was born with a broken brain, Mom. And later, shit piled on her, and her past wouldn't let go. I tried to help her. Honestly, I did."

Karol stepped closer to Bram. This time, she gently cradled and caressed him. She had lost her little boy and was beholding a young man evolving into being his father's son. She wept mixed sadness and joy.

Bram sensed this hug as warmer and more accepting than past hugs that often had felt obligatory or to drive a point.

Mathias stepped away. "I'll give you and Todd time alone together."

Karol held Bram at arm's length to examine him. "Todd?" She looked at Mathias. "His name's Bram."

Bram mumbled, "It's been a confusing ordeal, Mom."

"That's right," Mathias said. "His true name. I'll give you and Bram time together." He stepped farther away.

"No," Bram yelled. "Stay here. Mom? This guy saved me. Removed her ammunition. Mathias saved my life."

Karol stepped to Mathias and extended her hand.

"Thank you for my son, Mr. Mathias."

Bram whispered, "That's his first name."

Mathias and Karol grinned at one another. Karol reached to embrace the man, but Bram interrupted with rapid speech. "Wait Mom. Mathias is an Olympic fencer."

Karol turned to her son, still grinning, and asked, "Does that mean I can't hug the man?"

"No, Mom. Hug away. You have more hugs than one human can handle. Spread them around."

The two adults chuckled and embraced.

Bram did not know Lin and Luca, but saw one of them point at his mother, and the two of them become animated, jabbing fingers in one another's faces as if in an angry argument.

Francine and Aaron appeared from behind a van and simultaneously screamed Bram's name.

Bram's blanket slid off his shoulders as he ran to them with arms opened wide enough to hug both at once.

Bram did not know what the two detectives were wearing or had touched, but welcomed that even far on the other side of the planet, they smelled like New York.

Coming up for breath, Francine asked, "Is there anything I can get you, do for you?"

"Yes," Bram yelled. "Champagne."

Karol's head whiplashed. "Champagne?"

"Yeah, Mom. Me and Mathias survived—I mean Mathias and I. We survived."

Aaron held out a hand as if toasting. "I'm up for a glass."

"Okay," Francine said, making eye contact one by one to see if all were in favor. "After we finish debriefing, let's go for bubbly."

"Did they have champagne on that yacht?" Aaron asked.

Bram's eyes widened. "Did they ever. You won't believe all the shit—I mean things they had on that yacht. The toilets have seat warmers."

"Oh wow," Aaron said.

Francine watched Bram come to life with story following story and wished Jasmine could see Bram. See she was committed to this boy. See they all were.

Aaron grinned, picturing Colt one day being full of life, mischief, and smart-mouthed like Bram.

Karol felt Sol looking over her shoulder and smiling at what a great kid they had created.

Once Luca and Lin had obtained formal statements from Bram and Mathias, Francine pulled Bram to a quiet corner away from the circus of activity.

"Did you see the officers shooting at your captor?"

Bram nodded. "Yes ma'am. I saw clearly."

Francine looked at everything she could look at other than Bram before asking, "Did you see where the first shot originated?"

Bram took enough time before answering that his silence confirmed Francine's suspicion.

Even though they were far from the others, Bram lowered his voice. "There's a shooting range on 20th Street, between Fifth and Sixth Avenues, right?"

"Uh ... Westside Rifle ... We go there sometimes."

"I guess you know Mom's friend, Sonia, don't you?"

The blood draining from Francine's face confirmed Bram's suspicion.

Both stood silent as their worlds teeter-tottered for a moment. Life could go any of many directions.

Bram broke the silence. "My mother worked all my life to make a calm—sometimes dull—but excellent life for me. It was something precious she needed. I want her to be able to return to that. Not everything has to be said.

She lost enough. One day when I'm an actual detective—
or real estate agent—maybe she and I can talk."

Francine stared at Bram. Her lips began quivering and
she turned her head aside to hide her face.

"What's the matter?" Bram asked.

"You have the compassion of your father."

"You knew him?" Bram turned away to think, the two
of them standing with their backs to one another.

"Sol and K.C. were like an older brother and sister to
me," Francine said. "They were only seven or eight years
older than me, but we looked up to them."

"It's all true," Bram mumbled. "They really were case
officers." He swung around and grabbed Francine's
shoulders, pulling her to look at him. "You gotta tell me
everything."

Francine rested her hands on the young man's
shoulders. "Stay calm. Swing by my office. We'll talk."

Bram hesitated. "You mean make an honest to gosh
appointment with you?"

"Make an appointment. Call me. Drop in unannounced.
Doesn't matter. We can go around the corner for coffee."

"Yeah … Swell. I'll do that … But just so you know, I
don't drink coffee. Just green tea."

Francine laughed hard.

Bram appeared his feelings were hurt. "That's not
funny."

"Your father didn't drink coffee. Only black tea."

"Bram clutched Francine and cried hard. Amid sobs, he
said, "I'll drop by tomorrow."

Francine chuckled. "I think that may be a little
difficult. We're in Italy."

"Oh shit." Bram looked around, wiping his nose. "I
forgot."

Aaron arrived and stared at the woman and boy with

hands on each other's shoulders as if they were slow dancing. Aaron had the look of an eager child waiting his turn.

Francine noticed Karol watching and signaled for Aaron to join Bram. As she walked to Karol, she could hear Bram immediately spilling his guts to his friend.

Francine shook Karol's hand as if congratulating her for winning a hard-fought tennis tournament. "You've got a real winner of a young man there, K.C."

"I do," Karol said. "You opened my eyes to what I have." She sighed. "Life sure will be different—that's for certain." She thought about that upheaval for a moment. "I'll adjust."

Lin and Luca nodded at the hugger crowd, shook hands, and walked into the distance talking.

Once people were satiated with handshakes, shoulder pats, and hugs, the two muscular men, Aaron and Mathias, sized up one another.

Aaron said, "I heard you were quite the superstar in the Olympics."

Mathias shrugged. "I fenced. Years ago."

"Good job out there tonight," Aaron said. He buddy punched the steward's shoulder.

Bram yelled as loudly as he could, "God almighty, everybody."

All heads turned toward him.

"Enough crying and hugging everybody and everything. We survived. Somebody get me a damn glass and a damn bottle of champagne."

DC Fidler (Author)

A native of the North Carolina Appalachian Mountains, DC Fidler lives in Charlotte, North Carolina.

He has combined a career in academic psychiatry and cultural psychiatry with a lifetime of playwriting, acting, directing, composing music, and teaching creative writing and the dramatic arts.

He is an award-winning playwright, author of the textbook: *Psychiatry for Actors: Building a Character Using Psychiatric Principles*, author of short stories, and author of the novels: *Boogieban*, *Wood Whisperers*, *Dangerous Art*, and co-author with RJ Casey of *Green Lights of Baghdad*.

Appreciation

Thank you to my wonderful writing teachers: Doris Betts, Max Steele, Wallace Kaufman, and writers-in-residence James Dickey and Robert Anderson at the University of North Carolina at Chapel Hill. That was a half-century ago, but your caring presences continue to instruct me.

Thank you to Sandi Constantino-Thompson for your wonderful editing suggestions and your infectious enthusiasm that keeps me writing and rewriting long hours each day.

Thank you to RJ Casey, Travis Teffner, Paul Rashid, Ben Hogan, and Andrew Trumbull, my sometimes co-writers and writing consultants, who are consistently my audience when I write.

Thank you to Air Force Major RJ Casey, to an unnamed Manhattan homicide police officer, and to Charlotte-Mecklenburg Police Officer, Tammy Hunter, for answering my questions about operational procedures, about real-life experiences, and for encouraging my writing and research with compassion and enthusiasm.

Thank you to my numerous restaurant and coffee-shop buddies who keep me nourished with food and nourished with enthusiasm for writing.

Thank you to the Charlotte Writers Club for the many writing classes and critiques from club writers.

Plays, Novels, and Textbooks by DC Fidler

Novels and Textbooks
* Boogieban
* Wood Whisperers
* Dangerous Art
* Green Lights of Baghdad (With RJ Casey)
* Psychiatry for Actors: Building a Character Using Psychiatric Principles

Novelettes and Short Stories
* Recipient
* The Dust Portal

Plays
* Voices in the Woods
* Guilt by Association (With RJ Casey)
* Three Diaries
* Sir William Bowlinggreen and Company
* Shiraz
* Anniversary of Miss Nanette Pringle
* School Children Hiding Under Desks
* Grams
* Camp Uni
* Boogieban (Two-Actor Version)
* Boogieban (Seven-Actor Version)
* Ahulaqs
* Elk and Wolf (With Travis Teffner)
* Santee Delta (With Travis Teffner)
* Celtic Crossing
* Stone Touchin'
* Daugherty Park Merry-Go-Round
* La Dynastie

- The Last Farm
- Gyges
- Begat

Short Plays
- Persons
- Cruise
- Mobile to Where
- Oman Truce
- Second Amendment
- The Greek God Club
- Five X
- Microscopic Misconceptions
- Drone Guns
- Moon Bugs (With Travis Teffner)

Screenplays
- Green Lights of Baghdad (with RJ Casey)

Musicals
- Pied Piper (With Lauren Horacek)
- Healer Man
- Medicine Show

9 798986 461045